GOD HELP HIM

All three goons stood up and moved to corners. This time, when the deacon waved me to an armchair, I did sit down.

Leon brought coffee cups to the deacon and me. I sipped at mine. Straight hooch. Deacon Elmo lifted his cup to me and smiled. His silver mustache was the most magnificent I had ever seen, I admit. Except that when he drank it glistened with drops. The deacon studied me taking a second sip, then he leaned forward and looked me solemnly in the eye.

"My son, I feel something very special here this evening. You have come for a purpose, I know that. I will do what I can to enable God's will." He paused politely for me.

"Good," I said. His canned dynamism was making it fun to goof on him. "There is something you can do for me."

"You have only to speak it, my son, and if God's hand is visible to me in your request, then I am His humble agent, and yours. Wait, let me show His power: does what you are seeking involve a number?"

"Correct," I said and toasted him. Then I carefully placed my cup down, stood up, and took the pistol out of my pocket. . . .

Bantam Books offers the finest in classic and modern American murder mysteries. Ask your bookseller for the books you have missed.

Stuart Palmer
THE PENGUIN POOL
  MURDER
THE PUZZLE OF THE HAPPY
  HOOLIGAN
THE PUZZLE OF THE RED
  STALLION
THE PUZZLE OF THE SILVER
  PERSIAN

Craig Rice
HAVING WONDERFUL CRIME
MY KINGDOM FOR A HEARSE

Rex Stout
AND FOUR TO GO
BAD FOR BUSINESS
DEATH OF A DUDE
DEATH TIMES THREE
DOUBLE FOR DEATH
FER-DE-LANCE
THE FINAL DEDUCTION
GAMBIT
THE LEAGUE OF
  FRIGHTENED MEN
NOT QUITE DEAD ENOUGH
THE RUBBER BAND
SOME BURIED CAESAR
THE SOUND OF MURDER
TOO MANY CLIENTS

Victoria Silver
DEATH OF A HARVARD
  FRESHMAN
DEATH OF A RADCLIFFE
  ROOMMATE

William Kienzle
THE ROSARY MURDERS

Joseph Louis
MADELAINE

M. J. Adamson
NOT TILL A HOT JANUARY
A FEBRUARY FACE

Richard Fliegel
THE NEXT TO DIE

Richard Hilary
SNAKE IN THE GRASSES

Barbara Paul
THE FOURTH WALL
KILL FEE
THE RENEWABLE VIRGIN

Benjamin Schutz
ALL THE OLD BARGAINS
EMBRACE THE WOLF

S.F.X. Dean
DEATH AND THE MAD
  HEROINE

Ross MacDonald
BLUE CITY
THE BLUE HAMMER

Robert Goldsborough
MURDER IN E MINOR
DEATH ON DEADLINE

Sue Grafton
"B" IS FOR BURGLAR
"C" IS FOR CORPSE

Max Byrd
CALIFORNIA THRILLER
FINDERS WEEPERS
FLY AWAY, JILL

R.D. Brown
HAZZARD

A.E. Maxwell
JUST ANOTHER DAY IN
  PARADISE

Rob Kantner
THE BACK-DOOR MAN
THE HARDER THEY HIT

Joseph Telushkin
THE UNORTHODOX MURDER
  OF RABBI WAHL

Carolyn G. Hart
DEATH ON DEMAND

SNAKE
IN THE
GRASSES

Richard Hilary

BANTAM BOOKS
TORONTO · NEW YORK · LONDON · SYDNEY · AUCKLAND

SNAKE IN THE GRASSES
A Bantam Book / May 1987

For Betsy and Denise

Author's Note

Although this novel is set in a real city, it is entirely a work of fiction. A few liberties have been taken with geography and history. The characters, fortunately, are completely imaginary and resemblances to actual persons, living or dead, are entirely coincidental.

—R.H.

Chapter 1

Angel the Sex Change is kind of a sad case. Don't go getting me wrong now. I mean, who am I to pity anybody? But with Angel, all he ever wanted, as long as I've known him, was for the doctors to turn him into a woman. And after he finally got that, Angel did his best to change his name. And his life. Even toted around a little card proving he was a woman that he used to pull out for everybody. To this day, he still pleads with johns to call him "Angelica." But everybody who's known Angel for a long time just switched to calling him Angel the Sex Change. You couldn't say his life was actually all that different now. Except maybe sometimes the characters he runs around with don't beat him up afterwards any more.

The last time I saw Angel he was dancing up a storm at the Club Pimlico and batting his long eyelashes at this drunk police lieutenant who was crawling up Angel's legs. Angel makes a really sexy-looking woman, you got to say that, and a lot of men go crazy for a piece of it. The funny thing is how many cops follow Angel around with their tongues hanging out, almost as if cops got some kind of pervert hiding inside them. All those cops hanging around like dogs in heat makes Angel more than just the best police snitch in Newark. It also makes him *my* best source in the whole city for information about the cops.

But I wasn't all that glad to see Angel's head poking out the door of my apartment, smiling at me as I trudged up the stairs. It was Monday evening, about six o'clock, and my

1

stomach was aching from too much black coffee and too little food. I hadn't been to bed at all the night before.

Sunday and Monday I spent chasing down a fourteen-year-old runaway. Normally I kind of like looking for missing persons. You learn a lot about the city that way and you learn plenty about people. Start pulling on the strings of somebody's life and pretty soon you feel connected to everything they ever did and everybody they ever did it to. You start seeing the way the city is webbed and wrapped around with all those strings of different people's lives.

But this particular case had been more embarrassing than anything else, and, on top of that, depressing. The fourteen-year-old had a littler kid with her when she ran. Her own baby. Which she dumped in a flophouse while she kicked on her dancing shoes. Too young to grow up and take care of somebody else. Too young to take care of herself, for that matter. So she just leaves the baby and pretty soon the baby don't exist any more. Close your eyes and you float and pretend. And the pain just all goes away.

Except it never really does. Every time you turn around, there's something to remind you how all the pain is waiting handy for when your number comes up. That's what I was reminded by seeing Angel the Sex Change's head poking out my door.

"Hello, Papi," said Angel gaily. He had a big platinum wig on his head and a layer of pink lipstick on his wide mouth. Angel reminds a lot of people of the young Rita Moreno. Maybe it's the wigs or those flamboyant gestures of his, with two hands full of painted fingernails and a smoke rolled in yellow paper.

"You simply got to get yourself some decent threads, Angel," I said. "It's a crying shame, this homey way you let yourself run around."

Angel let out that peculiar laugh he has that ought to break glass. He was wearing a short tight skirt in black suede that showed off his long legs to best advantage. Under that he had on net stockings and tiny pink spike heels that matched his lipstick one-hundred percent. His blouse seemed to be made of tiny gold chains looped together, and

2

over that he wore a waist-length black-and-white fur jacket.

I pushed past him, and walked into my apartment. It's never a surprise when Angel shows up, because he knows I hide the spare key behind the old hall radiator, and we been friends since I took on a case for him a few years back—found a john that owed him two hundred dollars and stuck in his face until he paid up. Since then Angel has sent quite a bit of business my way, and I should have been happier to see him than I was. But at the moment all I really cared about was having a large drink. I rummaged around in the kitchenette for a bottle of Black Velvet I knew wasn't empty yet, then saw it sitting out on the coffee table with a used glass and a bowl of ice next to it.

"You bought me a drink, Sweetman," said Angel, swinging elegantly by so that his hip rubbed up against mine. "I knowed you would not mind."

My big square liquor glass was in the pile in the sink. I rinsed it out and bought me a highball to catch up. Angel arranged himself on the arm of a chair across from me with his skirt ridden up tight across his thighs so that I could have seen clear up to heaven if I wanted. Angel's been offering me free thrills ever since I've known him. I'm almost running out of polite ways to turn him down.

I poured us each another taste. That smooth liquor was like lotion soothing my mind. I took the joint Angel handed me.

"How you doing, man? *Qué pasa?*" I was holding a match to the tip of the joint. A big first drag put a little buzzing in my ears.

"Am doing very nice, Easy. But I been missing you. You been doing something?"

"You wouldn't believe me if I told you. You just wouldn't believe me, Angel."

"Okay. You don't got to tell me nothing, Sweetman. You having a hard day. I can tell. You want Angel to rub you shoulders, make them feel good for you?"

"First this mean old fat mama practically tells me to go spit in my hat, when I ask her real nice for my usual fee."

I looked to see if Angel would grin when I said "usual

fee." But he is a pretty nice person sometimes. He gave me the right kind of distressed look.

"I tell her one hundred dollars per day, plus expenses, for me to find her fourteen-year-old daughter. And the baby she was toting with her. Mama looked at me like I was spelling out possible side effects when I de-roach her apartment."

"The young girl, did you find her, Papi?"

"No trouble at all hunting down where the girl was holed up. South side, over by them unfinished projects on Clinton Ave? The first one of her girlfriends I asked told me right off. Only catch was, girl wasn't there when I got to the place."

I swallowed down a mouthful of barely cooled Black Velvet.

"The baby was, though," I said. "I mean, I was knocking on all the doors I could find in that tenement. But nobody's opening up today. Hard to blame them, I guess, considering the likelihood that it would only be the police, the bill collector, or some other kind of trouble, like me. So I go around into the alley, Angel. You would have loved this part. All dark and dripping wet from this fifth-floor clothesline. I climb up on some crates to look in the window. People'd been throwing garbage out their windows into that alley for probably thirty years. And nobody ever once came to pick it up, believe me. But I got up on some boxes and looked into the window."

"And you see this little tramp making love?"

"I told you she wasn't there, Angel. I didn't see much of anything, except a toilet and a sink. But I could hear a sound from another room. Real weak, like the little baby had cried herself almost out."

I put down the fresh drink Angel had poured for me, waved off the joint, and fired up a butt.

"Believe you me, there is nothing in that alley that I didn't bring with me that I would ever care to touch. So I took off my shoe and I smacked the glass flat with the heel. It broke mostly inwards. I shoved up the bottom sash and

4

go wiggling in across the sill on my belly. Then I pick myself up and walk through the bedroom toward the sobbing."

"It's gonna be awful, I can tell," said Angel. "Don't tell me no more, Easy."

"Baby's laying on her back in this filthy plastic crib. She's got this loop of cord around her neck, pulled tight, and the other end is tied to the frame of the crib. Little face and legs and arms're scrawny, like she hadn't had nothing to eat for a long time. Her belly was all fat and bloated. She was way too tired to scream much. Just kept letting out these little 'mews' once in a while."

Angel had put his long painted fingers over his ears and was humming to himself. That almost made me grin, but I was telling the story to myself mostly anyway.

"So I just naturally spent most of Sunday night and all day today at the Children's Shelter, which is not an easy place to slide in and out of with a battered kid. Usually they don't let you walk out without a cop handcuffed to each wrist, I think. It was no joke getting the baby treated and out of there, Angel. Without stirring things up, I mean. But I figured I owed the baby's grandmother that much."

Angel stopped humming and said: "The baby is okay, *sí?*"

"This oh-so lovely lady that works at the shelter talked to me for a while. And she took my ten-dollar bill, mind you. Then she wrote a few extra things on the admitting forms so I could leave with the kid. Which even though I don't like anything about this story is not my favorite part. Because naturally I got not one cent more from anybody for all my legwork."

"But the baby doing fine?"

"Even pulling off the case today put me way in the hole. I am not about to go back out looking for the baby's mother."

"Where is the father?"

"All I could find out about him was that he's some kind of spick, as my employer delicately puts it. He hasn't come around once since he found out the girl was pregnant."

"The baby didn't die or nothing. Don't you tell me that, Easy."

"Less than fifty-fifty, the doctor at the shelter said. Malnutrition. Something about the liver and kidneys."

"You don't know where is her mother? Maybe she is looking for her baby, crying her eyes out."

"Angel, you know and I know, they're gonna find that girl shacked up with some lover-boy she met at a disco club. She don't know that baby's alive any more."

"I fell terrible," said Angel.

"Made me feel like the cover of a matchbook, when all the matches're used up. You know what I'm saying?"

Angel cleared his throat. "Yas, they use you. Then throw you in the gutter when they through. I know how you feel, Easy. Angel feel that way too many times. Life is a long hard road for us, no? Us that live life our own way. A long dirty road. And lined with gutters."

"For God's sake, Angel, where'd you pick up that line of shit from? You got more money in your life than anybody I know. And more fun too, it comes to that. You hear that pitiful dribble in one of your soap operas or something?"

"Am missing something beautiful in my life." Angel lifted up his chin to show me he could be strong about something like this.

"Whyn't you go down Cosmo's shop or someplace, get yourself a poster of Diana Ross or something. Or maybe Michael Jackson, in your case. I suppose that ain't the kind of beautiful you mean, huh?"

"I mean true love," breathed Angel. I could almost feel his breath in my ear.

"That'd been my guess, somebody'd been here asking me. But don't tell it to me, man. We been through this before, I think."

"You prezudiced, Easy."

"I know you think that. Well, you may be right. Don't make no difference, though."

"You no think Angel is beautiful?"

"I don't think about it at all. I make an absolute point of

never thinking about you that way. I'm getting too old to change my point of view, Angel. I've told you that before."

"Piss on your old point of view," said Angel. But he gave me a dazzling smile to go with that. He has a lot of charm, when you come right down to it.

"What you been doing the last couple weeks?" I said. I fished four or five thin cubes out of the water in the bucket, stuck them in my glass, and filled it to the top with brown rye.

"You drink ice coffee, looking like," said Angel.

"That's a good way to think on it, way I feel. You want some too?"

Angel's glass needed some slivers of ice, and about an inch of Black Velvet, topped with fizzy soda water. When I handed it back, I said, "What's up with you since I saw you last?"

"Well, I got this friend I know," said Angel, making his face dreamy. "I got this man friend, and he got some kind of fearsome troubles or something. Nice looking man, too."

I raised an eyebrow.

"I mean, if he did got troubles, he could just bring them to Angel, *sí*? He don't need no detective. I make him feel so good them troubles just go right away."

"What's this guy want with a private cop?"

Angel shrugged. "I don't ask. Men come to see me when they are forgetting their troubles, not to remember."

"I bet. What's the name and address?"

"He gone call you tonight. His name is Walter Epps." It didn't mean a thing to me, but Newark is a big city.

"He know your name from when you was a fighter, Easy. Is not too often somebody remember you any more from you boxing?"

"Not too often. How do you know this character?" I tried lighting the joint again and at the same time keeping Angel from massaging my shoulders. Wasn't easy, but I did it.

"I go many places, Sweetman," said Angel gravely. Then he smiled. "Angel goes everywhere, *sí*? And I hear

7

many things." He leaned forward to let me smell the smoky sandalwood on his throat. "Could be Angel played some games with this dude sometimes."

"I don't doubt it," I leered, getting up to forage for food in the kitchenette. "What's your edge, though?"

Angel followed me over and arched back with his elbows resting on a counter. "Just always like to do you a favor, Ezell."

"And you want what for this particular favor, Angel?" Only thing worth eating in the refrigerator was a bowl of raw green beans, though they're one vegetable that profits from steaming. I ate a couple anyway, which made Angel wrinkle his nose. In the cupboard I turned up some corn chips that bent without breaking when I bit into them. I winged them bag and all past Angel into the trash.

"You don't want them chips?"

"I was gonna eat any of them garbage," I said, "I'd eat the cellophane bag first. You were gonna tell me what you had coming for this little favor you're doing me?"

"Don't you just know what I been wanting, Lover?" Angel's laughter tinkled like chimes. "You don't know, you don't been paying attention."

"I always pay attention when I'm around you, Angel," I said. "So you don't get your roving hands on my body."

"Fifty dollars then, Big Shot," said Angel.

"You get it when I get paid."

Angel closed then opened his forest of eyelashes. His voice turned husky. "You know you could pay Angel another way."

"Don't even think about it. And don't forget you promised to put in an appearance at the garden tomorrow."

Angel nodded regretfully. I lit a third cigarette. There was nothing fit to eat in the kitchen and I was too beat to go out again. After another drink and some more small talk, Angel picked up his handbag and left. I went to bed and dreamed I was chained around the neck and couldn't quite manage to bring the gun up to my head.

Chapter 2

"Yeah?" Ringing was still blurring the inside of my head.

"Is Ezell Barnes there?"

"Speaking. Who is this?" The bedside clock read midnight.

"Somebody that I know and you know said maybe you could help me."

"Who is this?" I repeated. Black prince of detectives, coming at you.

"I can't say nothing on the phone, you understand. I got to see you right away, though, man."

"You know what time it is? I been sleeping. Can't it wait until tomorrow?"

"No. Definitely not tomorrow. If I wait, there maybe won't *be* any tomorrow, you hear what I'm saying?"

"Sounds okay to me."

"What is this?" sneered the voice. "You work for a living or not?"

"Yeah I do. Where?"

I took down the address and walked through a shower and into my clothes.

Thirty minutes later I was steering through the dead center of Newark, through the huge DMZ in the central ward between Springfield and Clinton Aves that they call the Ponderosa. Not a scrap of life to be seen there. Just a big, empty, paved space carved out of the center of the city by fire, decay, and neglect. You've got an unobstructed view of the Manhattan skyline and not much else.

I pepped it up motoring along Belmont Avenue. Nowadays, they call it the Irving Turner Boulevard. But at the time I answered this call, 1978, it was old Belmont Avenue, just like it ever was and always will be to me. Same thing happened with High Street. Now it's Martin Luther King Boulevard; good name, means something. But they haven't got around to changing all the signs yet, and I can't think of it except as High Street.

The Ponderosa always gives me the creeps. Besides, I was getting curious about the case I was driving to. Not so much because of the peekaboo phone call. I get them all the time, what with my number in the Yellow Pages under "Investigators." Jealous wives get antsy when it's 2:30 A.M. and the bars are closed for the night and their men still aren't home yet.

What made me curious was the Weequahic address, which looked to be a much better class of customer than I was used to. Weequahic Avenue had once been Jew-prosperous, before the '67 riots sent all the Jews scurrying out of Newark and into the Oranges. It was still one of the tonier residential addresses in the city.

The house I was looking for was set far back from the boulevard, behind a couple of overgrown juniper shrubs and a head-high privet hedge that spanned the lot. Dark as a tomb, that house was. No car in the driveway. No lights in the neighbors' houses, either.

From my glove box I took out the thick aluminum flashlight/nightstick combo that I used to carry as a cop. I locked the car doors, switched on the beam, and toed through the narrow walkway between all that hedging. Already, the week after Labor Day, it was chilly enough to turn up my jacket collar.

The other side of the hedge looked neat and trim, from what I could see, though nobody was gonna think a gardening nut lived there. No kids' toys on the walk. No signs of a dog. Just a long, narrow lawn with deep pockets of rhododendrons fifteen feet high, with big caves of shadows in between them, along the sides of the house and the boundaries of the lot.

Halfway to it, I flashed on the house itself: square, big, three stories; white paint, maybe, or a light color. An old-fashioned sitting porch stretched across the entire front of it.

Damned place had not sign one of life anywhere about it. No porch light, no yellow seeping through the three door panes. Not a light in a single window.

The address was correct, though. The mailbox at the foot of the walk bore the number loud and clear.

Another three steps and my better judgment started telling me not to walk into a fishy spot like this without knowing more than I did. But me and my better judgment are barely on speaking terms, some days. The posh neighborhood whetted my appetite.

Ten feet from the porch, I cut right for the strip of lawn that swept around the side of the house, dancing the flash beam along the bushes, looking for God knows what. Keep myself from tripping in the dark, mostly. Casing for any old bogeymen lurking in the shrubbery.

At the back corner of the house, I cut the light and craned for a quick look in the backyard. Big contrast to the front. It was tiny, backing right up against the next lot. More over-fertilized bushes, plus a cyclone fence, both designed to repel riffraff. I padded back the way I came, hefting the flashlight, flicking with my thumb at its switch.

Which is when the bogeyman jumped out and got me.

A hundred-pound sack of cement dropped on my neck and shoulders from the third story. My head knocked off my knees. Then my knees accordioned. Halfway into a forwards sprawl, I stretched into a lunge away from whoever had snuck up behind me. Rolling onto my left hip, I jerked up, only to have screaming reflexes yank my head back from a boot that mushroomed inches before my eyes. Then up somehow, onto my two big feet, automatically hunching the big deltoid muscle of my left shoulder at my attacker. A giant black shape just three feet away blasted a right hand that deflected off my shoulder point and glanced against the top of my skull.

That's when my instincts took the wheel. My upper body curved to throw my right arm in front of the shadow's

11

left hook, my weight shifted to my left foot, and my left hand stapled a jab on his face.

This dude could take a punch. He glided off it, ducked to my left, and laid a second right fist over the top of my jab. I stopped it plenty quick with my chin.

My eyes filled with visions of what it must look like inside televisions. Then they cleared, and I yanked my head and shoulders back, back, back. He kept snapping left after left at my head, quick but stunning, like a trained and talented heavyweight. We both chased my head backwards, me backpedaling like a madman. *What* my mitts were doing all this time, I had no idea.

Then my back pillowed against a wall of shrub branches, which forced my sliding heels to dig into the dirt, and in turn bounced my cheekbone into his fist. But after that one lick I had my feet set. The next punch I picked off with a swinging forearm. Then I swung the other elbow up at his face. When he half-hopped back, I squared off and commenced teaching him the manly art.

The memory trained into my muscles from nineteen pro bouts cranked up my right fist, feinted with it, then feinted the left. When that froze him for a quarter-second, I bayoneted the right into his solar plexus. I delivered the whole package, from over the top, turning my wrist so it landed practically thumb-down, all the muscles of both legs and my upper body feeding into the punch. If I ever hit a man harder, I don't remember it. By rights, my fist should have come out the other side of his body.

Even that behemoth should have gone down gasping. But he only rocked back, like a punching toy. His arms gave little twitches. One circus strongman, to keep his feet under a train collision like that.

As he was swaying back into balance, I muscled up a left uppercut like a discus-thrower concentrating his every fiber into one ferocious swerve. The effort of it lifted me six inches off the ground.

Lifted my opponent a foot, though. Thudded onto his side and didn't move. Not even a groan out of him. It was eerie, the way he fell.

For a second, I hacked to catch my breath. When I could choke some air down, I hurt all over. Was he breathing? Yes. Did he feel worse than I did? Seemed likely. Did that last sock rattle his teeth? I fingered my own tender jaw. I fervently hoped so. But it was too cloudy dark a night to see really how he was feeling.

I edged a little closer and listened. Sounds like snoring were coming regularly from the big body. Holding my head and feet well back from him, I leaned in to pick his pockets for some ID.

It would have worked, too, except that this was one ranger that didn't know to fight fair. Just as I was stretching my fingertips, he jacked up with his arms and simultaneously swung his right leg around so fast I never even started to react. I absorbed the blow on the left temple. And down I went.

I wasn't out, I wasn't in. A pretty familiar feeling. Like waiting for the eight count, or the bell, or somebody's arm to pick you up.

Chapter 3

First definite thing I realized was, I was staring up into an all-too-familiar face from my not-so-distant past.

Dale Mooney, police academy classmate and sometime pal, grinned in my teeth and said, "Napping, Barnesie? Taking time out of your busy day to soak up a nice death scene?"

"Death scene!" For one second, my groggy imagination featured a severe delayed reaction to my uppercut. Then I calmed down. "Who bought it?"

Dale ignored the question. "You think it looks good, I don't—you lying out here counting the stars, with a dead fellow inside the house?"

"Dale," I said. "You could say I took a tough roll on a job tonight. Got this call, about midnight, setting up a meet at this house here. Place looked dead as your sex life, so I was casing it out some."

"Which is when you decided to catch forty winks on the crabgrass?"

"Uh-uh. That decision came after I got kicked upside the head. Real hard."

"Someone kicks you on the head while the suicide's going down inside, huh? That makes sense, sure it does."

"I'm dead serious. Some tough old mother was laying for me when I got here."

"You make this thug?"

"Too dark, Dale. Happened too fast. Great big dude, though. Strong mother."

"Oh, sure. Must've been Klondike Dan to take *you* out, right? You hear a shot, anything like that?"

"Nope."

Mooney had me on my feet by then and limping along the house stepping stones.

"Dalie?"

"Yeah?"

"Well?"

"Well, what?"

"Well, you're not going to dangle me in suspense, are you, buddy? What went down tonight?"

"Hmmm. I'm not sure what's okay for you to know."

"Come on!"

"Looks one hell of a very lot like a suicide. Who hired you to come over here tonight?"

"Name is Walter Epps."

"That's the dead item inside, all right."

"How long you boys been here?"

Mooney glanced at his wrist. "Maybe twenty minutes," he said. "Uniforms answered the call. Eddie and Griff and I drove in five minutes later."

The porch was all lit up now. A uniformed cop was parked by the front door. Through the gap in the hedge, I could see more uniforms, four cop cars, blue and red lights wheeling around, and a small crowd of the neighborhood curious, buzzing a little, but mostly just standing quiet or buzzarding over the hedge.

"You handling the investigation?" I asked Mooney.

Dale shook his head and ushered me up the four porch steps and into the house.

Inside, the hall was huge, the size of my living room, but warm-looking: dark wood shiny with new varnish. The floor was ancient hardboards that had been stripped, sanded, and revarnished through hours of expensive labor. On the left an enormous plate of stained glass, floral and greenery, was set into the wall like a window but was lit instead by lamps hidden behind it. Beyond that, two doors on the left, two on the right, led to other rooms or closets. All the little tables and hat-rack valets looked shiny and fragile and unused. The sculptured Oriental in the hall was exactly matched by the runner cloaking the steep staircase at the very back.

That's where all the activity was happening.

Two homicide detectives—dress pants, white shirts, narrow dark ties—were squatting with their backs to me, talking and pointing with pencils and fingers. What they were pointing at looked from where I stood like a man grinding out a one-armed push-up.

His body was stretched facing the floor at about a forty-five-degree angle, toes just touching the carpet, left arm tucked behind his back, other arm dangling straight down to graze the floor with his knuckles.

Two things set the scene off from a Marine gym. One was the yellow polypropylene rope, stretching tautly from the top of the staircase, holding the man's neck and head off the floor. The other was that the man wasn't wearing a jockstrap. Or anything else, for that matter.

Mooney gave me a little jab in the back. The two detectives stood up to look at us. One was a grizzly old dog. As we walked over I picked up on the younger one's square head and wide hard build. His hair was light brown, trimmed close around the ears, but with a big flop of it over his forehead, like Teddy Kennedy used to sport. Eddie

Dorey, Homicide's go-getter. Dorey was saying something I couldn't hear that made his partner snigger. Then all three cops were eyeing me.

"Found this item just outside the back door, Eddie," Mooney announced. "On his back, he was. Had his ticket punched, he claims."

"You're Barnes, aren't you?" Unlike my face, Dorey's was unsurprised.

"Yeah. How's it going, Eddie? You remember me?"

"The boxer, weren't you? I knew a couple guys you used to work out with down the police gym. What do you do now?"

"Got a private license."

"Oh, yeah? What's that like?"

"Little bit of this and a little bit of that. A living. I got some regular security jobs I handle, pays the rent. Trying to steer clear of the divorce work, but when I need the bread it's always there."

"Where do you know this poor chump from?" Dorey nodded over his shoulder at the corpse still half-suspended off the floor.

"Absolutely nowhere," I said. "Never even heard of the party until he called me tonight around midnight."

"What'd he have for you to do?"

"Search me. Man did not wish to discuss business over the telephone, you know?"

"Grab yourself a coffee," said Mooney. They had a cardboard tray full of Styrofoam cups on the desk. Couple of donuts and napkins, too. Made me feel funny, what with the corpse dangling there.

"This some new police department rule?" I said. "All the hard asses got to eat a bite before they permitted to leave the death scene?"

"Have a look at your late almost-client," Dorey said. "Go ahead. Just don't touch him. We're still waiting for the coroner to show up."

I bent down for a close-up look. Walter Epps had been a small man, nearly bald, thin mustache. Hair covered most of the other parts of his body, connecting his chest and groin. He looked angry in death, as if he were still feeling pain. His head hung crazily from his shoulders, vertebrae no doubt popped by the fall.

So as not to disturb the body's position, I squirmed around looking at Epps' arms from all angles. I found what I was searching for.

"What'd he shoot up with, you know yet?"

Dorey held up a plastic evidence bag. Inside was a syringe, two mostly empty little packets smeared with white powder, a throwaway cigarette lighter, and a kitchen spoon.

"Coke?"

"No, meth. Stinks like cat urine," Dorey said.

"Shit, two bags of speed," Mooney said. "He thought he was surfing on clouds, probably."

"Who tied the noose on his neck?" I asked.

"He did," said Mooney.

"Why wasn't it the hood that jumped me?"

Mooney looked at Dorey, who nodded.

"Come and see," Dale said. He opened one of the doors and flourished me through. All three cops walked behind me.

We were in the dining room. The ceiling was framed with a carved mahogany molding that matched the woodwork around the windows and set off the splashy wallpaper. The chandelier might play Sousa if a high wind ever hit it. It presided over a shiny walnut table where the entire New York Giants defense could sit in comfort.

Mooney headwaved me through an archway into a small fireplaced sitting room, then across a plush carpet into the living room. This was a big room, twenty by thirty. The windows on two sides ran floor to ceiling, all space between them filled with venerable bookcases. There weren't enough books to fill them now. An expensive-looking stereo filled some blank spaces, lots of components, with clear plastic shells showing off their multicolored guts. Professionally done portraits, and bric-a-brac, probably choice, filled other shelves. Not bad taste, really. But all the tiniest bit up-to-date and furniture-store-y, like the wall-to-wall mauve carpet, the too-coordinated sofas and armchairs, the

17

crystal table lamps. The mammoth rolltop desk, which had acquired some noble scars over the years, looked like a schoolkid defying the dress code.

Mooney was spreading a dozen or so color snapshots across a glass coffee table.

"Who lives here with him, do you know?" I asked.

Dorey flicked a finger at one of the bookshelf portraits. "Wife, no kids. We're out looking for her now."

Mooney called, "What do you see here, Barnes?" I stepped over and peered at the snaps.

"Batman mask on the big dude," I said. "And that's a Batman cape. But what is Epps there supposed to be dressed up as?"

"Easy." Mooney was disgusted by my ignorance. "He's Robin, the Boy Wonder. Except, of course, that he don't have nothing on but his ding-dong under the cape there and the mask."

Mooney and the other cop, Griff, hooted. I glanced at Dorey, who tapped the photo with his nail. "Walter Epps evidently liked to get his picture taken while he was tooting on old Batman's flute. What do you think, Barnes? That be the kind of blackmail would start a black fellow thinking about suicide?"

"That might do it," I said.

"Black guy'd never hold his head up, it got around he had a taste for other fellows' private parts," Mooney said. "Especially if the guy had a respectable life, government job, wife. But I suppose we don't have to tell you about black pride or nothing, do we, Barnes?"

Dorey flipped over each of the photos, one after the other. On the back of the ninth one, there was writing.

He held that one up. "Negatives cost a hundred-thousand dollars," he read aloud.

"There's your motive for suicide," Mooney explained to me patiently. Griff and Dorey's chins dipped a quarter inch in agreement. "Plus, the photos explain what your sweetheart outside was up to, Easy. He's the blackmailer. You interrupted his last sales pitch to Epps."

"Then why would Epps want to hire me?"

The three cops glanced at each other.

"Something different, could be," Mooney said. "Maybe something with nothing to do with these here pictures?"

"No. Probably he wanted you to find his body before his old lady got home." Dorey lifted his shoulders. "Blackmailer gives him the photos earlier in the evening, gives Epps until the witching hour to pay up or eat a bag of disgrace. Epps here makes up his mind to pull his own plug and calls you, Barnes."

"He got my name from a mutual friend," I said, "so he probably knew I live on the opposite side of town. Which gives Epps at least forty-five uninterrupted minutes to do the job on himself."

"That would be enough," Dorey said, still studying Epps' photo collection.

"Sounds right to me, Eddie," Mooney chimed in. "Griff, you?" Griff nodded and scratched a jaw that should have been shaved last Tuesday. "You, Barnesie?"

I shrugged. "Nobody can blackmail you if you're not ashamed of yourself. Did Epps make a big secret of being queer, you think?"

Mooney answered: "I knew who he was a little bit, because Epps worked over the years on any number of the projects in town. A cocky, arrogant little sucker, but I never heard anything but that he was straight as an arrow."

"He's smiling in the photo," I pointed out. "Don't look ashamed or secretive to me."

"No, that's wrong, Barnes," Dorey said. "Chances are gay photos would be pretty threatening to a married man's ego."

"Probably the time before this Epps was tricked up like Little Red Riding Hood," Mooney said. "Having the big bad wolf come up behind him and all."

"Then why wouldn't Epps try and pay up, if he could? Before he'd go and waste himself, I mean?"

"The key is, 'if he could.' Managing a federal project, Epps most likely made about thirty-five, forty grand. We don't think his wife works. With a house like this and all, I'd be surprised if he had two quarters to rub against each other in ready cash."

"Less than that, the way this house is tricked up," I said. "So that much sounds like suicide, all right. But what a sick way to kill yourself, man. He must have swan dived from the top of the staircase with that rope tied around his neck."

"Coroner's gonna find he was cranked to the eyebrows with speed," Dorey said in a monotone, stacking up the photos neatly. "He wanted the Dutch courage. Everything he did after that rushed by him like in a dream."

A uniformed cop poked his head into the living room. "M.E.'s here," he told Dorey, who said, "I'll be right there."

Mooney and Griff were poking around, opening drawers and peeking behind books.

"Give me a call tomorrow," Dorey said to me. "Downtown. Around noon. I'm going to need your statement. Afternoon be okay for you?"

"Okay, Cisco," I said. "I'll be calling you." I turned to look at Mooney. "Good to see you, Dale. Give you a call sometime."

As Dorey and I walked through the door, Mooney and Griff were chuckling behind our backs. In the hall we ran into considerably more cop types, including one man toting a doctor's bag. We threaded through and I took one last look at Walter Epps' body.

Next to me, Dorey said: "You win more than you lose?"

"Probably not," I answered, "you take a big enough sample."

"I mean when you were boxing."

"Eleven and six. Two draws. You don't get a shot at the Felt Forum cards with eleven and six."

"No, you got to do better than that," Dorey agreed. We shook hands. I left him standing there as the coroner scalpeled the yellow rope and Epps' body thumped to the floor.

Chapter 4

The next morning I was up and running through Branchbrook Park near my apartment just after the early morning commuter traffic poisoned the air. I needed it to shake off the pounding I'd absorbed. The side of my head felt sore, and my jaw was packed with sponge rubber, but a couple of aspirin took the edge off the ache. Sixteen years of boxing workouts, amateur and professional, train your muscles into resiliency, not to mention giving them a sharp craving for the blood flow of regular exertion. For seventeen years, since I left the army, still its light heavyweight champion at the time, I been trying to keep up the road work every day I could. Though most of the sprinting speed I had then is long gone, I've got more endurance now, enough to really pick 'em up and put 'em down when I hit the home stretch. As I get older I find myself looking forward to my runs. It's the only regular exercise I get. Seems to counteract having to sit on my ass so much of the time on the job.

A skinny beaten-dirt path, packed by hundreds of runners' feet, leads between two fat lilac bushes, under a draping maple tree branch, and down a series of little ravines. I exchanged nods with a fat jogger going the other way. He looked like a baked potato wrapped up in his silver sweat suit. It was the wrong time of day for a whole lot of other runners to be out, which was just my style. I like having time alone, to think. Oh, maybe once in a while, the last couple of years, I get to thinking I might be too alone all the time—some mighty drastic rethinking after all these years, let me tell you.

The path threaded through trees and came out behind

the baseball diamond. Three subteens were sitting in the tiny stands, taking hits from a toke they passed back and forth.

"Would you look at that," one of them said loudly. "It's a jog-man." He drew both syllables out long. "Hey, Jog-Man, how you doing, mother?"

I steamed on past them. "Yoo-hoo, Jog-Man," they yelled at my back. "You carryin' a load in your pants, baby. Shake 'um up, mama."

My steady clip, doing about seven-minute miles, had me out of hearing in no time at all. The path diagonaled the long way across the park, flat as a pancake now, with nothing interesting along the way until the end. The monotony set me thinking about the way I chose to make my living. Always scratching around for the odd dollar. Most mornings, while I'd be running and thinking, I'd reach a point where I was contemplating some other way to hustle through this life. Then some item of work would come to mind and distract me away from quitting thoughts like that. Today, unfortunately, I got to thinking about how routine was today's work agenda.

With about fifty yards to go, the path became bordered on both sides by round stones, behind which yellow and dark-red chrysanthemums had already finished their one big burst of blooms. Park system always puts them out too soon. I hit the gas and didn't pull up until I had run out of the park to the curb. Pausing for cars, I jogged easily across the street to my apartment building.

After a fast shower and shave, I dressed in navy blue dress slacks, a tan pullover sweater with leather collar and shoulders, and my over-the-ankle slip-on boots. In my tiny entrance hall I scooped up my poplin jacket and my Irish tweed hat.

At Al's Queen Street Grill I breakfasted splendidly—tomato juice, powdered-sugar donuts, and coffee—then drove over to my office on Branford Place. I hadn't been there for three days, but the street looked the same: a one-way alley that runs off Broad Street, which is enormously wide and noisy, a block away from Broad and Market, the hottest intersection in downtown Newark. I parked on No-Name Alley around the corner from the office building.

As I walked up the block I passed a jewelry store, a clothes shop called Marcello's, a Florsheim shoe store, the Ritz Theatre—currently reheating a little blaxploitation called *Penitentiary II*—a watch-repair place displaying all kinds of used watches in the window, another clothes store, and another shoe emporium. All the stores had contraptions of heavy metal bars that could be rolled out, swung to, or pulled down at night to cover the front windows. A record store trained its buzzy speakers at the sidewalk. Bob Marley was singing reggae.

> *Them crazy, them crazy*
> *We gonna chase those crazy*
> *Baldheads out of town.*

All along the sidewalk, pseudo-Muslims were hawking cheap rings, clothes, junk. Some of them gave me that "Brother" shit, a couple just stared at me like they do at whitey.

The ground floor of my building is a shoe store. For the last two years, since they built a newsstand in the old alley, I've had to walk through aisles of wing tips and sneakers to reach the service alley in back and then the stairs that lead up to my office.

There is no elevator, so I walk up two flights to the office suite I share with four other self-employeds. The landlord put random tenants together when no outfit big enough wanted the space. We split the rent on the reception area and on the ageless redhead who types and answers the phone for us all. Marlene's desk is ringed by the frosted-glass doors of our private offices. Most of the other tenants come and go—fast—as soon as they get up the bread for a better address. Only the painless dentist across from me hangs in.

Seven years ago, I had a sign painter come in and paint EZELL BARNES, PRIVATE INVESTIGATIONS in gilt on the glass panel. I felt a lot of pride when I first saw it, and I still like to see it scrolled up there, even though the gold paint is flaking off so fast that my name looks like BAINES.

Mail had piled up in my absence. One piece for each day in the tray on Marlene's desk. She handed it to me with a real smile, though. I closed the door behind me to read it. There was an electricity bill, and a campaign flyer from a state senator named Thornton, with a picture of him, heavy-set, short hair, Ivy League suit, giving me that solemn look that says, "Negroes can be intelligent too." I got a flyer announcing "Downtown Shopping Days" in Newark all this week, and a brochure from Woolworth's that I put away to look at later.

When I opened up the window to let some dust fly out, the noises of Branford Place belted me in the ear, along with some distant help from the Broad and Market jive.

Sitting at my desk, listening through the window, was like a dunk in a funky old city pool, washing me in the life of the streets. My office is a dump, but it's downtown, where I am more home than any place else. I feel locked into the noise and the smells in ways that run deeper than money, or schooling, or even color. Half an hour sitting there with the window wide open had me feeling full of spice and breeze. Time to take care of some business.

Out of my wall safe, I pulled my Colt .22 caliber automatic pistol, as pretty as a gun can be, just about the size of a pack of cigarettes, only six ounces fully loaded. Years ago I picked it when I first went on the job as a cop. A lot of officers carried guns like that as throwaways. You carry the throwaway just in case you turn somebody off by mistake one night in an alley, so you don't compound your mistake by getting tossed in jail. Nowadays, I use the little pistol to make bank drops for some of the local merchants on Tuesdays. I tucked it into my jacket pocket with my Chesterfield regulars.

Bank drops are my bread and butter. Most private detectives I know would give a thumb to be cashing the regular checks from my line-up of cash carries. I earned every one of them, though. For one thing, I keep my office downtown, when most of the divorce business has flown to the

suburbs. For another thing, I spent nearly five years court-
ing the local merchants, winning their confidence, before
they began taking their business to me. Those were lean
times, let me tell you. As soon as I moved into Branford
Place, I introduced myself around, let them know I was
licensed to carry firearms. Then I made the rounds practically every day, just dropping by most every shop in the
neighborhood, showing my face, like a cop on a beat. Just
so the local troublemakers would know somebody was out
there keeping an eye on things. After a month, I dropped a
business card on each shopkeeper, stressed to them how
local I was, right on the block, urged them to call me for
whatever reason.

After a while I started taking money from some of them
to make their bank deposits, and eventually, when we got
friendly enough, they let me arrange the work to suit my
schedule.

Now I bring receipts to the banks for nine of them
every Tuesday. Hazardous duty, requires a licensed
weapon, not to mention a substantial bond. The state li-
censing board recommends a fee of fifty dollars per bank
drop. I charge thirty-five. That's three hundred and fifteen
dollars for a morning's work every Tuesday.

My first pickup was for Feldman the Hatter. Feldman
is retired, gone to Florida, they say, though I see him
around on the streets every now and then. The hat store is
managed now by his son-in-law, Kelly, who is so Jewish he
could blow reveille with his nose. His real name is Marvin
Epstein, but everybody calls him Kelly. Kelly had gotten in
a new line of English suede driving caps. When he saw me
eyeing them, there was no denying him until I walked out
of his store wearing one.

Half a dozen more drops for small-time merchants on
Branford Place, and it was on to Cosmo's Optimo Cigar
Shop, a block away at Washington and Market. As I strolled
up, Fabulous Stan the Tattoo Man came out and strolled
down the sidewalk to his parlor. Stan was a walking adver-
tisement for his craft: he was lined red and blue from head
to toe.

"What's black and white and red all over?" I called to Stan like I always do. He ignored me like he always does.

The bell on Cosmo's Optimo Cigar Shop clanked as I pushed in.

"Give you the Giants and four points," Cosmo said without looking up. He was studying the *Racing Form*. "They're home, remember. And against the candy-ass Redskins."

"Cosmo," I said. "Got to grasp something to live for this weekend. Give me the Giants ten times. And don't forget you said you would help us out at the garden this afternoon. Three o'clock."

"Gotta leave by six," Cosmo said earnestly. "Tonight's card is special at the Meadowlands."

"No problem. Just don't be late. The government lady'll be there to count us."

From Cosmo's I crossed back to the Ritz Theatre. A payroll pickup and bank drop for them, and my chores were over for the day. I bought lunch from a taco cart and carried it through the shoe store. Up the stairs again to my office with dead time on my hands again. I hate sitting around worse than anything. Thank God it was time to phone Dorey at Homicide Squad headquarters.

When I dialed the number, though, the Police HQ receptionist reported that Dorey was away from his desk. She connected me instead to Dale Mooney, who told me the Medical Examiner wouldn't be posting Walter Epps until tomorrow afternoon. But his preliminary finding was sure-enough suicide, self-inflicted strangulation. Any time before then would be good enough for me to stop by, give my statement. Routine.

I hung up feeling more chipper. Case closed. That's about all she wrote. Shortest investigation I ever got called in for. Might as well start my weekend early.

I considered starting it off with a short glass of twelve-year-old Johnny Walker from this office bottle that a lady friend gave to me. The whiskey was as soft and smooth as she was before she left town on me.

But today was a big day for my neighborhood's community garden. I straightened up my desk and was handing Marlene the paperwork for billing the bank drops when she picked up the phone, listened for a second, then covered the receiver with her forearm.

"It's for you, Easy. I'm not sure you're going to like it, though."

I rolled my eyes and walked back behind my own desk to take the call.

"I done a foolish thing," said a woman's voice.

"What's that, Mildred?" No point in not sitting down again.

"I guess I should star at the beginny."

"Whatever you like."

"I really do need you help, Ezell."

"I don't doubt it, Mildred."

"You want me to star?"

"Whatever."

"Whar?"

"Wherever."

"You listening good?"

"Absolutely."

Last Sunday, Mildred told me, she was listening like she always does to her gospel show, *The Deacon's Beacon*.

"The Deacon, he pastor of the Church of Holiness Sanctified, see, and he announce to his flock how he making a special benefit of spiritual guidance and consultation available to the people of Nowork. Say he be staying in a fancy suite at the Robert Treat Hotel."

Mildred paused. She'd sit there forever until I said something. So I sighed, "What else, Mildred."

"Deacon say any of his flock can come by his hotel suite, receive the word of the Lord Almighty from on high. If you calls, they make a reservation for you. Then all you got to do is make a donation to his choich before they let you in, see him.

"I heard from my nephew, Charlie Walker, that some folks they donates as much as two hunerd dollars. For that much, the Deacon he bless a special place in the Good Book to help you in time of struggles. Charlie Walker he say the Deacon always bless the number."

"So the Deacon blesses the number, Mildred? You think God is maybe taking a cut off the numbers racket? Don't that sound suspicious to you?"

"Well, natchally it do, *now*," she said, as if I were the one who needed to get set straight. "That's why I be calling you, boy. Get my money back."

"So you went ahead and paid this hokey Deacon two hundred dollars for a holy number."

"Yef," said Mildred. "Matthew, Chapt twenty-five, Voice seven."

"And you played that number this week, I bet?"

"I don't like that tone of you voice, Ezell Barnes. You don't got to say nothing, boy. I know I sinned when I let greed get the better of me. I do not need you for to tell me that. And for that I know I deserves to be fleece by this false prophet in wolf's clothing, for inward, he were really a ravenin' wolf."

I let the pause grow on the line.

"Sheep's clothing, Mildred. Matthew, seven, Verse fifteen."

"Yef," said Mildred crankily. From experience, though, I knew she was pleased by my catechism.

"Did you go to the police to complain about this?"

"*Now* you talkin' like a fool, boy! How'm I gone go to a police, what with all them parkin' tickets they looking for me for! Hey?"

"Oh that," I said. "That still hanging over your head? Yeah, I guess the police are out of this, then. Well, did you go back and try to get your money from the Deacon?"

"How come you think they gone let me do that? Whar you brain, boy? Now you got to get right on it and do something!"

"All right," I said. I was thinking of my poor departed grandmother whose life was considerably shortened by having Mildred as her best friend. "I'll go talk to the Deacon for you. But I won't get anywhere, I can tell already. And if I do, I'm taking twenty percent recovery fee."

"Ten," said Mildred flatly.

"Ten percent of two hundred dollars is nothing."

"Ten dollars, I be saying."

"We'll discuss it after I see the Deacon, okay, Mildred? What's the number of his hotel suite?"

After Mildred hung up, I called the Deacon's suite and made an appointment to see him. First time slot they had open was seven-thirty that evening. Fine. Name? Mr. A. Gabriel, I said.

Chapter 5

When I parked in front of the vacant lot on Laurel Gardens which housed the community garden, the place was buzzing like a fire drill. Mrs. Pasquale was staking each broccoli and cauliflower plant with a thin bamboo rod. Mrs. Washington, upper arms bulging out of her dress, baseball catcher's shin guards strapped on, was on her knees viciously weeding around the carrots and turnips. Frail Mrs. Everett was clutching a hoe handle taller than her and scrubbing patiently at the paths between vegetable rows.

Two elderly men together were pulling coils of hose from the back of an old truck and attaching it to the faucet that the City had tapped for us off the nearest fire hydrant. On the other hand, the Field Marshal, decked out as always in his old army uniform, sat on the sidewalk in his lawn chair, eating hot dog after hot dog from the Sabrett's cart on the corner, drinking wine, and directing pedestrian traffic.

One, two, three, four, five, six, and me is seven. You need ten gardeners minimum to qualify for the national community garden contest. Too early for either Cosmo or Angel to show up yet, but I had complete trust in both of them. It was Ramone I needed to worry about.

"Mrs. Pasquale," I started, over by the brassicas. "You said you'd be responsible for Ramone showing up today. Althea's given us about twenty chances more than we deserve, you know. But this is the last one. Ramone's *got* to be here."

Her answer was to hand me a batch of bamboo stakes. "Shut up and get staking, Ezell," she snapped. "Ramone's out getting us all a cool drink. He'll be back shortly, I guarantee. Where is your friends that was going to be numbers nine and ten?"

"They'll turn up," I said.

One of the hose men yelled, "Lavinia dint write up the plant list the way they wanted it."

Little Mrs. Everett dropped her hoe, stuck her wrists on her hips, and I swear she blushed. "That's a lie," she screamed. "Make that lizard stop it, Ezell. I got the plant list right here in my pocket, just what they want."

"Snookie," I said. "You want to cool it for today, man? For once, we got to work as a team."

Snookie Izard laughed like a donkey. Two o'clock, he already had a major package tied on.

"Everything okay, Mrs. Washington?" I called. She nodded grimly and glared at the few remaining weeds around the beets. Made you glad you weren't on her weeding list.

Down the block came Ramone Pasquale, strutting and cool-hoofing it, paper-wrapped six-packs of something under each arm. He nodded to me.

"Ramone," I said. "Stick around, man. Don't get lost."

Ramone hefted the two packages. "Behind the fact we got beers to drink, man."

Between the sweet potatoes and the bush beans, Ernie Horton was trying to tug the sprinklers into place along with drunk old Snookie Izard, who was hindering more than he helped.

"Ernie, man," I said. "Why don't you get the Field Marshal to help you with that?"

Ernie turned his full indignation on me. "That fool! Sit there morning to night eating freaking franks, getting fall-down drunk!"

Snookie started giggling. "Field Marshal got a wiener on his back," he howled.

"That's right, baby!" hooted the Field Marshal. "I the man with the Guldens arm!"

I said, "Just so you're conscious, when Althea gets here to count us, make sure there's ten of us gardening like the contest rules say."

"Althea coming today?" shouted the Field Marshal. "Good! I like Althea. I got the official name of this garden all picked out, and it's a beauty."

"What you say?" Ernie said, getting belligerent.

By then, all eight of us had gathered by the sprinklers. Everybody looked at me.

"Go ahead, Field Marshal," I said. "What's your idea for our official name? You all know we got to pick one today."

The Field Marshal looked around. "The Laurel Gardens Gardens," he intoned proudly.

Ramone Pasquale sniggered. The ladies looked at each other.

"Asshole!" yelled Ernie Horton. "We go name the garden after you and the Snookman, we can call ourselves the Whiskey Sowers."

Everybody giggled at that.

"Wait a minute," said Snookie. He pointed to the street where Angel was wiggling out of his cab in toreador pants and high heels.

"We name it after Ezell's friend, we better call ourselves the Newark Hoers," Snookie said.

Ramone hee-hawed for a minute after everyone else stopped.

"Make him shut up, Ezell," said Mrs. Washington, "or I'm going to do it for you."

"How about it, Ramone?" I said, pinning him down

with my eyes. "You come up with a name for the garden?"

"Tell him that good name you come up with, Ramone," his mama said. "The one you told you parole officer about."

Ramone spat, large and noisy. "I got a name for you," he said. "You ready?"

"Yes," encouraged Mrs. Everett. "We do want to hear your suggestion, Ramone."

"Call it Eggplants up the Ass," he said.

Snookie and the Field Marshal roared. Mrs. Everett looked hurt and Mrs. Pasquale a little embarrassed. Ernie was angry, but Mrs. Washington had really had enough.

"Shut up, Fool," she bellowed. "Ezell, I'm waiting for the day you take this boy in hand. Better do it soon. I'm about ready to jump in his face."

Mrs. Washington then looked at Mrs. Everett, who looked at Mrs. Pasquale, then nodded to Mrs. Washington.

"We women talked this name business over," Mrs. Washington began. "And we agreed on what we want. It's gonna be the Newark Sharecroppers, and we don't want to hear nothing more about it."

"Newark Sharecroppers it is," I said quickly. "We'll tell Althea that when she gets here."

"I am here," Althea called like music from the sidewalk. "How are you all today? Garden's looking goo-ood."

Everybody started smiling and cooing at Althea, but I moved right in on her. Althea's light skinned, tall, beautiful, and nineteen years old. It's her summer job while in college to help coordinate Newark's part in the federal Urban Garden program. With her help, we'd gotten the water hook-up, free tilling, seeds, and composted leaves, and the group had grown to ten. Well, close enough, I hoped. At first, it was just Mrs. Washington and Mrs. Everett who had puttered unofficially in the vacant lot for who knows how long. For years, when passing by, I used to stop and shoot the breeze with them. Then, a couple years ago, they convinced me I ought to put in a couple tomato plants myself, and I was hooked.

The Urban Garden program really lit a fire under us,

and this year they were sponsoring a national contest. Ten thousand dollars for community improvement to the grand winner. Two thousand to each of ten runners-up. One hundred national semifinalists, and our garden had already made it into the semifinals.

Althea smiled up at me and slipped her arm through mine. "I think Newark Sharecroppers is a wonderful name," she said. My turn to smile.

"Are all thirty of your vegetable varieties ready for me to inspect? Yes? Then are all ten of your official community gardeners here? I only count nine of you."

"Cosmo's late," I said. "Probably weekend traffic. Let's go count the summer squash."

"Ezell." She tugged me to a stop. "I've already stretched the rules by letting you count the Field Marshal and Ramone as gardeners. I've watched them. The most they ever contribute is a few wisecracks."

"The Field Marshal helps keep the grackles out."

"There are no grackles in the inner city. And another one of your gardeners looks like a Broad Street hooker. Somehow I can't picture her dirtying her knees. Does she actually *garden*?"

"I told you. This is above board. Both Angel and Cosmo drop by once a week to help with the gardening. That's all the contest rules require."

Mrs. Everett trotted up to us, beaming. "Ezell! The lima beans are sprouted. I can see one! That makes thirty vegetables! We done it!"

"Isn't the ground cold for lima beans?" Althea grinned. "They'll never make it to blossoms planted this late."

"Don't matter," I said. "They're in there. And they count, sweetie."

"Well, why not?" Althea said. "You all are trying so hard." Mrs. Everett hustled back to the others with the good news. I was starting after her when Althea stopped me. "Ezell, before we get on with it, I want you to know something. I think you have done a wonderful thing for these people. You are a special man, you know that? Very few able-bodied, employed men in all Newark are willing to

33

help out with a project like this." She squeezed my bicep. "I just wanted you to know that I admire you for it."

"Then have a drink with me tonight."

"We've been through this. You're old enough to be my father."

"You got one boyish father, then, baby. Let's get a chance to know each other better. You know you like me."

"You are very nice-looking, for an older man. But I'm leaving for Wellesley next Monday. You know that. There isn't time to get better acquainted."

"Then we better start soon, huh? Where do you live, East Orange? I'll pick you up about seven-thirty. No, wait, dammit. I have business to take care of at seven-thirty. I'll pick you up at ten-thirty, eleven."

"Ezell!" Althea was laughing at me. "I don't go out at eleven o'clock. What would my parents think? Especially if a middle-aged man came for me in a pickup truck?"

"Then meet me somewhere. Meet me at the Chess Club on Washington Street. Eleven o'clock or thereabouts. Will you?"

Althea shook her pretty head, then grinned. "I guess I'm a glutton for punishment, Ezell. But, okay. Just don't be too late, or I may not be there."

Hot diggity. By now Mrs. Everett and Mrs. Pasquale were tugging at Althea's arms, too excited to wait any more for the official count. They started with the cole crops. I wandered out to the sidewalk to look for Cosmo. My watch said three-forty. He ought to be driving up any minute.

The first car to pull over on the garden block was a little silver Mercedes two-seater, carrying a woman. She swung her legs out, smoothed her tailored skirt, and high-heeled it straight for me. I watched her every step. This was a fine-looking woman in her late twenties, tall, clear cocoa-brown skin, cool features, bright eyes and a mouth made for sarcastic smiles or kisses. Her eyes moving up and down me made something tighten up my backbone.

"Hello." Off with my new lid. "You looking for me?"

"Who are you?" said the lady, with a trace of mockery. Her voice was low and educated. The tailored wool suit clung just snug enough, cut just above the knees.

"Well, I'm Ezell Barnes. How about you?"

"I'm Mrs. Epps."

"Mrs. Walter Epps? Wife of the man that killed himself last night? I'm sorry about your husband, ma'am."

"Your secretary told me you would probably be here. I've just come from Police Headquarters. I talked to someone named Detective Dorey in the Homicide Bureau. The police are reporting my husband's death as a suicide, pending the Medical Examiner's examination."

She paused. I nodded. "Go on."

"He told me you were present in our home last night just after Walter's death. Evidently Walter had called you for some sort of professional assistance?"

I nodded again. A low-rider steamed past us, stuffed with T-shirted kids. They yelled to the Field Marshal, who waved his frank at them.

"Just what did my husband hire you to do?"

I put my hat back on.

"You're jumping ahead pretty fast here," I said. "Last night, I got this phone call from a man that wouldn't identify himself, or even say what his problem was. Around midnight last night. He just gave me your house address and set up a meeting for right away. By the time I drove over and got into the house, your husband was already dead and the police were already on the scene."

Mrs. Walter Epps was giving me a look I didn't like. "Do I have to offer you money before you will talk honestly to me, Mr. Barnes?"

"Ouch! Dorey tell you about the blackmailer that clocked me in your backyard?"

"The murderer, is more like it."

I won't deny a pulse of interest.

"Walter was being blackmailed," I said. "Blackmailers don't often kill their victims. Too hard collecting the money from them that way."

"My husband would not have been frightened by those photos the police showed me."

"Oh? Why's that?"

"For one thing, Walter's sexual preferences were no se-

35

cret to me. Nor were they a secret to most of his acquaintances. The police naively assume that I should be shocked by Walter's bisexuality. Really. Do you suppose a woman can be married to a man for eight years without discovering something of his deepest needs?"

Two pig-tailed girls in tight jeans roller-skated down the slope so fast and so uncontrolled that I just snatched Mrs. Walter Epps off the ground and spun her out of the way.

Nice as it felt to touch her, I put her down and my hands back in my jacket pockets.

"Whew! Where were we? You sure your husband wasn't anxious to keep those Batman and Robin snapshots out of his friends' hands? He that shameless?"

The woman hadn't turned a hair when I grabbed her.

"I'm saying that the existence of those photos would not have driven Walter to desperation. He would simply have purchased the incriminating evidence from his enemies."

"Well, that's point number two. The police don't think your husband had a hundred thousand dollars."

"Don't you be an innocent, too," she said. "My husband lived in the city of Newark all his life. He managed government projects for twenty years. He knew everyone, and everyone knew him. His tiny thumb was right next to theirs in dozens of schemes and plots. The sources of his money would hardly bear the light of day, but he would find enough of it."

"Where did your mister keep his money?"

She raised an eyebrow.

Mrs. Washington and Mrs. Pasquale were making a racket. "Ezell! Come quick! Althea won't count the nasturtiums as a vegetable!"

I glanced over at the group. They were all having a great time squabbling, except for Angel, who was glaring at Mrs. Epps' outfit, and Althea, who was staring at me with a little coolness.

"Excuse me," I said to Mrs. Epps. "Nasturtiums count," I shouted to Althea. "You eat the pods like capers."

Snake in the Grasses

"Is there somewhere we can talk?" Mrs. Epps pulled out a skinny cigarette and let me light it for her. "I'd like to hire you to prove that my husband was murdered."

I thought that over. "Why not let it lie? Walter Epps wasn't doing much good for you, sounds like."

"Oh, true enough," she said casually. "I had no great love left for my husband. We lived our own separate lives."

"Life insurance, then? Walter have a suicide clause in his policy?"

"Something like that."

"Funny that you stayed together."

She shrugged and shook her mane.

"We had our arrangement. Walter was a more-than-good bread winner. He was always generous with me."

"Publicity worry you, his homosexuality becoming gossip column news?"

"I can do without becoming the laughing stock of Newark."

"What was your husband's edge?"

"Oh, he needed a woman on his arm at political functions, and a wife on his résumé for job appointments. Being photographed with a younger woman did something for his ego. Walter had plenty of ego, believe me."

"Well, that explains why he married such a beautiful younger woman, Mrs. Epps."

"Thank you," she said, still cool but more friendly. She hadn't puffed more than twice on her smoke, but was holding it decoratively. Now she tossed it into the gutter. Out the corner of my eye I caught Ramone starting for the good-sized butt, and I waved him away.

"What will it take to get you interested in me and my problem?" she asked, turning on a thousand-watt smile.

That smile had me spinning. What was I going to lose? Easy answer: I'd be annoying the hell out of two cops named Dorey and Mooney, who wanted this case closed and forgotten. I need to work with the cops in the city of Newark. What was to gain? A day or two's pay. A chance to spend more time with a fine-looking, uptown woman.

What I said was: "We got two concrete leads, then?

37

Walter's openness about his sexual preferences, plus his access to at least a hundred-thousand dollars. That's all mighty circumstantial, Mrs. Epps."

"Ruth," she said.

"What'd the police say?"

"They, they weren't listening to me very much, Ezell."

It was enough to go on.

"Okay, I'll help you out, Ruth." She smiled at me; I returned the compliment. There was another commotion from the gardeners, but this time I ignored them. "Of course, I can make no promises. It's doubtful I'm going to find much that's different from what the police got. But it's your money."

"Thank you." She lowered her eyes and said I-don't-know-what with them. "How will you start?"

"I'll start," I said, clearing my throat, "by looking over the police reports. And I'll show up at the morgue autopsy tomorrow afternoon. Two hundred dollars a day is what I get paid for this kind of work, and a retainer is customary."

"How much?" Not a trace of money worry in her voice. Maybe Ruth Epps did know where old Walter socked his nest egg away?

"How about three days' salary in advance?"

She just pulled bills from her purse, handed me six of them, and tucked the rest away.

"What's the best way to reach you, Ezell?" Two rumbling diesel-semis crossing where we stood forced her to shout. "Not here again, please!"

"I'll call you. Pretty soon, too. I'll need a list of your husband's friends and acquaintances, business and social. As many of them as you can think of."

Ruth Epps blew me another satisfied smile that made something in me howl.

"You'll be in touch, then," she nodded. Without another word, she walked to her car, shoulders moving beautifully.

I stood watching her until Angel jabbed me on the arm.

"Okay for Angel to go now?" he asked. "Is getting cold, Papi."

"Yeah, of course," I said, looking around. "Where is everybody?"

"They all go home."

"Cosmo show up?"

"Yas. He come and get counted, then go home too."

"Everything check out for the garden contest?"

"Yas."

"Well, thanks for helping out, Angel. I owe you."

Angel sighed. "Angel would do anything for you, Easy. You only gotta ask. You come watch me dance later?"

"Wish I could. Got to change out of these gardening clothes and go take care of some business in a little while."

"Yas. You got business with that dragon lady. With department store clothes. How come she got to hustle you at the garden, Papi?"

"Come on, Angel. That's a new client of mine. We were talking straight business."

"Sure."

"Well, I admit. I hope it won't always be straight business with me and her."

As usual, it took Angel only a split second to start fuming.

"Gotta run, man," I said, moving, "I'll come watch you dance tomorrow night, I promise."

Chapter 6

I scooped up a meatball sub on the way and finished it before I got home. To dress for shaking down Mildred's deacon I picked out a navy blazer, gray worsteds, and black wing tips. Striped tie. The soul of respectability. I figured the outfit would do for my date later with Althea, too.

Downtown, I circled until a spot opened up near the library, then hoofed it across little Washington Park to the Robert Treat Hotel. Somehow the traffic never lightens up in Newark, though half the stores are closed evenings.

A big-shouldered, deadpanned man in sunglasses answered the door to Deacon Elmo Toledo's suite. Behind him, lounging in the living room armchairs were two cookie-cutter imitations: close-cropped Afros, expensively tailored cream suits, inscrutable sunshade stares. I wondered if any of them was packing heat, but the suits were so well cut you couldn't tell.

As for me, my right blazer pocket was crammed with .38 Colt revolver, the police special I resigned with.

The room was urban-hotel standard: ceiling to floor drapery covered one wall of tall picture window, maybe a balcony behind it. Thin beige rug, two washed-out armchairs, a matching sofa, a tiny unusable desk pushed against another wall. Colorful touches, like orange lamp shades and framed floral prints meant to brighten the scene.

So far, nobody'd said anything. Nobody looked like they were going to say anything. I broke the ice. "Where's the Deacon, man? My appointment's for seven-thirty. My time is valuable, even if his isn't."

The twin scowls didn't twitch as they watched me stride over and knock on what I figured was the bedroom door.

"Deacon be coming in a minute," said the man who answered the door. "Whyn't you sit here, quiet, 'til then?" He gestured at a chair.

I grinned and shook my head. The boys looked at each other. Before I could start in really getting under these cats' skins, the Deacon bustled in, stocky, short, and as noisy as his henchmen were silent.

"Now, what do we have here?" he boomed, grabbing my hand and squeezing it. "A child of the Lord come here to pray and rejoice in His goodness with God's humble servant! Lord Almighty, how my heart fills with the kindness of

40

the Creator to all that he has made! Let me ask you, son, have you come a long way? Shall we break bread, or perhaps take drink together, before we pray together to the Lord God Almighty that His will for you be done?"

"Well—" I started.

"What say, son, to the kindness of the cup? Leon, bring this pilgrim a libation, if you would, my boy."

All three goons stood up and moved to corners. This time, when the Deacon waved me to an armchair, I did sit down.

Leon brought coffee cups to the Deacon and me. I sipped at mine. Straight hooch. Meant to loosen up the vocal cords and the purse strings, no doubt.

Deacon Elmo lifted his cup to me and smiled. His silver mustache was the most magnificent I had ever seen, I admit. Except that when he drank it glistened with drops. The Deacon studied me taking a second sip, then he leaned forward and looked me solemnly in the eye.

"My son, I feel something very special here this evening. You have come for a purpose, I know that. Let us pray to God Almighty that your prayers can be answered at this time. I will do what I can to enable God's will." The Deacon paused politely for me.

"Good," I said. His canned dynamism was making it fun to goof on him. "There is something you can do for me."

"You have only to speak it, my son, and if God's hand is visible to me in your request, then I am His humble agent, and yours. Wait, let me show His power: does what you are seeking involve a number?"

"Correct," I said and toasted him. Then I carefully placed my cup down, stood up, and took the pistol out of my pocket.

Chapter 7

The next morning I skipped my habitual roadwork through the park. I needed something more soothing while I took stock of the night before. So I pulled on my oldest ratty khakis, let a faded flannel shirt ride tails out, and plunked a soft round hat on my head. I picked up my ultralite fishing pole, just a skinny five feet long, with its tiny reel. Into my breast pocket I tucked a one-inch square box of no. 9 gold hooks and split shot and a small plastic bag.

Out my front door and around back to the garden, where two shovelfuls out of the compost bin filled my beer can with thick pink night crawlers. Snake-worms, Ernie and I called them. None of the other Sharecroppers were around yet. Just as well. If Ernie and Snookie saw me going fishing, they'd want to tag along for sure. This morning, I could use some alone time.

Where Park Avenue runs over Branch Brook Lake, that skinny pond widens to about a hundred twenty feet. It's the deepest pool too, maybe ten feet in the middle. The feet of fishermen and winos have beaten down the banks there to bare clay. But you can still catch fish, if you know what to do. And if you have some patience.

At nine A.M., the spot was deserted. I let the rod butt touch the ground, while I threaded the biggest crawler until the little gold hook was completely hidden, even the eyelet. Fumbling in my breast pocket, I scooped out two BB split shots and clamped them twelve inches above the hook with my teeth. Then I flipped over the spinning reel's bail and cast right at the center of the pool, directly under the Park Avenue bridge.

Lots of people who fish there fix bobbers to their lines

and lay their poles down to crack open a beer. You don't
catch much fish that way, as far as I'm concerned.

Overhead, cars and trucks whooshed and rattled over
the bridge. I studied the transparent floating line and gave
the worm a tiny twitch every few seconds. Wasn't twenty
seconds before the surface line coils began straightening,
then came the tugging on the rod tip. I tugged back to set
the hook, let him play himself out, then cranked him in.

Out flopped a yellow perch, beautiful gold belly. Be
good eating, too. A real prize, though I never mind whatever I catch, pumpkinseed sunnies, bluegills, sharp-lance
old catfish, even a leftover hatchery trout, now and then.

The sun was out clear and making my forehead sweat. I
gutted the fish, pared out the gills, and wrapped it in a
plastic sandwich bag.

I cast again. I watched the thick stream ripples turn
glassy and reflect the sun in different colors.

Last night's work had been inconclusive, all around.
But not without promise. The Deacon's boys hadn't batted
an eye at my revolver, the Deacon had faked elaborate surprise and sorrow and then vehemently denied that
Mildred's two-hundred dollars represented anything but a
donation to his pastorship, freely given.

It ended in a temporary stalemate, me threatening to
annoy Deacon Toledo as often as it took to retrieve
Mildred's money, him calling down God's forgiveness on me
over and over as I left, like a man possessed.

My date with Althea afterwards, also inconclusive,
wound up at three A.M. on the doorstep under her parents'
bedroom windows. After three hours of trying, I couldn't
talk her into going home with me. But there was lots of
laughing and a sweet, not-too-short kiss at the end. Maybe
I'd see her again before she left for school, we agreed.

My line had been soaking in the stream for a long time
with no action. I eased it in, twitch by twitch, without luck.
I looked at the sun again; high enough now for me to get a
move on.

After my shower, I dipped the perch in cornmeal,

browned it in butter, and cooked two jumbo eggs sunny-side up. Fried fish is better than bacon for breakfast. After two cups of hot brew, I was off to Police Headquarters.

That boxy gray fortress, a city block long, is hunched just behind City Hall. Detective bureaus are on the third floor. Courts are in there too, on the fourth floor. Across an enclosed fourth-floor walkway is the city jail. The "Dead House," it was called in the old days when justice was swift, though no more certain. Arrest them, try them, and march them across the covered bridge to the jail house. No revolving doors back then. By the time I joined the force, those days were changing once and for all. Now the locked-up street punks yell mouths of shit down at passersby from the cellblock windows. God help the female who picks her path to work between those two buildings.

Just inside the main entrance to Police HQ sits an information desk, leaned on by the standard-issue alcoholic cop. Humming to himself, he'll be, and making hard faces at the civilians who wander in. There's plenty of cops they just got to get off the street and behind a desk where they can't hurt someone. The rubber-gun squad, they call them. The trick is not to pay a desk man like that any mind at all. I took my cue from the plainclothes detectives ahead of me, beelined for the elevator at the rear of the lobby, and rode it up to the third floor. Another desk there, where I told the drunk that Mooney was waiting to see me. For that, I got to cool my heels twenty minutes or so.

The old building was even more tired than I recalled, with that cheesy tan or green glossy paint, all chipped up and filthy, like it was covered with a thin coat of gritty vaseline. Pink-flecked linoleum floors were worn through to the subflooring. A locked iron door on the right led from the reception area to the Bandit Squad, Fraud Squad, Auto Squad and the District Squads. A bigger door on the other side let you into the shadow world of Homicide. I clocked it. Twenty-seven minutes before that door opened and Mooney popped his head out.

"Won't take but a minute, Barnesie. Follow me, will ya?"

Homicide boys lived in a single big room. Maybe fifty feet by thirty, it was semidivided into two squad rooms by beige metal and frosted glass partitions that didn't reach much above a man's shoulders. Maybe eight men sat in each half of the room, looking as if they called it home. There were a couple of makeshift offices, probably for lieutenants.

Mooney led me past the men's and women's room doors, then past another door on which was taped a poster listing the Miranda rights in two-inch letters. Sort of an eye chart for the legally blind.

"You been up here before, right?" said Mooney. He was sitting behind his desk. I took the aluminum chair alongside it.

"Couple times when I was in uniform. Picked up characters wanted on homicide warrants, had to drop them off up here."

"Coffee?" Mooney picked a mug off his desk and was heading off.

"Why not? Make it black, though. No sugar. Just the caffeine."

"Right," Mooney called. "Don't confuse nutrition with drugs."

I swiveled around to take the place in. Probably fifteen desks in all, doubled up on by team partners. Each with its own beat-up manual typewriter. Never did see a police typewriter that had the top part of its housing still in place. They have this way of breaking when they get thrown at suspects.

Not much else in the room. A few mug shots, some out-of-date calendars, pictures of girlfriends, and a whole lot of gummy, unventilated air. Couple of homicide sergeants sat two desks away, shooting the shit. You could almost see the invisible wall between them. The lines in their faces spoke of how much they'd seen in their time. Steady diet of stiffs'll make anybody strange, I guess. A lot of homicide cops strike people as tight-lipped and defensive because of how much they like thinking well of themselves. They're just making sure nobody will ever get the chance to make a fool of *them*.

Dale Mooney sloshed a Styrofoam cup of coffee down in front of me. Then he propped his Hush Puppies up on the edge of his desk. That surprised me. Toughboy dress code did not include either red cardigan sweaters or Hush Puppy loafers. Maybe the Pat Boone look was coming back in hard-boiled circles?

"Jeez, is this a piece of candy. A statement from you is not even necessary any more, the finding being suicide and all. Might as well do it, though. In case two months from now some idiot starts hollering murder or something." Mooney was scrawling on a legal pad in his lap and dripping steaming coffee from his mug.

"About that," I said. "I just finished talking to one person who thinks it was a murder."

"Epps' wife?"

"The same."

"Figures. Some people take it as a family disgrace, old Waldo whacks himself."

"She asked me to look into it for her. That a problem for you?"

"Oh, shit," said Mooney, reasonably. "A job is a fucking job, Barnesaroo." He wound the form through the carriage of his typewriter. "Long as she's meeting your asking price, why not string her along for the buck? Of course, you seen the photos of Epps making like the Caped Crusader. Not to mention him swinging in the breeze *au naturel*. Nobody has to convince you this is one guy that did it his way."

"That's pretty much how I see it, too. You talk to the lady in question?"

"Eddie did. We talked over everything he got from her."

"She doesn't think her husband made a big secret of being gay."

"What she means is, *she* more or less knew what tricks he was up to. That don't mean the whole city of Newark, including the government folks that employed Walter Epps, were up-to-date on it." Dale grinned like a jack-o'-lantern. "Besides," he said, "it's one thing to come out of the closet.

46

It's something else to come out wearing a Batman costume, you know?"

"Where'd those pictures come from, you find out yet?"

"Just made them half an hour ago. This degenerate that manages a porn palace on Washington Street ID'd Epps' masked friend there. Didn't recognize Epps in the slightest, by the way. Pics were snapped at this sex club in Manhattan, The Blastoff Pad. Guy'd seen a million like them. Said some of these perverts go in there and pay up front to get the photos taken of them in the act. Get their rocks off that way. Sometimes, this guy said, they take pictures of the shy types with a hidden camera, and then squeeze the poor fools. Like Epps."

"You trace the photographer? Or the model posing with Epps in the pictures?"

"That we did," Mooney said between sips of coffee and sharpening his pencil. "And guess what we found? Dead. Both of them. Couple months ago. Lovers' pact, it was. Romantic. Gave each other poisoned lambrusco. Word is, soon as the news leaked out, place they had uptown was ransacked for these kinds of pictures. Thousands of them, they had. Somebody, or maybe a bunch of somebodies, looking for blackmail scores."

"Mind if I look over your file when we finish with my statement?"

"Course not. Be my guest. Got all sorts of personal data on Walter Epps there. Jot some of it down and impress the widow. Make her think you're out there pounding the bricks for clues." Mooney tossed a manila case folder across the desk to me.

"Other thing Epps' old lady laid on me is how he's got so much off-the-record money. Swears he could buy off the blackmailers, no sweat."

"You ever talk to a wife didn't think the old Turk didn't have the mattress stuffed with fifties? Is she talking about a bank book we could look at? Or just her personal feelings?"

"The second, I think. Medical Examiner look at Epps yet?"

"One o'clock this afternoon. You looking to come along? Glad to have you. That'll clinch it, of course. Can't close any case out officially as a suicide until we get the old verdict from the coroner. Hey, going to the autopsy's gonna look just great with the widow! Ever been to one?"

"What, autopsy? Nah. But I seen plenty of blood and guts in my day as a cop. And over in Nam, too. I be all right."

"Yeah, I figured you would. Just wanted to lay fair warning on you, is all. This's a little different, is all."

"Thanks for the helpful tip, Dale. How different?"

"Let me put it this way to you, buddy. Try not to lick your lips."

"What?"

"During the autopsy," said Mooney. "All this crap is floating around in the air and sticking to your lips. Don't lick your lips. You do, you're gonna taste it all. Which is sure to make you toss your cookies."

"And they say friendship is a lost art."

"At your service, buddy. You want to lay your statement on me now?"

For the better part of the next half hour I talked. Then, while Mooney typed up my version of Walter Epps' death, I thumbed through the folder on Epps. The police file contained little. As for money, Epps made $37,500 a year as director of Family Planning Services, Inc., a federally funded project. No other sources of income listed. No substantial bank accounts noted. As for his sexual preferences, statements from Epps' friends were few and tight-lipped.

When Mooney finished, I read my statement over, initialed one corrected typo, and signed it.

"First assignment I ever handled that I could honestly say was a caper," Mooney announced. He was playing with his empty Styrofoam cup.

"How long you been in homicide?"

"I made Detective about two years ago," Mooney grinned. "Making my move up in the world finally."

"You must miss being in the Mobile Crime Lab, though. Camera work and all."

"Yeah." Mooney sighed. "I do. That was a job I really liked, I was seeing one out every three homicides in the city."

"You were born for that job," I laughed. "Freaking ghoul is what you are."

"How's about you, Barnesie? You making ends meet out there in the private sector?"

"Same old same-old," I shrugged. "It's one-third bank drops and payroll pickups, one-third motel-watching for divorce cases, and one-third waiting for some merchant's stockboy to back up to the loading dock after hours. Maybe twice a year something more interesting rolls in."

"You were how many years on the force before you packed it in?"

"Eleven and change."

"So your pension had vested at least."

"Sure. I'll spoon up a heaping twenty-five percent of the salary I resigned at, if I live to age fifty-five."

"Why the hell did you quit with only eight years to go for a full pension?"

"Remember that sergeant's list they killed a few years back?"

"Nah." Mooney shook his head. "I never give making rank any thought so I don't pay no attention to those things."

"Yeah, well, I gave making rank a lot of thought and time too," I said. "Even enrolled in John Jay College and got my bachelor's degree in Police Science. Anyway, I took the sergeant's exam and did real good, fifth. You know they normally name forty or fifty sergeants off each list. I came out high enough to get made for sure."

"But the bastards killed your list before they were forced to promote a black guy to sergeant's rank?"

"I could read the writing on the wall," I said. "I quit."

"Yeah, but you should have hung on, Barnesie," Mooney said. "Times changed in the department. Plenty of black guys in the upper ranks now. Sharp college guy like you would have soared to the top."

I grinned and then changed the subject.

"You got to be somewhere, Dale? You want to eat lunch or something?"

"Got a better idea. We got two hours to kill before the autopsy. We'll head over to my gym. Work out. Sound good?"

"All I do any more is run in the morning a little. Ain't sparred in years, or weights or anything like that."

"Aw, come on. You're my guest today. You don't got to jump in the ring or nothing. Jump some rope, do a little bag work, toss the weights around some. We'll take some steam, spend about thirty seconds in the sauna. You'll feel like a million bucks. Come on."

"Maybe I'll take you up on that," I said. "I got a gym bag in the heap, as a matter of fact. Where you working out these days? You're not taking me to the police gym, are you?"

"That dump? Hell, no. Place was like a dungeon. Department didn't keep it up." Mooney threw on his leather jacket and holstered his revolver on his hip. "Quite a few cops got memberships at the Turkish Baths. You know, that joint on Mulberry Street."

"Place is crawling with Muslims," I said. "The hell are white cops doing over there?"

"No more," said Mooney. "Used to be. Used to be a club for fighters. Mostly Muslim boxers. But when the health boom came, the owner jumped right on it and split the place up in two. He's got half for his stable of boxers to train in. And he's got a new section for the body beautiful crowd. Easy way to turn a buck."

"Owner's name is Fahriq, right? Hassan Fahriq?"

"Yeah. Know him?"

"Used to, way back when. Want me to drive over, meet you inside? That way we can each drive to the M.E.'s office from the gym."

"Sounds good. Just tell the broad on the desk that you're my guest. She'll put you on my tab. Meet you in the locker room."

Chapter 8

Sign said TURKISH BATHS now, and they'd angled the roof line to look modern, and covered the outside with orange formica or something. But the place had been known as the Mulberry Street Gym to the army of pugs waiting for their big break to break. Shot at fighting on the card at St. Nicks, Jersey City Armory, or maybe, if you really got lucky, a prelim at Madison Square Garden. Me, I was twenty-one years and a good twenty pounds trimmer then. Plenty game, pretty damned savvy, but definitely limited as a puncher. No more lucky than the others, either.

I checked in at the carpeted lobby. Mooney was waiting in the locker room.

"Place is really different now, huh, Barnes." Mooney was beaming.

"You're telling me. Don't remember nobody wearing a powder blue jogging suit with racing stripes last time I was here. You do any sweating, Dalie? Or you just walk around the gym and pose?"

"I am gonna take a walk, right now," said Mooney. "Them clothes of yours smell like you been mopping up the gym floor with them."

"I can meet you out there, if it bothers you, Dale."

Tattered sleeveless sweat shirt, short frayed cutoffs, old lace-up boxing shoes. That musty old smell that never quite washes out of my gym clothes dredged up a warm memory of workouts gone by. I looked at the stained hand wraps wound up in my bag, then figured I wouldn't be sparring and tossed them into the bottom of the locker.

Out on the gym floor, the equipment looked good, shiny and complicated, but like you could raise a sweat just the same.

51

"This is the general public side of things," said Mooney." Exercise bikes are behind that partition. Nautilus, free weights, mats're right in here. Racquetball courts, indoor track're downstairs."

"How do I get to the other side?"

"That door over there. But they probably won't let you through. They don't like to let the nonfighters in unless you know somebody."

"What you talking, nonfighter? Used to work out here, my man. Probably still know some of the players. I'm gonna try my luck."

"Sure. Meanwhile, I'm in here on the machines, Barnesie. Soon's I'm finished, I meet you over there, okay? We'll go for steam. You see this gorilla in the ring ripping people's heads off, that'd be Ray Velnarsky. Guy we work with at Homicide. Works out with the fighters, which is not too popular with them. I'm gonna introduce the two of you later."

At the door, I got lucky and ran into this old corner man on the boxing gym door. We swapped a few memories, hee-hawed for a while. You had the best left hand I ever saw on a light heavy, he told me. Could not punch myself a time card, I said. But it was nice of him to lie, anyhow.

Inside was like the dark side of the moon compared to the body beautiful side. The close sweet stench of old sweat hugged me like a warm, wet blanket. A big two-minute clock in the room's center ticked off the seconds left in the round. Two twelve-by-twelve-foot rings filled opposite corners. Two sets of boxers ground away at each other, dull thuds caroming off the tan tile walls, mixing with the machine-gun cadence of the speed bags.

Next to me, a tar-colored beast worked the taped heavy bag with jolting hooks and short rights. The bag lurched slowly after each shot. And this was the extra-lead bag. You got to hit those things a ton to jar them at all. He was grunting, targeting each and every punch, sucking down air like a steam engine through the mouthpiece clamped in his jaws.

Two shadow boxers worked their mirrored foes from side to side. Up and down and in and out. Others skipped rope, some mechanically, one or two crossing hands and double-twirling.

The bell sounded an end to the tougher of the two matches and the couple in the ring climbed out. The mauler working the heavy bag next to me straightened up to watch when the new fighters climbed between the ropes. Me too. It was a classic match-up. Boxer versus a walloper. The round started, and the dude with the heavy punch unloaded on his opponent right away with a flurry. Hoping for a quick KO, he pinned the quicker man to the corner ropes. Corralled in a small ring like that, you can't maneuver worth a dime. The puncher worked the body over with liver and kidney shots, waiting for the arms to drop to protect the gut. Then he'd move up top to the head with uppercuts and hooks.

At least that was the plan. But every time the puncher bore down, a hissing jab licked out at his eyes. Third time, he pulled his head back, and the boxer was free and out into the ring. Across the ring the puncher stalked him, and soon blood began to trickle from a deepening gash over one eye.

The bell clanged. I gave that round to the boxer. But over the long haul, if you can't knock a puncher out or stop him on cuts, more times than not, you're gonna hit the canvas with your face. I should know, that being why I gave up prizefighting and became a cop.

I grabbed a rope dangling from a row of hooks and commenced to twirling it, just stepping at first, letting the loop rub the floor under my soles. When the lower legs began to loosen up, I set that rope to whirring some. I was way too rusty to get fancy, and soon enough the old legs would be lead to pick up. But at least I handled the rope well enough to show a few of the young bloods around that I was no stranger.

The timekeeper yelled, "Let's get in there, Velnarsky. We got a gym to run here."

The locker door opened on the far side of the gym, and the light in its frame was blotted out by a massive rawboned head. Short red curls on a skull that looked two inches thick, one of those Frankenstein skulls that the Slavic people sometimes have. Looked like you'd need a sledge-hammer just to dent him.

Crossing the gym floor and up through the ropes, Velnarsky moved on his toes, pro linebacker–style. No headgear for him. Not even a mouthpiece. He just rolled that thick neck and shoulders and waited for his opponent to get ready.

Other boxer that climbed into the ring was the tar-colored water buffalo who'd been working on the heavy bag. Even bigger than Velnarsky, he was. Built like Hercules, too. Slabs of leg muscle, shoe-box sized. He stopped to pull on the headgear, though, and slipped his mouthpiece back in. Both men stuck padded guards over their shoes and came out at the clang of the bell.

Velnarsky moved straight into his man, while the other circled to his left, keeping his body turned, then all at once moving to Velnarsky's opposite side, hoping to catch him swaying in the wrong direction, leading the way with a driving thrust at the white man's nose.

Velnarsky leaned his upper body back so naturally you'd think he was shadow boxing. With his left fist, he batted the water buffalo's face, lunging in, three times, fast. Then he broke clear and stood alone for a second, bobbing a little and rolling his gloves over each other like he was revving up.

The bigger man hopped on his toes a few times, edging closer, a pretty nice side movement. They circled a time or two, Velnarsky almost standing in place, letting the buffalo spin him around. Half a dozen jabs on both sides.

I'd moved right over to the ring to see this, and now I took a quick look over both shoulders. There was nobody doing anything in that gym but watching this bout.

Old water buffalo was looking pretty sharp. You'd never think he could shuffle like that. What's more, I'd seen him jolt that lead bag shot after shot, with both hands. He was giving old Velnarsky the big upper body weave now. One minute into the round.

Both fighters were faking leg kicks, jerking up a knee quick and often. But nobody had swung the extended leg around yet. I had watched kick boxing a couple times before. And you always knew what was coming.

This time it came when the buffalo cocked his left fist and sent it up low, at Velnarsky's chest, leaving a big hole over his guard for that red-haired ape to come in through. Velnarsky could have driven his car through that hole.

To an old pro, it was an obvious enough trick. Big black man left that hole on purpose, hoping for Velnarsky to lean towards him. Already he was arching back, starting to swing up the left hip and whip the left leg around, concentrating the full force into his foot, and aiming straight at Velnarsky's thick head. When that foot smacked home, the buffalo's body would be turned completely around, back thigh muscles lined up for the mule kick.

Which never landed. Without blinking, Velnarsky routinely picked off the chest punch and stepped neatly inside the other man's stretched-apart legs. Right then Velnarsky could have neutered old water buffalo for good. Instead, he dug a short twisting punch into the stomach. The huge man just crumpled from the force of that blow. But he didn't completely lose his feet. That happened a second later when Velnarsky stepped back, one, two, three, then powerdrived a leg cruncher to the back of the black man's knee. You could hear the cartilage ripping up, water buffalo hollering his way to the canvas. Two swift leg flicks, to the side, to the head, settled his hash for a long time to come.

That gym was totally silent. The trainer was slapping his fighter, rubbing the salts under his nose. Velnarsky climbed out of the ring and unlaced his gloves. And then walked towards me.

The reason, as I suddenly noticed, was that Hassan Fahriq had slipped in next to me at ringside. All those young hopefuls went back to what they'd been doing, clearing out for Velnarsky.

"When are you going to get some decent fighters stabled here, Fahriq?"

"Your ass," Fahriq spat back. He deliberately lit a cigar with jeweled fingers. As always, he moved with more grace than you expect even in such a short, slender man. Who else could look relaxed and elegant wearing a dinner jacket in a noontime gym? "I wouldn't dare let any of my million-dollar prize fighters get in a ring with you, Ray. If you want to work out here, strictly hamburger is what you'll get."

"Woolley was no hamburger."

"No, Woolley was all right. Until somebody showed him odds he couldn't refuse. Used to be money in my pocket until a minute ago. You're not eating any more of my cash makers, baby."

"How about *you*?" Velnarsky swung on me. "You're big enough. You looking to spar? No kicking, just straight boxing between two heavyweights."

"Oh, Ray," Fahriq said. "Now you've gone and terrified the boy. Think he's stupid enough to climb through the ropes with you? This boy's been to college. Ain't that right, Barnes?"

"Ray Velnarsky."

"Ezell Barnes. Pleasure meeting you."

Velnarsky wrapped my hand up in his. Nothing vise-like, but enough to leave no doubt about the man's enormous strength. He felt as hard as Chinese arithmetic.

"Came down here with a fellow from your office, Dale Mooney," I said. "He's riding exercycles on the other side. I was giving him a statement on that Epps case."

"You were the one counting the stars at that death scene last night." Velnarsky's face looked grim even when he sneered.

Feeling the chill, Fahriq said quickly, "Listen. You want to step into my office and talk?"

Velnarsky shook his head. "Got to shower up and get a move on. You change your mind, Barnes, decide you want to mix it up, I'm always available."

We both watched his big muscles power Velnarsky into the locker room.

"Stir clear of that motherfucker, goddam animal," Fahriq said quietly. "I'm half-surprised he didn't lift his leg and piss on your feet." Fahriq eased out of his tux jacket. Under it, he was wearing a white silk shirt with puffy

sleeves and French cuffs. Black velvet arm bands pinched
the shirtsleeves back at each bicep. The onyx studs matched
one of his many rings. Only the silk navy blue bow tie was
standard Muslim dress.

"Those last two little kicks were cute."

"White man like that got no nerve endings in his body.
Heart of pig iron."

"He's itching for a piece of me, ain't he?"

"Shit. I'd give the numbers handle for a week to see
you straighten out that gorilla in the ring, buddy. Nothing
but a street fighter, you take away that kick boxing. That's
just shit he picked up in the commandos, or something."

"Looked pretty impressive against that big boxer of
yours."

"You don't see the kind of garbage that's taking up boxing these days. Ten, fifteen years ago, half the boys in this
gym could take that ape to pieces in the ring. Especially
you, with that speed of yours."

"What makes you think I still got it?"

"You look in shape. Let my boys bring you some big
gloves."

I squared off against the extra lead bag, because it was
free, shaking my shoulders loose. Then stabbing two right
hooks, two left ones. Trying to look nonchalant and praying
to rock that bag at least a little.

Fahriq was propped behind the bag, leaning into it so
it wouldn't jolt away from me too much. A compliment.

"You still starving in the land of plenty?"

"You got it," I said. "What's happening with you?" All
my roadwork gave me a decent wind. But my arms already
felt like cement.

"Same old shit with me, Barnes, just new flies is all. I
never have no trouble. Here, try and hit through the bag at
me. Aim it for my head. Now my belly. That's more like it,
buddy. Now you look like a fighter."

"Feel like cherry in a bowl of Jell-O."

I uncrouched to shake my shoulders and give a quick
look around. Every last soul in that gym was stopped in his

tracks, watching the big boss actually holding the bag for this over-the-hill palooka. Came in a has-been, but I was going out a legend, probably.

"You put on thirty pounds, looks like. You hit any harder than you used to?"

For answer, I laid into the bag with all my shoulders, and to my relief really made that lead bag jump. Hassan gave a little grunt.

Then he smiled. "Come on into my office, buddy," he said.

Two tuxedoed flunkies with matching dark shades were lizarding in Fahriq's big office. The shorter one was wide enough to confuse with a major appliance. Both jumped to their feet when we walked in.

"Praise be to Allah, brothers," Fahriq laid on everybody, not one trace of smile on his thin face. "The beneficent. The most merciful. Lord of the world who knows all things."

"*As-Salaam-Alaikum*," murmured the penguins, but they had their dark sunglasses trained on me.

"Praise be to his holy name. For he has brought us light, brothers. That we may see our way in the darkness." Fahriq looked at me.

"Show 'em you like 'em," I said.

"Welcome back, oh lost and found brother. And know that my house is your house. For our house is the house of Allah."

Fahriq swung a hand towards me and said to the blues brothers: "This is Brother Barnes. Please leave us alone now. For we have much to discuss, brothers."

The two grunted in unison, jammed black, short-brimmed hats on their heads, and penguined out. They'd be standing guard outside.

"This is pretty nice, Hassan," I said. "Couch feels like real leather. Last time we met, you were hawking watches off a tray on Branford Place."

"I had to hustle my ass off, too," Fahriq said, sitting down on a four-cushion velour sofa. "Or I'd still be on the corner."

"More like jail, the way I see it," I needled. "If you hadn't hustled your ass into my office that night, you'd either be dead or in stir for murder one."

Seven, eight years ago, I used to see Fahriq when he was working the streets around Branford Place, king of the two-bit scores. Then the scores got a little bigger, until Fahriq's partner smelled a double-cross in their tiny numbers operation. The ambush was set up for the Ritz Theatre across the street from my office. But even then Fahriq had more informants than anybody in Newark; he caught wind of the trap at the last minute, banged his shots off first, ducked out the fire exit under the big screen, and walked to the nearest refuge: my office.

No innocents hurt; just one less mob creep pimpling the streets. Who knows when a Fahriq favor will work magic for you? I let Fahriq hang in my office until I could sniff a clear coast, and off he scooted.

"So, Ezell Barnes." Fahriq smiled. "There something I can do for you, old friend?"

"Now that you mention it, there probably is. I figure you sniff out more of what's going down in Newark than a police dog, right? Got those mob connections and all. You still got those connections, don't you?"

Fahriq was enjoying this. "As far as the civilians are concerned, I *am* the mob, Ezell."

"Black mob."

"That's right. Just the black mob."

"Ever hear of a nobody named Walter Epps?"

Fahriq was busy getting a cigar lit. When he finally blew a jet of rich smoke across all the rings on his hands, I said: "He died last night, and I got the job of poking into it for his old lady. Ever hear the name?"

Fahriq added an inch to his smile. "Of course, I have heard the name before, baby." He circled the cigar with two fingers and waggled the other three. "These fingertips are on every last wiggle that gets wiggled in this city."

The dull thud of boxers working out in the gym thumped through the glass door of the office. Framed pictures of Fahriq's fighters challenged me from the walls.

"Sit down, would you, man? You make me nervous."
But Fahriq's big grin told me it would take much more than
me ever to jitter his nerves.

"Well?"

"Epps was no one important, just a flunky. Another
Indian in that tribe that runs City Hall. I buy and sell bigger fish than Walter Epps every day of the week."

The real Muslims turn sick every time they even think
about hoods like Fahriq.

"You ever buy or sell this Epps character?" I asked
him.

"He have anything worth buying or selling?"

"Evidently, he did. His ever-loving manhood. Know
anybody wanting to sell Walter Epps his reputation as a red-
blooded lady killer?"

"Man was a fag. Blackmail?"

"That's it. Seems some enterprising types caught old
Epps on film. Laid the photos on him with a demand for
one hundred large."

"Ain't that engrossin'." Fahriq was thoughtfully rolling
his cigar.

"Was Epps holding a hundred grand to pay off the
blackmailers?"

"Not a chance." Fahriq frowned. "Anybody has that
kind of stash, I'd know it. Besides, once the milk men start
in with a shakedown like that, they're out to pump you dry.
You don't get them off your back until you are dead and
buried."

The phone on Fahriq's desk rang. He hissed orders
into it in this money voice he has. Then he stood up from
behind his desk and matadored a velvet jacket around his
shoulders.

"Got to go tend some business arrangements," Hassan
said. "Really nice seeing you, old buddy. You stop down
whenever it suits you. Always welcome to work out with my
boys. You sparring any these days?"

"Just with you, old buddy. Otherwise, a little roadwork
is all."

"The offer stands. Come down even if you just need to

touch base on something. Any time. I still owe you for a thing or two."

"You owe me nothing, after all this time."

Fahriq gripped my arm just above the elbow. He was a slender, tough man, not a powerful one. But I could feel that energy of his connect us.

"I happen to know something else, Ezell. This Epps person no doubt took himself out, all right. But there are some people he was doing business with that will take offense at you snooping in his affairs. I would steer clear, if I was you. These are very short-tempered people I'm talking about."

"That so?"

Fahriq walked us to the outside door and reached for the knob.

"And they shoot in the back," he said.

Out on the gym floor again, we went our separate ways.

Chapter 9

A quick shower at the gym, and I scurried over just before one o'clock to the Medical Examiner's office next door to City Hospital on Cabinet Street. Sprinting in from the parking lot, I flashed my credentials on the blonde-bobbed receptionist who looked me over like I was sweating on the furniture. I gave her this big watermelon grin. When I asked for the Epps autopsy, she frowned and dialed up a Doctor Butterfield, icing me over her slim shoulder the whole time.

Down a long wood-paneled corridor. Mounted on the walls between office doors were autopsy photos somebody had carefully selected to turn that passageway into a ghoul's gallery.

Outside Butterfield's office was a specially revolting photograph. A young air force pilot, still in uniform, with this six-inch part in his hair. And in his skull. Next to him on the morgue slab was the propeller blade that did the parting.

"You ask me, Barnesie," Mooney's voice startled me, "I think it was the barber that killed him. Not the butler, not the maid, so it's got to be."

Dale was watching me from his chair just inside Butterfield's door. Behind the desk sat another man wearing seven hundred dollars worth of navy chalk-stripe over a gray silk shirt. The cuffs of the shirt were shot out from his suit cuffs to show the on-color embroidery stitching. When I stepped up to shake his hand, I got a gold-ring bruise on my knuckle and a quick whiff of something subtle and expensive. But oh so manly.

"Barnes here used to be a Newark cop," Mooney said.

Butterfield let go of my hand. His barber knew how to cope with a hairline in full retreat, I had to give him that. Still dark tan, in September, over an olive complexion. Quick, strong handgrip. Lean and maybe agile, not too tall. Handball puts you in that kind of shape. Squash, maybe, whatever that is. Butterfield was in his early forties, but looked the type that spends a lot of weeknights in the Manhattan dating bars, weekends in Vermont or Cape Cod, trying to hold at a virile twenty-five.

And doing a superb job, by the looks of it.

He said: "Coffee, gentlemen? Soft drink, maybe? My girl will get you something, if you like."

"Not for me, thanks," I said.

"That's the ticket, Barnesaroo. Go easy on the old stomach. It don't know what's coming up, does it?"

"Yes, I think that's wise." Butterfield's grin made slits of his eyes. "Especially if postmortem analysis procedures are new to you."

Butterfield and Mooney swapped a look. Seasoned hands. Virgin Barnes.

I was shifting around feeling uncomfortable. The

leather chair I'd plopped into had a big depression in the
seat bottom, so your butt sagged way down below your
knees. I wondered if old Butterfield had it fixed that way on
purpose. You never know. Some folks grab an edge wherever they can get it.

"Detective Mooney has been telling me that Mrs.
Ruth Epps has retained you to investigate her husband's
death. She isn't really claiming a murder, is she, Mr.
Barnes? *You* don't buy that, do you?"

"She is, Doctor," I said. "Me, I don't have an opinion
either way. Looked like suicide to me. But until I hear your
verdict, I'm officially on the case for the family. And open to
the evidence."

"Well, we'll have the certain evidence soon enough,"
Butterfield said, looking from Mooney to me. He pushed
back his chair and stretched to full height. "Follow me, if
you will."

Before Mooney and I could clamber after him, the
desk buzzer sounded off. Butterfield wheeled back and
picked up the phone. Prep school BMOC's grin seeped off
his face. He spat into the receiver, oily as could be:

"Well, all right. If the blockheaded bitch is too stupid
to know her own good, we're not going to stop her. Go
ahead. Put the boy's body on display for her. . . . Either
way," he ordered. "The boy is a mess from both sides. Mag-
gots on the left side of his face, and the other side's half
blown away. You get to choose, Larry. However you want to
show her." Butterfield lightly cradled the phone and played
with the third open button on his shirt.

"That the drug dealer, Doc?" Mooney asked.

"His grandmother. Doesn't want to believe the body is
her grandson's." Butterfield turned politely to me. "We re-
ceived a young man's body this morning. Shot in the head,
close range, .20 gauge shotgun. He wasn't found for several
days. Detective Mooney tells me it was some kind of drug
vendetta, isn't that so?"

"That's our information, Doc. No doubt on the ID, either. Prints match his arrest record. Nineteen-year-old kid."

"The boy's grandmother refuses to accept that her grandson is dead." The material in Butterfield's suit rode particularly well when he shrugged his shoulders.

"It's hard to let go of somebody you love," I said.

"Or someone you felt guilty about," Butterfield shot back. He mocked me with an expert's smile.

Then he peeled off his suit coat, tugged on a dazzling white jump suit in place of a lab coat, and springy-footed out of the office so quick that Mooney and I were still hoisting out of our chairs.

Halfway down the corridor from Butterfield's office a draped-over rectangular window was built into the wall. Charging by, following the doctor to the autopsy room, first Mooney then I passed the boy's grandmother. Neat as a pin and just as tiny, she stood there, quiet as a whisper, clutching a Bible with her head bowed. Waiting for the drapes to open like she was ready to be executed. As we edged behind her, the low hum of an electrical motor brought the corpse up before her eyes. I risked a glance. Horror show, like the doctor said. When the first whimper bubbled out her lips, an attendant swiftly moved out of another office and propped her up by the arm.

By then we were passing through a metal fire door and down a staircase to the deepest basement floor. The temperature dropped ten degrees. Butterfield ahead of us slid between two stainless steel swinging doors. I swear his jump suit fit like tailor-made. Mooney plunged right through after him. I sucked in my gut and followed.

The cool sweet-and-sour air of refrigerated meat smacked me in the face. Some kiss of death. Butterfield and a wizened man in a white coat rotated a gurney through the narrow doorway of a big refrigerated vault. Inside it, neat rows of bodies rested on low platforms. The dead were stocked in all shapes and sizes, it seemed. From babies to old ladies. White bodies were looking like old wax. Blacks seeming dusted ash gray.

Butterfield wheeled Walter Epps' body past me. The attendant closed the vault door with a thud that blew cold breath on us all. Epps' corpse was naked except for a rain-coat-green plastic tag dangling from one big toe.

I followed Butterfield and Mooney past six stainless steel tables. At the second one, two white-coats were rapidly carving up a fat woman's body. Mooney's voice boomed unnaturally off the tiles when he said:

"How's she look down there, Doc? Maidenform city or what?"

The man with his rubber-covered fingers up the woman's vagina grinned. "No way, Dale. One big one. At least. Or maybe a lot of little ones."

Mooney laughed, turned his head, saw me, and winked.

My feet kept moving after Butterfield, though my heart was less and less in it. A kind of numbness was keeping the stomach sickness from boiling up. At the third dissection station, an emaciated man's body, toothless and filthy, was getting scrubbed with alcohol sponges. His toe tag read, JOHN DOE. FRELINGHUYSEN AVENUE.

"What happens to a nameless body like that?" I questioned Butterfield.

"Indigents are buried in paupers' graves in the City cemetery," Butterfield said shortly.

At the last stainless steel dissection station, Butterfield and his lab assistant flopped Epps' carcass onto a slab of marble, like a sack of rags dumped into the Goodwill bin. They shoved the body around until it was sagging in the outline of a human form hollowed in the cold stone.

Butterfield stuck a hard rubber block under the nape of Epps' neck. His assistant began clipping hair specimens from the head, mustache, and crotch, putting them into envelopes.

"Joint like this really brings out your appreciation for the human body, huh, Barnesie?" Mooney sounded serious. "Reduces life sorta to the bare bones."

Butterfield began his monologue into the microphone suspended over the table, squinting down at Epps' features as though about to paint a portrait. He pressed down on the mike pedal below the autopsy table and rambled out some mumbo-jumbo about the eyes, nose, ears, and throat, then backed off for a breather. We all just stared at the late Walter Epps in silence. Dried yellow puke in his mouth clashed with his purple lips and gray skin. The ring of close-cropped hair around his bald top looked smeared with gray. So did his bushy eyebrows and pencil-line mustache.

Butterfield launched back into his monotonous description of the contusions on the subject's chest, face, and neck. Finished, he walked to a cart his lab assistant had shoved over and fussed with cutting tools and towels that lay on top of the cart.

"Now the fun begins, Barnesie," Mooney elbowed me.

I took a step closer as Butterfield walked back to the table.

"See these marks here, Gentlemen." Butterfield tapped at Epps' Adam's apple with a slender probe.

"Rope burns, right, Doc?" Mooney piped up.

"No, not exactly, Detective." Butterfield held Epps' chin and rolled his head from side to side. "What's your guess, Mister Barnes?"

Crime school was in session and Butterfield couldn't resist playing professor.

"If I have it right, there are three causes of death from hanging." I looked at Butterfield, who said nothing. "First, Epps here might have strangled to death if his wind pipe was closed or his larynx crushed. Or he could have lost consciousness and then punched out if the blood flow to his brain was cut off. Or, third, he could have broken his neck when he leaped from the second floor staircase and the rope tied to the banister was too short."

"And?"

"He broke his neck."

"Why's that?" Mooney asked.

"Swelling at the nape of his neck," I explained. "In most hanging deaths, a sudden jolt on the rope jerks the victim's chin upward and snaps the neck at the base."

Butterfield's amusement burst into full bloom then. "So you're a forensics expert, are you, Mister Barnes?"

"Yeah, where'd you learn about this stuff, Barnesie?"

"Book somewhere," I replied.

"Well, I'm just gonna have to try that some time," Mooney said. "Book, you say? What do you know about that?"

"So the cause of death was a broken neck," Butterfield announced. "On that we're all agreed."

"Yeah, but how'd his neck get cracked?" I asked.

"Suicide by hanging," Butterfield lifted his shoulders. "No signs of a struggle here, no tissue beneath the deceased's fingernails, no contusions elsewhere on his body not attributable to his fall."

"Why?" Mooney asked me. "You still think maybe the guy that bushwacked you in the yard might've strung Epps up to die?"

"No, but there are one or two loose ends."

Butterfield snorted.

"There's always one or two loose ends," Mooney said. "Christ. You're lucky if there're only one or two."

"The rope he had tied around his neck was way too long," I explained to Butterfield. "Epps' chest was almost flat on the floor. That doesn't mean he didn't tie the rope to the banister and leap off and topple over and break his neck, but you'd think Epps would make sure the rope was plenty short enough so that his feet wouldn't reach the ground and his neck would snap clean."

Butterfield shot Mooney with his eyes.

"Yeah, but Barnesie, you saw the meth we found in the house—guy cranks himself up on that shit, he's liable to do a lot of crazy things."

"Do you seriously doubt it was suicide?" Butterfield looked at me incredulously as he picked up Epps' left arm and poked at the injection mark to highlight Mooney's point.

"No, I don't," I confessed. "It's just that his wife paid me a lot of scratch to cover all the bases for her. I'm just thinking out loud here."

"For once I think Detective Mooney may be right." Butterfield sneered at Mooney. "Methamphetamine is a very powerful stimulant that often induces irrational violent behavior. And Epps' suicide would certainly fit that pattern."

"Are you going to run a toxicology test on his blood?" I asked.

"Most definitely," Butterfield nodded. "That's routine procedure. As soon as the lab has the results I'll forward them to you."

"Thanks," I mumbled.

"Good. Now that we've talked that over, let's get down to business." His smile set my gut on edge.

Butterfield picked up a scalpel in his right hand like a claw. Then the scalpel dipped and he brought the glistening point into Epps' shoulder. He drew it down to the center of the chest, then back up to the other shoulder.

The cream-colored "V" carved in Epps' chest gleamed under the fluorescent lamps and pink juices started pooling up in the hollows between his ribs. Butterfield opened Epps up from his chest to his groin. Blue-veined intestines swelled from the gas-gorged abdomen.

Oh God.

I tightened my stomach muscles and tried to think about Epps like he was only a frog in a high school science class.

Butterfield was cutting away the center section of Epps' rib cage with what looked like expensive poultry shears. I had heard that it takes tremendous effort to dismember a human body. But the doctor was clipping away at the rib bones with the silvery shears.

"You better step over here, this side of the table," he said to me and Mooney. "Some material may fly your way."

Grunting once, Butterfield wrenched loose a spider-like piece of ribs and muscles. He inspected the transparent membrane that surrounded the organs in Walter Epps' chest cavity. He cut that too.

The lab technician started snapping a few Polaroids of the cadaver in all its multicolored horribleness. He took one of me and Mooney looking on, too.

Then Butterfield disconnected the folds of intestines

from the stomach and anus, running the mucous-coated length of them through his hands before dumping them into a metal bucket.

"Still with us, Barnes?" The medical examiner grinned at Mooney and he smirked back. "You don't have to be here, you know."

"Oh, I'll stick it out. Seen plenty of blood and guts in Vietnam," I said. "And a certain amount more on the streets of Newark, when I was a cop. You get used to the blood. What does throw me, though, is just thinking that one day somebody's gonna dump my guts into a pail."

"You saw action in Nam, did you?"

"Uh-huh. You?"

"Saigon. A little field work. What about you, Detective Mooney?"

"Me? I was one of those guys that flunked the old blood test and had to get married. Of course, that's action, sort of."

"That how you got started in this line of work?" I asked Butterfield.

"Unfortunately, yes."

With more exactness than he had used up 'til now, Butterfield sliced through the bronchial tubes of both lungs, then held the pinched stem of each lung upright like the neck of a full wineskin, weighing them in the trays that dangled from the clock-faced butcher's scales. The smooth outer linings of the lungs shone like the tight red skin of an apple.

The recorder whirred again. After he finished his spiel, Butterfield went on about Vietnam.

"My first year of residency, I got drafted. Put in charge of the Eighth Army Forensic Laboratory in Saigon. Worst job in the military services, I thought at the time. It meant I was in charge of shipping the corpses back stateside."

"Goddam. That must've been lovely," I wagged my head.

"Some cadavers were so badly decomposed, we could never embalm them arterially. We'd just sprinkle powdered formaldehyde over them and pack them up in body bags. 'Shake and bake,' they call it, in the trade."

"You used to hear stories," Mooney said. "About how the soldiers'd stick a Russian rifle, one of them AK 47s, inside of a corpse. Stitch it back up. Have it shipped back to the States in the coffin. Sometimes even smuggle dope back to the States inside them corpses."

Butterfield emptied the contents of Epps' stomach into a plastic bag along with a couple of other things.

Forcefully, almost violently, he peeled back the death mask of skin from Epps' face, exposing a web of sinews and strands of muscle. The high-pitched whine of a small electric saw sent chips of skull bone spattering across the table. With a chisellike claw, Butterfield pried the cap of Epps' skull loose from the membrane inside. Pink fluid oozed from the brain.

Butterfield took time out to catch his breath. Then he slid his gloved hands inside Epps' head and detached his brain at the stem. With a long, thin blade, Butterfield butterflied the brain on an acrylic cutting board. Without thinking I flicked my tongue across my lips.

Mooney's warning flashed back too late. Made it past all six examination stations, through the swinging doors. Desperate to find a men's room, I lunged up the stairwell and about halfway down the corridor.

Chapter 10

The mannequin receptionist came scurrying out into the paneled hall when she heard me.

Just in time to watch me puking helplessly on the carpet's geometrical pattern. "What do you think you're doing?" she shrilled. But I was too far over the edge to get smartass with her.

By the time I got my act together enough to push out past her to take the air, she'd started in making these little cries of alarm. To no one in particular, not even to me.

Outside, I took about twenty deep breaths, then went to sit with the windows open in the pickup.

I lit a cigarette and nursed grudge thoughts about the way I spent my life.

Still, by the time I'd smoked that butt down, my next move was looking clearer to me. What this Butterfield character had determined about suicide made perfect sense, if you were not an unreasonably suspicious type. Which sometimes I am. And sometimes I just want to earn my pay.

Start by asking Epps' friends and co-workers about the likelihood of blackmail driving him to suicide.

My new El Camino growled instantly, blew out of the City Morgue parking lot, then graveled to a stop at the first phone booth I saw.

I caught Ruth Epps just going out of her house.

"My spare house key?" she said. I could picture her eyebrows lifting. "Were you under the impression I had invited you to move in?"

"Need a list of your husband's co-workers. There's got to be one among the business things in his desk drawers."

"I'm going out for the evening." The breathy voice gave me goose bumps. "Why don't you come by tomorrow night, and I can give you whatever you need. And I'll order some dinner for us?"

Hi-dee-ho, my heart sang. Dinner with Ruth Epps sounded better than whatever I had planned for the near future. Including the rest of my life.

"Can't I use the key now?" is what my voice said. "I want to get right on something."

"I'd rather be here," Ruth said definitely. "Tomorrow. Nine o'clock?"

"I can make it."

"Have you turned up any relevant information yet?"

"Nothing in particular. But I'm still interested enough at this point to snoop around some more. Folks mostly do not come forward and volunteer their stories, you know."

I hung up and drove straight for Weequahic Avenue,

which was free of cars in mid-afternoon. I was not about to
twiddle my thumbs a whole day on this case, no matter
what Mrs. Epps wanted. I made fine time across town. My
truck was conspicuous enough in that neighborhood to park
a full ten blocks from the Epps house.

To disarm snoopy neighbors, I made a point of hiking
straight up the front walk to the house, as if I had a right.
Meter man here, old Mrs. Neighbor. Fellow's over at the
Epps house to fix the plumbing or something, George.

One-third of the people in this world keeps spare
house-keys under the doormat. Another third hides its keys
somewhere else near the front door, like me. The other
third knows better. When I brushed through the collection
of Swedish ivies and strawberry begonias, one of them, just
one, was a plastic replica. When I lifted the "plant" and
Styrofoam root-ball out of the pot, there was the key at the
bottom, twinkling at me.

Inside, I tracked straight for the living room. The
mauve rug looked richer in the slanty afternoon light. I
swiveled into the chair behind the big oak desk and
scooched back to slide open the middle drawer. That re-
leased the catch on the side drawers. Epps had been a
pretty neat man as far as organizing his business affairs. It
was easy enough to spot his business ledger inside the third
drawer on the right.

It was a large green canvas-backed binder, the kind
accountants use. Epps' outfit was labeled Family Planning
Services. From what the ledgerbook told me, it was a sort of
Planned Parenthood operation, abortions, counseling, birth
control, and all that jazz. Epps had fifteen employees listed
on the books, with social security numbers and other personal information that nobody but the nosy federal government and me would be interested in. I jotted down the
names and addresses on a sheet of paper. The ledger listed
the operation's accountant as the firm of Carp, Brian &
Rabinowitz. New to me. Could have been a high-wire act,
as far as I was concerned. I put the ledger back in the
drawer.

Family Planning Services, my ass. Where were they

Sunday when my fourteen-year-old noosed her little babe to its crib?

On my way out I stopped to look at a couple of family portraits on the bookshelves. Ruth Epps took a terrific picture. I found one of her in a strapless evening gown, hair done up, that was a showstopper.

That's when my curiosity started getting the better of me. I just had to take a look upstairs in the Eppses' bedroom. Maybe I'd find something that would give me a feel for both of them.

There were four rooms upstairs, all large, every one dusted and polished to a fine sheen. Damn! I'd never thought about running into a maid. But anyway there wasn't one around now. Even the closets were neat and fresh. Two spare bedrooms looked vacant as motel rooms, so I gave them just the once over. Another bedroom off the hall had been converted into an all-purpose store room. Gave that the same treatment.

Big bathroom was papered in silver and black. Lots of mirrors. All brand new fixtures in jet black. Tub was fixed up with a whirlpool or Jacuzzi or something.

In the master bedroom, a new, fat-pine canopied bed held court in the center of the floor. I flicked on the wall switch. Mrs. Epps' signature was written everywhere. It seemed that for Walter Epps this had just been a guest room.

My guess was, long ago that bed had been a battleground.

So strongly did her personality ooze from everything, I found myself wondering if the elegant Ruth Epps with the delectable cakes had ever entertained other guests in that room and in that bed. Thoughts like that have a way of stirring when you're snooping around a lady's bedroom.

The long walk-in closet was loaded with clothes from the finest shops in Newark. A sharp brown borsalino, very today, nestled in a hat box on the shelf. More unscuffed shoe leather perched on a shelf of that closet than I had worn out in a lifetime.

A tall dresser stood up against one wall, two sets of

drawers dividing the front vertically. Walter Epps had pack-ratted his clothing, unlike his business books. His top drawer was stuffed with all sorts of junk, from jewelry to pipe cleaners. But what caught my eye were the skimpy nylon bikini pants. French designer underpants. According to the label, they were "Napoleon Boner-Pants." Man had to be a gay blade to swishbuckle through life in those things.

Ruth's side was a well-ordered system of sweaters, stockings, shirts, bras, and panties folded neatly and filed away. In a top dresser drawer, behind a little geometrical pile of handkerchiefs, there was something else. Under two cardboard trays in a velvet-covered jewelry box, a letter had been folded and stuffed in.

The scrawl on the outside was a man's. The postmark was more than a year old and Jamaican. No return address. I shook the sheets out of the envelope and sat on the edge of the bed. A letter addressed to "Ruth" from her lover. Signed "Always."

Always seemed like a pretty literate dude. Romantic enough, too. Especially on the subject of their condo in old Jamaica.

The condo part of the letter was interesting.

> This place is paradise, baby! I got here yester-day afternoon, and I've already caught six hours of sun. Right now, I'm sitting on the deck, and Con-chita is going to bring me another Planter's Punch. That Conchita is incredible about serving all my needs. (Hah-hah, just kidding.) The government is pretty incredible, too. They seem happy to let you do whatever with your cash, as long as you don't try to take it out of their country again. Sweetheart, this condo is safer than a Swiss bank account, and it's all here waiting for you. Hurry up and dump your chump!

The rest of it got explicit, just about clinical, in describing what *Always* planned to do with Ruth Epps' body when he got her alone in their tropical Eden.

Hard to believe the cool and classy Ruth Epps I met yesterday would be turned on by sexual details like that.

I read it over again. Not much clue to their relationship except plenty of physical jazz on both sides. How much pressure was this Romeo putting on her to leave Walter Epps? Was she still making it with him?

Everything got tucked back the way I found it. On the way out, eye-sweeping the room one last time, I was startled by a grim, angry face in the dresser mirror. My doubts over the suicide view of Walter Epps' death weren't putting that look on my face. Reading Ruth's love letter had me smoldering inside. If I knew the lady better, I guess what I was feeling could be called jealousy. But I hardly knew her at all. Stranger yet. Instead of getting excited that the lady liked to get it on with men other than her beloved husband, I was feeling—I don't know what. Some kind of disappointment was mixed in with it, though, whatever it was.

Feeling kind of lost, I wound my way down the stairs and out the front door.

Chapter 11

Time to interview some of Walter Epps' former employees. Several addresses on the list I'd copied from Epps' business books I recognized as being in the Columbus Homes Housing Project. So that's where I drove. The late afternoon smog floated the group of ten gray buildings off the asphalt paving like gravestones. Commemorating years of stupidity and indifference, more than likely.

In a tar lot strewn with shattered glass and crumpled cans, I left my truck and hiked past four rusted skeletons of cars picked clean and left to collapse. When I glanced back at it, my ride seemed begging me not to leave it alone there.

Crossing between two of the buildings, my ears commenced ringing with the weird booming echoes coming at me from all sides. Voices going on in endless bickering. Going nowhere's more like it.

In the lobby of the nearest highrise I pretty near gagged on the stench of ancient urine and rotting garbage. From four feet down, the walls were all yellow and brown from people pissing on them.

The mailboxes in that lobby were battle-scarred veterans. Over the years, their cheap bronzy finishes had been gouged and twisted from routine screwdriver attacks. Not one of them locked any more. Two of the names on the list of Epps' employees were printed on the boxes, though. So I stepped to the elevator, pressed for the eighth floor, and ricketed straight up. I was positively relieved when the car shuddered to a stop.

Then down along the stained and filthy corridor, looking for apartment P. Richards, John, was supposed to live there, said Walter Epps' employee list, designated as Epps' "administrative assistant," along with two or three others. Those probably weren't real jobs at all. Just pushing pencils around all day, picking up Uncle Sam's paystub once a week. But I was curious as to the opinion Walter Epps' underlings had of him.

The cinder block wall had been finger-painted over by somebody with shit-covered hands. I hugged the opposite wall, even though I had to hop a pile of garbage at the foot of a clogged trash chute. Cops who work the projects always wear heavy gloves. This was the first time I ever forgot to bring a pair. Getting old, I guess.

The trail of broken letters on the doors was easy to follow from "A" to "N." No apartment P at all, though. I retraced my steps to the elevator and the stairs, but there were no other apartments on the eighth floor. I picked my way back to apartment N and knocked on the door.

"Yeah," the door barked right back, as if somebody inside'd been watching me all along through the peep.

"Looking for a party that lives on this floor," I said. "Could you open up a minute?" Slow and clear.

"Who that you looking for, Mister?"

"Man name of Richards," I told the glass eye in the door. "Mr. John Richards, supposed to be at apartment P."

"Never heard of nobody by that name."

"Well, he's supposed to live in apartment P, up here on this floor."

"Ain't no apartment P."

"Well, what about the other apartments?"

"Don't know nothing bout no other apartments, Mister. All I know is ain't no Richards in here, and you ain't coming in here neither."

"No need go getting yourself all riled up there, partner. Seems to me there's some kind of mistake on the mailboxes downstairs."

"Only mistake's one you making right now, chump. Go on, move you ass out a here, I call the cops or worse. Hear?"

Can you jab somebody in the peephole? I sure was tempted.

Then I laughed. "Hey, you have yourself a nice day," I called through the door.

I weaved on back to the stairwell, passed up the elevator, and walked down two flights to the next apartment on my list. Stokes, the name was, according to Epps' books. I rapped on that door and caught the tiniest movement on the other side. Peephole treatment again. Only this time I must have passed the test. Because the door cracked and two weary eyes checked me out. Then the chain started rattling and next thing the door swung all the way open.

So did my glass jaw. It dropped around my ankles and pretty near shattered on the concrete floor. The woman I was looking at had stopped moaning since I last saw her being led away at the City Morgue. But it was definitely the old lady who'd stood there grieving over what remained of her grandson's body.

"Yes?" Her voice was hoarse with the grief.

"This the Stokes residence?" I said, knowing damn well that it was.

"Are you with the police?"

"Not exactly. I used to be. Working as a private detective now. Name is Barnes." I fished in my pocket for some ID.

"Well, please come in." She stepped to the side so I could enter. She wore the faint scent of synthetic violets.

Behind me she swung the apartment door shut. I stood there watching her try to close and latch the chain with those frail blue-veined hands.

"Martha," she said over her shoulder. "This is Mister . . ."

"That's Barnes," I said again, like a dope looking all around the room before I fixed on the wire-haired terrier sitting obediently at her side, bright eyes fixed on me.

"Sit down, Mister Barnes."

I plunked myself down in a doily-laced armchair.

"I'll fix you a nice cup of coffee, Mister Barnes."

"No, thank you."

"Didn't I see you this morning, at the morgue? I was there to identify Kelvin's mortal remains."

"I didn't think you had noticed me. I'm sorry about your boy, ma'am."

"My grandson. Such a good boy. I raised him exactly as if he were my own. My daughter died early on and Kelvin lived here with me until lately. Always a good little boy. How can you understand something like that, Mr. Barnes?"

"Police told me he was killed over drugs?"

"Well, they said that, all right. But I doubt it very much, Mr. Barnes. Kelvin would not get involved in anything dirty like that. He was working a good job and all."

"Worked for Mr. Walter Epps, didn't he?" I asked softly.

"Oh yes. A real gentleman, Mr. Epps. It's queer that he killed himself so close to when my Kelvin was murdered."

"That's it, Mrs. Stokes. It's very queer, those two things happening all at once."

"I think when two men work together, then both of them die at the same time, they got to be connected."

"Seems likely, doesn't it? But I just came from the coroner's office. And it looks like Mr. Epps' death was most likely just a suicide."

She plucked at the doily pinned to the sofa arm.

"I was planning to ask Kelvin a few questions about Mr. Epps. I guess there's no point in wasting more of your time, Mrs. Stokes."

"I'm afraid I only met Kelvin's boss the one time. Seemed such a nice man to me. Kelvin didn't talk about his job much to me."

"How about Kelvin's friends? Maybe a girlfriend who might know something about his job working for Walter Epps?"

"Kelvin didn't bring many of his friends around for me to meet," she said, looking at her frail hands again like she was surprised they were empty. "He worked other jobs part-time, you know." The dog moved to her side. "And he was way too shy to date many girls. When he was a baby, he had a touch of polio that withered his left arm. Left him feeling uncomfortable around most people, especially girls."

"I understand, ma'am." Then I immediately felt like a heel for wondering if Kelvin Stokes had ever played Boy Wonder for Walter Epps.

"There was this one thing that seemed peculiar, sort of," Mrs. Stokes said softly, stooping to scratch the dog behind one ear. "This white man come knocking at our door a few days before Kelvin went away and disappeared. Said he was looking for someone else and had the wrong apartment by mistake. But I could tell by the surprise on his face when I opened the door that he was lying. He was expecting to see Kelvin, I know it."

"What did this white man look like?"

"Oh, he was frightening to look at. Giant man. Looked like a gangster the way he kept his hands in his pockets. Had red hair."

"Curly hair?"

"I'm sorry. I couldn't tell you. He was wearing a hat and these sunglasses."

"Thank you a lot, Mrs. Stokes," I said, standing up.

"Are you sure you wouldn't like something to eat? Wouldn't breadsticks or cottage cheese go nice?"

"No, really. I got to be running." I stepped to the door and unlatched it. My haste shamed me some. Felt like I was abandoning her.

"Mr. Barnes, I hope you catch whoever it was killed my Kelvin and that Mr. Epps." Her mind was set on murder. "Lord forgive me, but I don't have much faith in the police these days."

"You'll be all right alone?" I asked.

She nodded. "Martha's here."

The two of them watched me from the apartment doorway, while I waited for what seemed like forever for the elevator to come. "Latch up good now," I called to her. We waved good-bye then. As I rode to the ground I felt ashamed again, as if somehow I should be taking her out of there. Ezell Barnes, the Black Knight. A familiar feeling from when I was a cop. But you just know there is nothing in the world you can do.

Beads of sweat were rolling off my neck and back by the time I pushed out the lobby door and into the thin sunlight and the sour air.

I came up dry on the other names on Epps' list. Except, of course, for more carefully planted and doctored-up mailboxes.

I didn't loiter over it, because there was a hunch I wanted to play that afternoon. I drove crosstown to the Bureau of Vital Statistics and walked up to their desk two minutes before five. Grumpy old buffalo of a woman dug through the graveyard of records there to ice what I'd already figured out. Even so, what she told me hit like a slap to the nose.

Sure, I knew that plenty of other crooks had raised the dead to shave a little cash off the books. Been going on long before Walter Epps got his start. Improving your edge is the American Way, right?

Just, the idea of resurrecting fourteen dead children,

80

ages one day to three years, as ghost employees, spooked me.

Chapter 12

At my regular diner in the Frelinghuysen industrial district, I ate a dish of potatoes and gravy billed as "Salisbury steak." When I stepped outside, it was raining lightly. The dashboard clock said 7:35; I set my wristwatch by it. The Club Pimlico was probably open for early business by now so I set the 350 V-8 to belting me way across town to North Newark. For the past six or seven months, Angel had been hanging there most nights, flirting and hooking until two o'clock and past. For the last week, he'd been the featured go-go dancer, and I had promised to catch his act. More important, I needed quick information about Walter Epps' public and private life. And Angel the Sex Change is the best in the business for that kind of dope.

I sailed past Washington Park. Even in the drizzle, gay men were out cruising. Some posed on the sidewalks. Others trolled the streets in their cars. Every once in a while, you hear about a gang of tough south-side street kids swarming into the park and savaging up a couple dozen gays. Every couple of years the mayor vows to clean up the city, and the press regurgitates protesting newsprint. But this evening, the rainy skies were strictly for lovers, looked like. Boys that couldn't be older than sixteen were parading on the sidewalks as I drove by.

From the outside, the Club Pimlico has the same charm as a Forty-Second Street massage parlor. The stucco front is washed harsh white by floodlights. The cluster of broken bulbs looks like a growth on the trunk of a neon tree above the door. The avenue always reminds me of Saigon under siege, half burned out but half-trying to hang on. The fronts of the stores still in business had metal shields—one notch up from grills—pulled down over their plate glass windows. Under the metallic orange haze of the street lights only hookers sauntered along, except for the red-eyed traffic in and out of the Pimlico, that is.

I sucked in a deep breath of wet air before I crawled into that cave. The Club Pimlico is a hangout for losers and perverts of all shapes and sizes, but definitely not all colors, except for some of the black hookers and dancers. Four years ago, some black fool went rushing in there, lead pipe in his hands, looking for a dude he thought was messing with his woman. The regulars at the bar took that pipe and broke his foolish heart and head, too, right there on the floor of the bar. Self-defense was the way the cops reported it.

Me, I kept my black hands open and clear and free of my body going in.

Inside the door sloshed the usual humidity and tension of a dive crammed with chumps who haven't been laid for a month. I've been in a hundred joints like it. But the Pimlico itself I had only been in once before, to watch Angel dance, at his request. Like a cockroach in a toilet bowl I had slugged down a quick drink and scurried out of there before somebody squashed me.

Tonight, as my eyes adjusted to the light, I could see a really fine light-skinned sister moving it around behind the bar, not wearing more than high platform heels and fishnet stockings over her purple G-string. Matching purple scarf twisted around her top barely covered her tits. Discreet. She wouldn't be wearing anything at all for long.

I scanned the bar for Angel, but he was not to be seen. I did turn up a face I never expected, though. Eddie Dorey was perched on a chair-back stool at the far end of the semi-circular bar, left side completely shielded by the safe wall. His gun side had an unobstructed view of the room. The man was a professional, all right.

Because I didn't figure he had seen me, I watched him for a second. When the music faded, the dancer let her body slow down, then she scooped up her show clothes and stepped off the platform, threw on a silk wrap and arranged her legs on the stool next to Dorey. Not very close to him, not far away, both wearing that weatherbeaten look of long-time lovers.

Some of the barflies had taken to staring at me by then. Without warning, Dorey lifted his eyes and met mine matter-of-factly across the room, as if he'd known all along I was there. He flicked a finger towards himself.

Weaving to him, towards the stage lights, I could see the blue coils of thick smoke in the air.

Dorey leaned and said something to the long pair of legs beside him. She unwound and high-heeled behind the bar to talk to two other mostly naked women.

"How you doing again, Eddie?" I said. "What brings you here?"

"Sit down, Barnes." Dorey wasn't smiling. "Question is, what brings *you* in here? I hang in here all the time. And I never seen you here before." Dorey's white dress shirt was open at the throat. Over that, he wore a summerweight pale blue suit that had years of mileage on it. His on-duty clothes, geared to look and feel off-duty by the necktie being stripped off. But Dorey would always look kind of on-duty to me, tie or no tie.

"Thought I would take myself out on the town tonight, for a change. Single dude like myself likes to catch a little local color once in a while, you see."

Dorey grinned then, more to himself than to me. "Uh-huh. Tell me about it. In case your eyes ain't changed to the light yet, the only local color in here is ivory snow white."

Twisted my head around and slapped some fake surprise on my face.

"Shit-toast," I said. "What's a nice plantation boy like me doing here at the white folks' party?"

Dorey sipped at something hard on the rocks. "You're with me. None of these toads are going to mess with you."

"Thanks, but I don't plan on staying long enough for trouble to brew." Through the smoke-laced air I squinted at the next dancer on the runway, a hard-looking redhead in a fishnet body suit that didn't hide her hairdresser's secret. "I'm looking for Angel. You see him around tonight?"

"Yeah, she's out, probably hauling some john's ashes." Dorey drained his drink. "Wait a couple minutes, she'll be back."

I nodded.

"Paulie." Dorey lifted his head as the bartender drifted over. "This here is Barnes. Friend of mine, okay? Give him whatever the hell he wants to drink and put it on my tab." Paulie hefted a silver eyebrow at me.

"First a phlegm-cutter," I said. "Brandy up. After that a Black Velvet rocks."

"You like all them bubbles in your scotch?" Paulie was saying to the next customer in a choirboy's tenor. He poured my drinks, with a scotch and very little water for Dorey, and moved off.

"Where do you know Angel from?" Dorey lit up a smoke with a gold-plated lighter and I followed suit.

"Did a couple jobs for him, few years back. You know. Bill collecting, that sort of thing. We been friends ever since then."

"Good enough. That's what she told me too," said Dorey. His voice was matter-of-fact. I made a face.

"What's the matter, Barnes? You don't think I check up on people? Maybe you didn't think I'd check you out after you fell into a death scene, middle of the goddam night? Of course I checked you out. So don't sweat it none. Just run-of-the-mill stuff, hear? You got a clean bill of health, as far as I'm concerned."

We both drank up. The BV tasted watered down.

"I always go straight to people like that Angel for information," Dorey was telling me. "I absolutely got to rub elbows with that type of person if I want to do my job the way it should be done." I nodded.

"You know, the best description I ever heard of people like Angel was, a guy once called them street chameleons. You ever heard that? Because they got to survive out there. On the street. Every day. To do that, every day they got to be diming people out. Got to. Right and left, believe me. If a character like Angel is squealing *to* you, all she needs is the same opportunity with somebody else, she'll be squealing *on* you.

"You don't believe me, do you?" Dorey's face went sour. "There are precious few people in this life you can count on, Barnes. For your own good, you got to keep somebody like that Angel at arm's length. That way she can never hurt you. You can't count on none of these people."

The first dancer, all legs, worked it around the bar towards us, shimmering green silk shawl wrapped around her bare shoulders. She slid an arm around Dorey and hugged herself up against him. He said nothing to her. She speared me with a half-second look. Black man comes sliding on into this here all-white bar, her eyes said, and gets hassled by nobody, must be somebody special. Somebody worth knowing. I said nothing.

The beauty untangled herself from Dorey and drifted off again, the sweaty-sweet smell of her perfume lingering behind.

"Who's the trim?"

"My main squeeze." Dorey took a pull on his scotch. "Beverly and I got a crumb-snatcher, a little boy."

"I heard you're married." I made it up from the wedding band on his finger.

"Yeah, sort of," Dorey scowled. "But not to her."

"Sort of married is like sort of dead, ain't it?"

"Yeah." Dorey sucked on a swizzle stick. "Not to change the subject, hah-hah, you see the toxicology results from the medical examiner yet?"

"No, Doctor Butterfield said he'd let me know as soon as it was done."

"Well, it's done, and it shows Epps was cranked up to the Twilight Zone on methamphetamine."

"Figures."

"Suicide, case closed." Dorey lifted his glass to me.

I wasn't so sure. Dorey seemed straight goods and all. But I hardly knew the man well enough to pour out my heart to him. I decided to keep under my new hat what I found out about Epps' tombstone employees and about the coincidence of Kelvin Stokes' murder. At least until I could check Dorey out with Dale Mooney. I might need a ten-gallon hat by the time I got through.

Angel stepped long-limbed onto the platform and began to shake it at twice the speed of the previous dancers. He moves great—everybody says he should join a big-time revue in Atlantic City, but he won't. I know his secret. The go-go joints have stricter dress requirements, breasts must be covered, which suits Angel just fine. He's working on his development up there. That night he moved like Lola Falana.

About a minute in, Angel spotted me, beamed like a kid, and blew me a big kiss. Good old Angel, right in the middle of an exotic dance number.

Behind the bar Beverly was watching the shaking and sending conspiratorial smiles my way. When I caught one, she switched to different smoke signals. And the invitation was definitely being delivered to my address, I could see now. Dorey had eyes only for Angel as he twirled off his little skirt to get down to bikinis. I threw Beverly a noncommittal smile and turned back to Dorey.

"You looking into the attempted blackmail?" I said fast.

Dorey snorted. "You crazy? I'm working my head off on real homicides as it is. Now I'm gonna chase around after some shakedown that never happened?"

"Thought you might want to tie up all the loose ends." I swirled the booze around in the bottom of my glass and then polished it off. "Think Vice will investigate it?"

"Not a chance. They're as asshole deep in work as I am. Last year, you know, I caught more squeals than any other detective in Homicide."

"You really found yourself a home there, brother, huh?"

"You bet. It's nothing like working in the precinct, believe me. Too bad you never got the chance to work the Detective Bureau, Barnes. You'd probably still be with the department."

Paulie wandered past us with a white wine bottle in his hand. Dorey and I along with half the barflies craned our necks to see who'd be drinking that swill. Dude in a business suit buying it for a toffee-colored hooker.

Dorey said: "What I mean is this. In Homicide, we got twelve dependable detectives. No fuck-ups. Each man pulls his own weight."

I nudged him. "And some guys pulling two men's weights."

"I mean it," Dorey said. "There is no damn deadwood like you got laying all over the precincts. Nobody fucks around with anybody else's work unless you need the help. Everything is very tight in the Homicide Squad, like a brotherhood."

"The hell you say?"

"How we take care of each other." Dorey appeared fish-eyed, looking through the ice cubes at the bottom of his glass. "Everybody gets taken care of by the department. Commissioner Manouso's got exactly the right attitude towards this. No horseshit. You do just what you have to do. Nobody gets crucified for doing his job too well."

"Nobody was taking care of nobody, I was working as a cop." I shook my head. "I didn't look after myself, nobody was gonna come along, do it for me. Nice to hear you fellas are minding each other's store over there. Manouso's a hard man, I hear."

"Bet your ass," said Dorey. "Scumbags're everywhere, right? Fucking city's totally run over with shittem scumbags. They got their rights, you think? I'll tell you what their rights are. With the Manhattan fucking phone book on the neck, they'll get their rights."

Paulie came by, silently set us up with another pair of drinks.

"You know Sammie Macky?" Dorey said.

I shook my head.

"Me and Sammie Macky're driving around down along the Ironbound last winter. February, I think it was, and cold enough to freeze the fucking doorknobs off City Hall. Hookers're standing over the manhole covers, so the steam'll blow up their skirts. We get a call to check out this corpse that somebody found behind a big dumpster in a gas station.

"So me and Sammie go driving around down there. And the corpse turns out to be nobody else but the late Roger L. Percy, Esquire. A defense attorney that a lot of us knew from cases we had testified at. Nice guy, was Roger. Never busted your balls on the stand, in front of the judge. Asked you the tough questions, but with a little respect, so you didn't wind up looking like a horse's ass, as when some of the other lawyers start asking *their* questions.

"Now I don't say that old Roger Percy was a straight ace through and through. I really didn't know the man all that well. But he was perfectly all right to go to court against. He didn't make a point of dealing out any shit. And he didn't particularly want none from anybody else."

Dorey rattled the ice cubes in his glass until Paulie surfaced with the scotch bottle. I nodded okay to another, too.

"Well. Sammie and me don't recognize old Roger at first, because behind the dumpster there Percy has got his pants yanked down to his ankles, underpants and all. And he's got this big brown shopping bag pulled over his head. Right where the Shop-Rite label is, the bag's got a mouth drawn on it in lipstick or something. And there's this hole torn out where the mouth would be. And there's stains and come and shit all around the hole. After we take the bag off and we see who it is, Sammie and I flip the body over to see what was the cause of death."

Paulie glided again down the bar, and scotch reappeared in Dorey's glass. I shook Paulie off. I was already pie-eyed enough, which was mostly okay with me that night. I'd had a hard couple of days, and besides I couldn't have sat sober for a story like Dorey's.

"So what would you guess was the cause of death?"

I shook my head. "Heartbreak of psoriasis?"

"Be serious," Dorey said. "That poor jerk had a Pepsi bottle, one of them long thin ones, stuck up his asshole. Jammed in tight and then snapped off. He cruised a couple of tough queers and they savaged him and he bled to death in the cold."

"They ever find who did it?"

"At the autopsy," Dorey spat. "They found about ten prunes shoved up his ass too. Imagine that? The kind of slime that would think to do something like that?

"Well, we didn't have to do any imagining," Dorey's face was poisonous. "We made a point of finding those particular scumbags. And we took care of that particular situation, Sammie and me, couple other guys. And if I'm not mistaken, before the end, there were two scumbag queers very sorry they had offed Roger Percy.

"The report got sent directly to Manouso, and the department took care of me and Sammie on that. And that was all she wrote. But it teaches you a few things, something like that, Barnes. About the kind of people that're out there jerking off on the world."

"Ray Velnarsky a part of this brotherhood, I suppose?"

Yeah," said Dorey, but he was scowling. "Where do you know Velnarsky?"

"Mooney and I worked out at the gym today, watched Velnarsky mutilate some poor palooka in the ring."

"Well, that's one bastard you don't ever want to get mad at you," Dorey said. "I am eternally glad he's on my side of the action."

"Look to me like he enjoys fucking people up."

"He lives for it. Ray was over in Vietnam for three tours of duty. Couldn't get enough of it. He was a LURP, you know what that is? Elite of the elite. Long-Range Reconnaissance Patrol, this special branch in the Green Berets. Go out into the bush solo for two months at a crack, wearing tiger suits and grease paint on their faces. Hide in the bushes and ice whatever comes by. I would think, you live like that, like an animal, you never get it out of your blood."

Chapter 13

At that, I stuck a tenspot under Dorey's glass and said something to him about being in touch. He just nodded, sitting up there against the wall, and turned to watch Beverly move and slide again. But he was also keeping one eye on Paulie the bartender and all the other night creatures in the Pimlico. Not in any way participating, but still a part of everything.

On my way out the door, I seemed to bump into every person and table in the joint. It didn't help my concentration none when Beverly blew me a kiss from the dancing platform that Dorey'd have to be blind to miss. Then Angel came up, as if he'd been keeping watch on me the whole time. Without saying a word he took my arm and made like he was propping me up.

It had stopped raining, but the air felt wet and cool. I shook free of Angel and staggered a little way down the block to lean against a streetlamp, and suck in a chestful of refrigerated air. I lit up a cigarette. Angel's little high heels came tapping up besides me.

"You drink too much, Papi," he was clucking at me. "Now you gonna feel pretty bad, I think."

I did my best to make the expression on my face resemble a headache. Angel looped his slender arm through mine and snuggled up. I could feel his padded bra press against my arm and that made me squirm loose.

"You know. It's really wonderful and all, having you here to nag at me," I said.

"I seen you was talking with Eddie Dorey," Angel changed the subject.

"Yeah, he told me how you gave him my life story." I

glared a little at Angel. Who could take a hint. And get mad about it.

"You think I'm gonna tell somebody something you no want me to say? Go piss on you, Easy. Why don you never truss Angel?" Angel pretty near stamped his little foot. But he was too ladylike.

"Dorey, he maybe is okay. Not like none of those other cops. But I never gonna say too much to this Dorey. And I don say nothing to nobody else."

"Right," I said, remembering what Dorey had said about street chameleons. "I'm needing some of your time, Angel. You got to tell me some things about this Walter Epps character you put me on to. Right away."

"Oh? Sure thing, Mister Big Shot. Right away? Time is money to me, Sweetman. You know that. And the night-time is very much so."

"Well, look. You eaten yet? I could use some food myself here. So how about I buy you dinner while we talk? That be money enough for you?"

Angel looked at me sadly and held my arm as we walked over to my truck.

Angel insisted on doing the driving over to this place near his apartment on Orange Street. Orange Street is where the Puerto Ricans live in Newark. I often thought the name was pretty suitable, because Puerto Ricans eat more damn fruit than anybody I ever saw. They got pretty good food all around, actually. Especially the fried stuff and the side dishes made out of fruits. But what you see most of in the summer when you drive down Orange Street is these vendors with carts, selling fruit drinks and a sort of sno-cone covered with all different kinds of fruit juice they called *piraqua*.

My dashboard clock clicked off 10:30 as Angel pulled over at the corner of Orange and University, in front of the Zion Church. Across the street was Torrez Cuchifrito, the best *cuchifrito* joint in Newark. And I got that opinion from Angel, who should know.

As with most joints in Newark, you can't tell from the

outside what it looks like on the inside. There's a big turquoise six-sided sign out front, plastic, lit up from the inside, that says TORREZ curved across the top, and CUCHIFRITO curved around the bottom. I tilted my lid down just right and Angel and I sashayed in.

Maybe fifteen people were standing around, listening to *salsa* tunes. Everybody turned to ogle like they always do, Angel being at his ravishing best. He just ate up that attention, too. If I'd come strolling in there with any other Puerto Rican woman, I would be eating some trouble, looked like. At least, I could hear some of them youngbloods muttering about *taita*. Which is supposed to mean nigger in Spanish.

With Angel along, though, everything was gonna be cool. He has that kind of style.

At the counter you could watch the fryman work. So we sat down there. I nodded at Torrez when he came bustling down the counter to put knives and forks and paper placemats with a map of Puerto Rico in front of us.

"We haf *bacalaito* tonight." He checked over his shoulder to see where his wife was behind the counter and then winked at Angel. Torrez is maybe five feet five, heavy, with dark brown skin. He wears a short mustache, and his hair is thinning and brushed back with some kind of oil. He is really your properous businessman type.

"What you gonna haf to eat, Onn-hell?"

"*Cuchifrito*," said Angel, looking around Torrez's head at the gold-veined mirror behind the counter. "And *tostones*. And *viandas*." After each item, Torrez turned his upper body in the direction of his frycook and barked the order.

"You wan *guanabana*?"

"*Si.*"

"And you?" he said to me. "You wan the *bacalaito*? Is very good tonight."

"Yeah, sounds good," I said. "*Bacalaito* and *sofrito*. And give me some *malta* to drink, okay?"

"Very good." Torrez turned his whole body and shouted "*Malta!*" as if taking a parachute jump out of an airplane.

He bustled off up the counter. Angel casually studied his face in a little silver pocket compact he carried. Torrez's fat wife brought the malted drink for me and the fruit punch for Angel. For a while we sat there without saying anything. I was watching the frycook do his thing.

Out of a plastic bag he shook little bits of pork that Angel once told me were pieces of the pig's stomach or ear. That's why I never eat *cuchifrito*. Frycook dropped them into a huge shallow steel bowl full of a mixture like bread crumbs, and tossed them with his hands until they were coated. Then he dropped handfuls of the stuff into the fryolator and the fat boiled up dark brown almost to the rim, popping until the pieces of pig floated like golden corks on the surface.

Frycook snatched a big piece of white fish meat out of a bowl of water and did the same treatment to it in a different vat of frying oil. He sliced up bananas into rounds and mashed each slice with a wood mallet. Then he breaded them too and threw them in with the pork. He dished up a whopping spoonful of rice into a china bowl, added some red kidney beans, and covered all of it with the *sofrito* sauce, which was all red with tomatoes and a spice called *achiote* that I like a lot. From a pot on the back of the range he ladled out some white starchy stuff, almost like boiled potatoes, that I had never seen before, and poured olive oil on it out of a cruet. He put that in front of Angel and the *sofrito* in front of me. Then he lifted the fry baskets and hung them to drain over the vats. With a slotted spoon he scooped out *cuchifrito* and *tostones* on a plate for Angel, and the fried codfish fritter, *bacalaito*, for me.

Very delicately, Angel picked up a *tostone* with his fingers and bit into it. Flakes of crisp fried coating fell onto his plate, and hot oil oozed where he bit in.

"You know that friend of yours that was supposed to call me last night," I mumbled through a mouthful of hot *bacalaito*. "Well, he did. And then he got dead right away. Did you know that?"

"Yes," said Angel gravely. "Rose told me. And then was in the newspaper. We all gonna miss that little man pretty much."

I shoveled down two heaping spoonfuls of *sofrito*, wiped off my mouth, and looked at Angel. He was lighting up a long slim cigarette. And he was pointing his chin in the opposite direction from me.

"What's the matter with you?"

"Nahthing."

"You not gonna eat your food?"

Angel shook his head of expensive wig.

"Well give me one of them *tostones*, would you?"

"All the time you wanting Angel to do something for you. You just like a pimp sometime, Easy. You always taking, never give nothing."

"Cheer up, will you?" I said. "I'm gonna need you to help me out. Can't afford no temper tantrums. Eat your food, why don't you? This *bacalaito* sure is looking mighty tasty."

Just like that, Angel grabbed up his handbag and stormed off to the ladies' room in back. From down the counter Torrez raised an eyebrow at me. I shook my head at him in exasperation. Nothing to do but finish off my food, then start in on Angel's plate, picking off the *tostones* one by one.

It took Angel a while to come back. But when he did, he was wearing fresh lipstick and exaggerated calmness. I turned to him:

"Your playmate's wife hired me to look into the way he got dead, Angel. She thinks he didn't kill himself. And a couple things got me thinking the same. What should I know about this Walter Epps?"

Angel swiveled on his stool and shook his thick mane-of-the-day.

"Come on. Why would the man want to kill himself?"

Angel gave me one of those little Latin shrugs of the shoulders.

"The night he talked to you about hiring a private detective, did he seem strange to you, any way at all?"

"Always the same, he was. Every time I see him," pronounced Angel. "Bossy. You know. He like to be the big shot all the time."

"How long did you know him?"

"Long time," Angel said, getting dreamy on me. "Five, maybe six years. I meet Waltie when I go to Human Resources Institute."

"The what?"

"You-man Ray-*sources In*-stee-tood. You know. For my condition. To get the operation." Angel glanced down at his lap.

Took me a second to wire the connection. For the last ten years, the only real money coming into Newark has been federal money. Lots of that around. And lots of it going straight to the Public Health Department.

Every year, it seems like, Public Health in Newark goes through another facelift. After every election, another wave of charlatans drums up new names for the old social problems. Along the same lines as convincing a starving man he's only got a vitamin deficiency.

Now the same thing was true of all the other city agencies, too. Police Department was now the Department of Public Safety. Public Works they now called the Office of Structural Maintenance. Sanitation Department, which used to be just plain old "Garbage," now was Refuse Disposal and Reclamation.

New names, same old problems. Nobody was ever fooled.

On the other hand, nobody ever did nothing to stop the merry-go-round, either.

"Walter Epps wasn't a doctor," I said. "The hell was he doing down at a Public Health agency?"

"He just one of them hanger-ons," said Angel wisely. "They all sliding from one fat paycheck to the other." Then Angel made a frown and said something you hear from every person who ever lived in Newark: "They don't do nothing but stealing the city blind."

"I hear you. What work did Epps do down there?"

"Nothing, I think. He don't do nothing. And nobody at that Institute ever do nothing for nobody. I was going there for one year, almost."

"You were trying to get your operation done."

"Rehabilishun," Angel said. "They was going to re-habilishun me. They says. Then the operation I can get for free, right here in Newark, Papi. The operation going to rehabilishun me and take me off the streets, they telling me.

"But nobody don never do nothing, ever time I go there. Sometime, nobody is even in there at that Institute when I go. You got to have many talks with the psychiatrist, they says. Before the operation can be. Take a long time. Like they think I gonna give up, not come there no more. But I am keep showing up and waiting there. Got no maga-zines for waiting in that office. Except maybe one, two. But only in English. And never one time I see no psychiatrist. Never see nobody at that Institute except this Waltie Epps. Maybe one, two more."

Angel was waving his hands around in the air. He stopped that, and folded them on the counter so he could lean towards me.

"Pretty stupid to wait around there, Papi, no? Angel could never change her life, wait around that Institute. For nothing. Have to go Chicago."

"Yeah. You already told me that part of the story. About a hundred times, maybe. And you ended up paying for the trip to Chicago, and the operation, and the recuperation time, all that, yourself. Right?"

Angel nodded.

"Was it worth it to you, do you think?"

Angel smiled.

"Really think it changed your life, do you?"

Angel nodded again. He had no doubts.

"Tell me something. What's so different now about the way you live, Angel? You doing anything now you didn't do anyway before the operation?"

"You got too many questions for Angel." He was lip glossing himself in the gold-veined mirror behind the coun-ter again. "Maybe you think Angel some kind of answering service, something?"

In the mirror I gave Angel my hard-day look. "Epps was managing a different project when he died, did you know? Name of Family Planning Services. Your Human Resources Institute probably ain't still in business."

"No." Angel was positive. "When I come back from Chicago, I go to that Institute, give somebody piece of my mind. But nobody there, and office is all closed up. Everybody gone away."

"So you think the whole agency had nothing behind it? Just a front for some kind of scam, maybe?"

Angel shrugged again. "They did nothing all day, Papi."

"But you kept in touch with Epps after that, right? Played around with him some, you said?"

"Yas."

"He ever talk to you about his wife?"

Angel looked at me like I had two heads.

"Course he had troubles at home, what you think, Easy? Waltie didn give her no love so unless she were some kind prune or somethin I don think she was very happy."

"You mean prude? No, you saw her, she's one attractive woman."

"She had another loverman," Angel said. He bit down lightly on his lower lip, shiny with red polish. "Thas something I can guess always."

"What do you know about that? Well, you are right on the money, this time, amigo. I tripped over this letter from some dude to Epps' wife, there. Sounded like they was getting it on pretty good."

Angel perked up, like the idea of an unfaithful wife pleased him.

"Yesterday I seen Bette Davis and her loverman kill Bette Davis' old man. Because they were so much in love, and he was so much in the way." Angel reached over to grab my arm. "You think Waltie's wife and her loverman maybe kill Waltie?"

"Well, I sure haven't thought about it that way so far. But it's not much less likely than anything else I got so far. The police think Epps pulled his own plug while screaming high on drugs."

"Love is like drugs sometimes," Angel mused. "I know. People lose their mind to it."

"Was it common knowledge around town that Epps was hitting from both sides of the plate?"

"Do these blue jeans got Calvin wrote on them?" Angel tilted his head back for effect.

"*Everybody knew?*"

"Papi, words travel fast, you know?" Angel said. "Who didn't know? He don't, Waltie, care, I don't think."

That one had to soak in awhile. Blackmail was out if Walter Epps was out of the closet. Angel popped a mint in his mouth and hummed something that was probably the theme from *The Young and the Restless*.

I finally said, "I got two more things. First, what about Epps' assistant, kid named Kelvin Stokes?"

"Most work he done for Waltie was after hours," Angel giggled. "You know how most men got a secretary, Papi? Waltie has his little Kelvin."

"Ever meet him?"

"Course, he's kind of cute," Angel smiled.

"Well, now he's kind of dead," I said.

"Him too! Ooh, that's so sad!"

"Next item, you ever heard of a Homicide cop named Velnarsky?"

Angel wrinkled his nose. "He is very mean. And very much man. Very strong. Very manly. But he like too much to hurt ladies. He so big there and so strong he should give much love. But he only give much hurt. No girls I know like to go with Velnasty. Even ones that like to be hurt."

"You know Eddie Dorey, the same way?"

"No." Angel made a proud flip of his head. "And Angel like this Eddie very much, too. But I work with his old lady. And Angel never take no man from my friend or nobody I work with."

"You think Dorey's an honest cop?"

A Latin shrug from Angel. "Papi, you mean money? They all are snake in the grasses. They all is living a lie."

"Epps a snake?"

"Could be. Federal big shots was dragging him before the Grand Jury."

"Epps was before a Grand Jury! Testifying about what? Epps tell you?"

"Nobody supposed to know," Angel winked. "But Waltie can't keep so secret when he's in trouble."

So the U.S. Attorney had himself a nigger by the toe. He would never tweak Epps loose until he hollered out some other names. Whoever knew that had plenty of reason to shut Epps up in perpetuity.

"Listen, keep your ear to the ground," I said and dropped a tenspot alongside the greasy empty plates in front of us. "If you hear the names of people mixed up with Epps, let me know."

Angel and I left Torrez Cuchifrito to the thousand hostly handwaves of Torrez. Driving across town, neither of us said much. But just before he climbed out by the Pimlico, Angel rummaged in his handbag, then handed me a cocktail napkin.

"I most forget," he said. "Beverly give me this for you in the ladies' room." Angel snapped his purse shut and clicked off like he was mad.

But a block away, when I looked in the rearview, I could see him waving his beaded handbag good-bye to me.

Under the first street light, I pulled over and read the scribbled note. Beverly was suggesting that I stop by her place when the Pimlico closed at two A.M.

Dorey apparently was headed home to his wife. I thought the offer over for all of two minutes. What did I owe Eddie Dorey? The guy was playing both sides against the middle. Probably Beverly was also free to see other men.

I slipped the pickup into gear and barreled over to her place.

Beverly's address was a door on the third floor of an apartment building rapidly collapsing into a plain old tenement. She waited just enough before answering my knock, letting the anticipation build. The lady knew all the tricks.

When the door floated open, I thought I was back in Southeast Asia. Incense hung in the air, and she was dressed in a blue and red silk robe gaping to show her smooth flesh underneath. When her black hair was combed straight out, it hung around her shoulders and, light skinned as she was, she looked strangely oriental with maybe some French blood mixed in.

Her smoky smile was the only invitation I needed. I stepped in and locked the door behind me.

Chapter 14

At one-thirty the next afternoon I was parked in my Chevy kicking three empty mocha containers, waiting for my two o'clock appointment with Mr. Carl Carp, of Carp, Brian & Rabinowitz, the accounting firm listed in Walter Epps' books. Wanted to chat about some ghosts.

At the moment, I was haunted by other ghosts of my own. I don't make a practice of sleeping with girlfriends of men I know. Not that the night with Beverly hadn't been worth it, and, after she told me she and Dorey were free to see other people, I didn't hesitate. It's just that Dorey had more or less introduced me to the girl, and I'd breezed with him all evening long, like an old homey, then gone off and snaked his trim.

I didn't feel all that bad, I guess, until I was in the bathroom afterwards, fixing to leave, and Dorey's four-year-old kid walked in on me, wearing my tweed hat and toting a toy M-16. I cleared out plenty quick after that.

Two rings of the Baptist Church steeple beside Lincoln Park, and I plunged through the solid door of Carp and Henchmen. Inside the reception area, I reminded the secretary how reporter Elwood Leroy from the Newark *Star-Ledger*, which was me, had called for a two o'clock appointment. A couple minutes later she ushered me into Carp's inner sanctum.

Carp's private room had wall-to-wall carpeting, plush

to your knees, and real old-fashioned hardwood wall panels. But his desk looked manufactured by Corning Ware, and it was festooned with all the machine-age business tools, desktop computer terminal, high-power calculators, intercom, and designer phone.

Behind it a troll out of 1930s cartoons puffed his cigar at me and tried to wheel his chair back. Carp's three-piece suit was stuffed with Carp to the point where he had no choice but to leave the bottom two vest buttons undone.

"Please take a seat," he wheezed and gave me a sweaty, nicotine-stained hand to waggle.

At seat level, the acrylic wedge on Carp's desk was poking me in the face, which for some reason made me feisty as hell. It proclaimed in etched letters that its owner was CARL L. CARP—CERTIFIED PUBLIC ACCOUNTANT, as if bandits like Carp had so many different faces for their clients they needed a name tag to remind them of something.

"The *Star-Ledger* wants to do a story on my firm?" Carp was saying. "Naturally, I'm flattered. But I don't see what interest it could have."

We both smirked at his modesty.

"So your angle is what, Mr. Leroy?"

"Well, it's maybe unusual, I admit." I worked up a little cub reporter pep for the man. "But we think this story's gonna have tremendous appeal to the average reader." I leaned forward in my leather sling chair. So did Carp in his.

"What is the story?"

"Just recently," I said, "it got to our attention that your accounting firm was working hand-in-hand with some of the federal projects in Newark. Advising them on their financial problems and the like? Well, I personally think, and my editor agrees with me, that it is pretty damned impressive the way you and your associates have been taking a strong hand in the welfare and administration of these public projects." I smiled encouragingly.

Carp said, "Sort of a marriage between the private and the public sectors."

"Exactly." I paused.

"Can you be specific?" he said.

"To be perfectly up front with you, Mr. Carp, although I am acquainted with a few of your federal projects, I don't want this story to wind up just about a list of names on a balance sheet."

Carp began looking as if his tie tack was caught in his throat.

"Take Family Planning Services," I said. I flipped a couple pages in my notepad for effect. "What I'd like to do here is not only discuss the financial structure with you, but also interview some of the employees, get the workingman's view. Color like that goes over, you see."

Carp didn't know whether to shit or go blind.

"How do they feel about the program's management? I mean, you take some of these federal projects, the employees are just working stiffs, right? In so many words."

"I don't think." Carp could hardly move his teeth. "On second thought, I really don't believe a news story would be in order. Not in the best interests of our clients."

"Oh, you're being too modest, Mr. Carp. You gave these workers a new lease on life. A little exposure is just what you've been deserving."

Carp did more than catch my drift, he nearly gagged on it. He squashed the end of his cigar in the ashtray like a drunk aiming his car key at the front door keyhole.

"Who are you?" he choked out. "Who told you to come here?"

Now we both knew what we were talking about. Carp scooped up a ballpoint pen and clutched it like a dagger.

"Normally, we journalists don't like to reveal our sources, but this particular source's got nothing to lose now." I stood up over Carp. "Walter Epps put me on to you. And don't bother telling me to get out. I was just on my way."

At the doorway I swung around and looked at him. His hand was already making a move for the space-age phone, but he froze when I looked back. "I'm just looking to get your name into the newspapers," I said. And left.

Outside, I waited in my pickup on the opposite side of Washington Street, sipping my last cold coffee. At the side of the building Carp's Cadillac sat like a parade float in the spot named for him. By five o'clock nobody had yet scolded me for sitting in a "No-Loading" zone, and I'd smoked six cigarettes. I admit I'd played my hand slap-happy with Carp. That man was not about to give me piece one of information. All I'd done was spook the pants off him. Anything that happened now should happen plenty fast. If Carp did panic enough to play the fool, I'd better be right there watching him do it.

My shoulders wiggled against the elastic band of tension around my chest. Every so often I had to blink my eyeballs off the entrance to Carp's office, or they would water. Lincoln Park behind me was ringed with stately brownstones, reminders of Newark's golden years. Before I arrived uptown, unfortunately. Mind you, Newark had never been Manhattan, but it still showed traces of its own special class. Take the three thousand or so cherry trees that were planted in Branchbrook Park near my apartment. On any Sunday in late April, there'll be maybe ten thousand people in the park, looking at and smelling the cherry blossoms. I never missed it, even years I had no lady to go with. Which had been the case once or twice lately.

Traffic was picking up by the minute. I started planning how I could get my wheels out fast when I needed to.

Suddenly the gold Eldorado whipped out of the alley next to Carp's office and really motificated around the park. I could just glimpse old Carp puffing like mad on his cigar as he gunned it past me.

For a couple of blocks I laid back, then picked up his zigzag course through the bumper-car traffic up the western slope of the city and into the Oranges. Half a dozen times the gold Caddoo darted and almost lost me in the low sun. With Carp pulling at the wheel like a crazy man, I was lucky to keep him in sight at all. He dragged me through a maze of narrow potholed streets, between rows of rickety wooden tenements. Then, without warning, the streets widened into tree-lined ribbons of smooth concrete. Gas lanterns flickered in the dusk.

Carp had towed me across the Newark line into the upscale suburb of South Orange.

Not much farther on, the gold car slipped into the three-car driveway of a colonial house with a low-cut lawn rolling down to the cobblestone curb. Carp hustled into that big house, and I sat for a long time across the street. Waiting and feeling disappointed. Some big desperate move Carp was making. Looked as if he'd just belted home to tuck into his lamb chops and potatoes. Nothing to do but camp out some more, hope Carp'd remember to panic after dinner.

I thought about my own dinner, which I was not tucking into. Just got to roll the dice sometimes, I told myself. I settled in. Would a car-styled pickup attract undesired attention in such a posh neighborhood? Mental note to order a few different magnetic repairman signs for the doors. Tonight at least, the big houses behind their big lawns just sat there unperturbed.

When I found myself toying with the ignition keys, I got a grip on myself, sat back, and forced myself to watch the sun go down. One advantage to all the pollution in New Jersey's air is the cinerama sunsets of purple, pink, and orange neoned across the sky every clear evening. Really set off the lily-white and gray houses of that fat neighborhood.

I was still Ferdinanding the sunset when Carp waddled back out to his car. He streaked all the way back up the street while I was firing up my short. His trail was child's play to pick up, though. Carp highballed it straight to Interstate Highway #78 and pointed his car east, back towards Newark. I whomped along after. When carburetor barrels three and four powered the pickup past sixty, my heart dropped down a notch and I caught my breath again.

At the foot of the Port Street ramp Carp belted off, me following a quarter mile behind. Below us, Port Newark sprawled like a beachhead. As far as the eye could see were rows of lighted warehouses, battalions of imported cars and trucks, and packing crates standing at attention. A long line of freighters rose ten stories above the piers as I drove down Craneway Street to the City Channel. Running lights on their bows and bridges silhouetted the cargo cranes against the night sky.

Snake in the Grasses

I cut my lights on Neptune Street and watched Carp's car rumble across a railroad spur that dead-ended at an enormous warehouse door. No sooner had he doused his lights than he was hopping out and trudging into the side door of a warehouse the size of two football fields. Faded brown letters stretching across the building's crown announced it to be the UNION OVERSEAS TERMINAL.

I backed my truck into the shadows of a loading dock about two city blocks away, diagonally across from Carp's warehouse. It felt long abandoned. I dropped down my glove box door and fished out the compact 8 × 20 binoculars I keep there for snooping. Angel had been playing with them. I reset the right eyepiece, then used the center ring to set the left. On the window sill I propped the glasses and eased my body into a position I could stay with. If the lenses didn't bounce back a stray light beam, nobody was gonna notice me.

Another long wait. You always expect a dead-fish stink down the Port, but that night the air blew strong and fresh. The clear day had passed into a bright-moon night. I killed some time watching car-carrying trucks shuttle back and forth with shiny Datsuns strapped to their backs and craving two extra-thick spiced beef sandwiches on rye from Weintraub's, with sides of both potato salad and cole slaw. Half a six-pack of Heineken and a Chesterfield, too. Bag of chips, maybe.

Pretty soon another car graveled into the lot, a black-walled, no-chrome Chevy sedan that spelled C-O-P-S. It stopped next to Carp's Cadillac, and out stepped a bull who threw down his cigarette and toe-soled it out. Even without his boxing trunks, the movement of his bulky shoulders and neck gave him away. In fact, even Velnarsky's tight waist-length windbreaker showed his muscles shifting around. Watching him, my own belly muscles tightened. He turned towards the warehouse and disappeared through the lighted door without once looking back.

My natural move would be to glide out of my truck, through the shadows to a window where I could listen inside the warehouse.

Except that the street light splashed right on the warehouse door and the wide-open approach to it. Besides, all the windows I could see were heavily frosted. Velnarsky could step out at any second. I stayed put.

The dock that terminal was perched on was littered up with all manner of harbor debris, discarded equipment, broken down forklift, rusted cables and such. My mind cataloged spots in the shadows behind the huge derrick foundation, or up against one of the big hawser moorings, where a man could hide, if he needed to. If he weren't too weak from hunger to hide.

A buoy's blinking red beacon bobbed in the wash of a tugboat heading up the channel. You could hardly hear the sea rat rooting through the garbage pile thirty feet away. But you could see him, all right. Rats like that hunted alone, I remembered hearing. Wharf rats are the size of small dogs and twice as fierce. Bastards don't have to hunt in packs like their smaller cousins in the projects. Most any one of them's more than a match for the junkyard canines that nose through the marshlands around the Port.

An autumn wind blew through the crack in the passenger's side window so I rolled it up tight to cut down the cross-ventilation. Too early still for a killing frost, but if the Newark Sharecroppers made it past the semifinals and into the finals, we'd have to buy plastic covers to drape over some of the vegetables at night to protect them. Cloches, they called those covers. You peel them off in the morning, stick them back on at night. Put Snookie and Ernie in charge of it.

By eight o'clock I knew my nine o'clock date with Ruth Epps was in trouble. Maybe Carp and Velnarsky would give me a break, make a move sometime soon, so I could get to a phone and push the time back.

Then the warehouse door cracked yellow again, framing Velnarsky and Carp side by side for a minute. Velnarsky lit Carp's cigar for him. The wind blew their laugh together at me. Then a second laugh. Velnarsky's shadow swallowed Carp. The squat troll had to peer up to see Velnarsky's face.

The two of them started wandering chummily down

the wharf apron, toward the water, chatting away and smoking up a storm. Once they stopped. Carp frantically slapped at his pockets, maybe searching for car keys. After a second I could hear him laugh nervously.

Velnarsky laughed with him. I heard his voice mix in with Carp's. I saw his arm snake around and drop buddy-style on Carp's shoulder.

I realized then what was about to happen.

My forearms started trembling so I could not hold the binoculars on them. Somehow I got the door open, kicked out of the truck, and slouched along the roadside shadows. I half-wanted to yell a warning, but my heart was pounding so hard even my feet were on automatic pilot.

When danger is menacing you, the adrenaline powers you clearheaded and strong. But when you peeping-tom at death stalking somebody else, you can't draw your breath, you keep floating off from the scene.

By the time I reached the pier itself, the background noise level took me by surprise. The whole thing was creaking and being slapped at by waves.

Moving as fast as I could without tipping off Velnarsky, I closed ground on them slowly, catching peeps of the short man and the big man strolling past heaps of shattered planks, stacks of old packing blankets, rows of white-painted oil drums. Is it bulkheads, they call them? Whatever, they walked past maybe ten of them. Most of the time I was catching up, one or the other was out of my sight, and half the time they were both concealed by wharf clutter. Every time they reappeared I was relieved to see Carp still walking. Maybe I was wrong about what might happen next.

Just past the derrick mooring, long before I was close enough to make any move, Velnarsky did the most horrible and near-impossible thing I ever saw a man do.

Obscured by the ten thousand different shapes on that wharf, Velnarsky slid his hand off Carp's shoulder, onto his left bicep, as if he was gonna whisper Carp something confidential. But then the Homicide cop flexed his right knee, wheeled his huge body with unbelievable force to his left, still gripping Carp's bicep, and whipped Carp's whole tubby body four feet off the ground and into a revolution in the air.

As Carp came flying halfway around, head first, Velnarsky strained his upper body further to the left. It was almost a genuflection. With those brute arms fully extended, he belted Carp's unprotected head into a sick collision with the iron bulkhead at the middle of the pier. The only sound I ever heard like that was the fleshy splat of a traffic-light-running Chevrolet, just pouring on the speed, knocking a pedestrian up over the windshield and onto the roof. Carp's corpse just collapsed, like a sack of grass seed.

Another second, and Velnarsky had Carp's body slung over his right shoulder. Moving as though Carp's fat body were light as a cat hair, he walked clear back up the wharf, right at me crouching behind an old elephant crate.

Then he was past me and, a second later, he cut left to the rear of his own unmarked cruiser. With one hand he unlocked the trunk. Then he dipped his shoulder and dumped Carp's body next to the spare tire. One foot dangled over the tip of the trunk before Velnarsky stuffed it back in. He fumbled with Carp's body until I heard keys clank.

Then Velnarsky pocketed his own keys and stepped to Carp's car, next to his. He cranked down every window in it.

Driver's door open, Velnarsky stuck in the keys to unlock the steering wheel and levered the gears into neutral. Bracing his shoulder on the doorframe, he shoved that Cadillac along without a speck of trouble. Where the parking lot gravel met the boardwalk, he reached in to turn the wheels and heaved all eight thousand pounds right up onto the pier.

Along the apron's edge a ten-foot path was fairly clear of major debris for the entire length of the wharf. Velnarsky rolled the Cadillac that entire route, stopping three times to toe obstacles over the side. He pushed past me again, five feet away. He wasn't even breathing hard.

Peering around my packing crate, I could follow Velnarsky's progress clear as day. He took no more than three minutes to push that dinosaur the whole two hundred yards. To the end of the pier he pushed, until the car bucked forward, went tail up, disappeared.

Chapter 15

Three times is a charm. As Velnarsky turned to walk towards me for the third time, I braced myself to settle his hash. The .22 automatic in my pocket barely filled my hand when I pulled it out, but it would do the job, providing I combined it with total surprise and a shitload of savvy. I peeked around the crate edge again: Velnarsky was striding back like a man with a clear conscience. I'd let him blow past me, two, three steps, then step out, freeze him, disarm him.

And then what?

I had no handcuffs, no phone nearby to call the cops. And Velnarsky wasn't going to be too damned cooperative. Or much afraid of me holding that mickey-mouse gun on him. He'd killed Carp with his bare hands, but no doubt his shoulder holster was full of something the human body doesn't much care to eat.

I decided to force him onto his knees, hands behind his head, stretch him on his stomach for a pat-down, hands still clasped, then roll him on his back. I'd keep well out of kicking distance, his specialty: I was pretty damn certain that I'd eaten one of Velnarsky's kicks already, that night Walter Epps died. Then, when I knew he was clean of weapons and keys, I'd march him back to his car and make him climb into the trunk with Carp's corpse. Then I'd drive the two of them, killer and evidence, to Dale Mooney at Police HD. Mooney not there, I'd ask for Eddie Dorey. Barnes, Hero of Newark.

It was a pretty good plan for the two minutes I had to make it in. I froze and sipped shallow breaths. The tip of

109

Velnarsky's spaghetti-strand shadow poked into my field of vision, bobbed, moved forward. No earstrain to hear his footsteps slap at a regular but nonchalant pace. My legs shook from the tension, and my stooped back ached sorely. Always a mistake to try timing the footsteps—just makes you concentrate too hard so you freeze. I aimed to hang on until I saw all of that broad back. Then straighten up, take the big step out. Don't forget to point the pistol at him with two hands.

More of the long shadow revealed itself, hands, knees, feet. . . . The footsteps clunked loudly all of a sudden, and Velnarsky's whole body was in plain sight, toeing athletically past my crate.

I stretched the big stride out behind Velnarsky and opened my mouth to yell Freeze! As I brought the pistol up, though, a third car cornered the warehouse and lurched next to Velnarsky's cruiser, spitting gravel. Velnarsky instantly pivoted and began trotting towards the car.

Nary a split second to choose. Taking down Velnarsky with my present firepower would be tricky, at best. Tackling a second thug was impossible. Like a gopher, I dived back behind my crate.

Without much ado, Velnarsky turned over his motor and screeched out of the lot; the other car was right on his tail.

I jammed the little Colt back in my pocket, angry as all get out. They'd fade out of the Port before I could scramble back to my car. Velnarsky would spend the night losing Carp's body as only a Homicide detective can. Where it would never be found.

I stamped across the pier to the warehouse. Carp and Velnarsky had met there for a reason important enough to get Carp dead.

Fire escape on the left side hung its old ladder low enough for me to stack three crates, leap, and grab onto the bottom rung. Rusty hinges screamed as I dangled, but eventually the jammed counterweights swung the rail of iron stairs vertically. I clambered on up to the third-story

metal landing, while that ladder slowly retracted like a
swamp creature sucking in its tongue.

Fist wrapped in a handkerchief, I punched in a pane of
glass in the fire door, pushed the inside release bar, and
stepped inside, onto a plank catwalk running the length of
the warehouse. V-shaped suspension struts gleamed white
as ribs in the moonbeams filtering through the old skylight.
Three stories below me, the warehouse floor was a desert
plane of concrete, except for clusters of thrown-out pallets
and other rubbish in the corners. The air was moist and
funky; a good spot to grow mushrooms. From way up where
I was perched, the whole floor looked dusted with talcum
powder.

Edging my way along that catwalk, I teetered like a
high wire aerialist. Down the iron stairs at the end, I shook
and reverbed my way to the floor. The skylight softly lit the
center of the floor, leaving the edges in shadow, like for ball-
room dancing. But what was really unbelievable was what I
could hear. Sounds of me totally filled that enormous space,
every tiny slap of shoe leather on cement floor whacking
louder and louder as it bounced back from the giant tin
walls and roof.

At the back middle of the floor hunched a sort of shack,
maybe a one-story office, completely enclosed by the warehouse. Years ago, when this joint stored more than air and
dust, it had probably been the operations room for shipping
and receiving clerks. Its single door was heavy metal, double, no, triple locked. Clear burglarproof, even to me.

If I hadn't been nursing such a grudge I might have
given up then and taken a chance on calling in some cavalry.
But I'd pumped up so tight for jumping Velnarsky, something I now knew I'd been building to for the past three
days, that I was still jazzed to the teeth with frustration and
violent anger.

That's probably why I vibrated back up the iron stairs,
onto the catwalk. Gripping a roof strut, I swung out, holding by my hands, three stories above the cement floor. It
was four struts, about six feet apart, to the one over the

shack. Dropping my left hand, I kicked my legs, got my whole body swinging, and reached my left arm as far as I could to grab the next strut. Then I kicked the swing up again and stretched to grab a strut with the right hand, then swung to the left again. When I was hanging over the corrugated sheet metal roof, I let 'er drop, twenty feet down.

Boomed and crashed and bounced uncontrollably, spilled onto my knees, then my face, tin sheets flexing and yawing. When I could get balanced, I crabbed around on hands and sore knees, searching for a seam or hole or weak spot. Which I found, no trouble, when the section holding me caved inward on a sudden. For one long second, I clung there. Then, with a last up and down shudder, the roof ripped itself free of the beams it'd been tacked to, and tipped me with a hideous screech down to the cement floor.

Did my elbows and knees ever smart! Ripped and stinging from the stuck-out nails. I cursed and brailled my way along the walls until I touched a light switch. My eyes were tearing like the devil. But not from the sudden fluorescent glare. The harsh edge of ammonia soaked the air. Before my eyes squeezed shut, I saw two trestle tables made out of plywood sheets and sawhorses, on which some entrepreneur had spread out a chemical laboratory.

Once you've seen a lab like that, you never mistake it. A money-making item: in Newark, usually two hundred and fifty bucks per eightball packet, about three grams; an ounce costs around nine hundred. But I never saw a meth kitchen as high tone as the one I was in now, at least not since the Oriental Street police raid in 1968. This one was by no means your typical fly-by-night soup kitchen manned by some dental-school kid scooping fast pesos on the side.

I forced eyelids apart a crack to spot the row of hooks holding army gas masks, pulled one on, and pretty soon I could see okay. My breathing cleared up enough for me to poke around the setup. That equipment and all that flaskware alone probably retailed for over two and a half grand. But after that outlay what remained was mostly gravy. For two hundred and fifty dollars, anybody can buy all the chemicals, except one, that you need to get going. The steps are easy, too.

Meth labs are always called kitchens. This one had a pretty good store of preserves. Stacked against the walls were two and a half dozen fifty-gallon drums of wood alcohol, hydrochloric acid, mythlamine, acetone. And, sure enough, I sniffed P-2-P. A weird concoction; smelled just like piss. P-2-P is nearly impossible to get hold of—only one or two legitimate medical purposes for it. But this outfit had stashed a fifty-five-gallon drum of it, enough to pave the sidewalks of Newark in meth.

Someone had thoughtfully labeled everything with red grease pencil. In the center of the kitchen sat a giant cast-iron caldron, maybe sixty quarts, where all those poisons would be poured together and seasoned with a pinch of mercuric chloride and a few strips of aluminum foil.

Like any good stew, this stinking mess is simmered over a low, low flame for eight hours. Stir it up constantly until that sludge turns brown-green, and it'll get the consistency of cake batter. Then it goes in small batches into a triangular flask, where it gets sucked through paper filters and wire mesh by a suction pump. The liquid meth that ends up in the flask gets poured into a shallow Pyrex dish, laced with liquid ether, and then put out to bake under a sunlamp. Never, ever, over an open flame. Meth kitchens blow up all the time. Looking over that equipment, I could picture the incinerated corpse we found of a careless seventeen-year-old meth chef who had made one fatal mistake in the recipe just before he left this world. In a puff of smoke.

The whole evaporation process takes maybe sixteen hours. Usually the joint is left unattended during this. Just too damned risky to hang around while all that volatile vapor is in the air. Like now.

The batch I was looking at had arrived at the late evaporation stage. Slowly crystallizing, it was heated from underneath by a low-heat automatic electric warmer and from the top by the funnel-shaped sunlamp.

I poked at the sediment in the tray. Tan-white in color,

it didn't lump up when I dabbled at it. Definitely high-class stuff. Bad meth has this gray-green tinge to it. It kills more junkies in Newark than all other drugs put together. Liver disease, it gives them.

I was probably looking at fifty thousand dollars worth of high grade meth. Sounds funny, but I found myself feeling relieved that the stuff looked okay. First corpse I ever found, when I was a rookie, was the body of an old speed freak in the crapped-up bedroom of a condemned house. His face was every bit as green as the bad meth he'd punched out on. Being green myself at the time, I'd blown lunch all over him.

That office door had double-keyed locks. So I just had to hoist myself back out through the hole on the roof.

Hustling back to my car, I put some of the pieces together. Epps, Carp, and Velnarsky were partners in the meth kitchen. Not hard to figure how Velnarsky was hooked up to the others: he'd muscled in and was taking his cut for dishing out "protection." When Epps got targeted for a Grand Jury, Velnarsky had shut his mouth good. Then, when Carp spooked from my needling, Velnarsky killed him, too.

Other pieces of the action were still mysteries to me. Who supplied so much P-2-P? Cops and accountants and civil servants don't have access to a chemical so scarce and tightly controlled. Another thing, who moved the drugs out and tied into the street pipelines? Not fat old South Orange Carp, that's for sure. And not likely Walter Epps, who lived the uptown life and got his picture took with the mayor. Least of all Detective Velnarsky, who'd be way too well known to the Vice Squad and undercover cops who patrol the drug scene in Newark.

Who else was I up against?

Chapter 16

Without Carp's body to unveil in Velnarsky's car trunk, I'd be risking life and limb to go crying to the cops at this point. Hell, even with Carp's body I'd need every power of persuasion and all the luck. Velnarsky's word against mine. And him a Homicide Squad superstar?

What next? If Carp's blabbing was threatening enough to Velnarsky that he iced the little troll, then probably Carp kept records in his office that would be even more worrisome. Maybe they'd even ID the other parties in this unholy alliance. It was worth the risk: I'd be better equipped to cover my own ass.

Across from Carp's office, I parked and sat tight for twenty minutes. When I was reasonably sure the coast was clear, I crossed the street and scooted down the alleyway to the rear of the building.

First I climbed on the window sill closest to the door, leaned over, and unscrewed the naked twenty-five-watt bulb that threw the only light. I left it threaded in its socket.

The back-door lock was the flush-plate Yale tumbler I'd seen on the front doors when I blew through that afternoon. Brand new, but the same kind they made fifty years old. Easy pickings, if you've done that kind of work before. Now, if a deadbolt had been there, I would die of starvation before I crashed into that building. This looked good, though. None of the doors or windows showed any tape or contact alarms.

The ballpoint pen I keep clipped in my glove box has hollow guts, and my lock picks fit neatly inside. Nothing's foolproof, of course. While an average beat cop would never think to look inside a pen for burglar's tools, a good street-wise detective would probably check there first thing.

What faint light filtered in from the street was enough. The next-thickest pick fit, and those large tumblers on the older locks make them usually a snap to flick over. As long as they're brass and not rusty. The minutes felt long, but only a couple creaked by before I could turn the handle and squeak the door open. Picks back into the ballpoint, ball-point back into my pocket.

In that pitch-black hallway, I clicked on my little pen-light, but held it in my left hand, at arm's length from my body. If there was a trigger-happy guard in the building, his aim would be dead on the flashlight, not on me. My gunhand would also be free to return the fire. Only trick in this case was, I wasn't toting a gun with me. I was going to look like a real superstar returning fire with my cigarette lighter, but no experienced B & E man would dream of carrying a gun, which, in case you do get picked up, zooms the charge to Armed Robbery, for which you do serious time. Besides which, if anyone gets hurt, for any reason, the old Armed Robber takes the whole weight.

The layout of Carp's office was fixed in my mind. Even in the dark, I made no noise getting there.

No sounds of life from inside. Time for some Master-charging. Another outdated lock, this time spring-loaded. I wristed the card until the semi-hollow door popped and opened, sweeping the thick carpet's nap.

The mercury vapor lamp on the street outside filled the reception area with a metallic orange haze, letting me move around the desks and chairs without cracking my shins. What I was looking for, information on Walter Epps' federal rip-offs, was not likely filed away under "R." I soft-shoed it into Carp's private office where it was much darker.

Only an interoffice memo addressed to C. Carp lay on the bare ceramic desk. The clever drawers and lone file cab-inet turned up zero. I rooted around in the paperwork stacked neatly on the bookshelves and even in corners on the carpeted floor. The only books on the shelves were a book-club-bound series of American classics, third shelf from the top. That caught my eye right away. For one thing, they were all well-known works that I had never read. They also looked plenty out-of-place in an accountant's office.

I took down *The Sound and the Fury*, *Walden*, and *Leaves of Grass*. In the thin orangey light, I ran my fingertips along the planks behind them. Not a thing. Grabbed *The Confidence Man*, *The Marble Faun*, *Education of Henry Adams*, and *Riders of the Purple Sage*, layered them on the carpet, and put my fingers to work again.

This time I could barely feel it. Almost too thin for my thick fingers. A hairline crack tucked into the seam between two boards. I unfolded the long blade of my penknife and slid it into the crack and almost halfway around a square section of woodwork before I got the click I expected. With the tip of the knife, I pried up the section and reached in to caress the metal door of a wall compartment planted behind the bookshelves. Not a safe, it felt more like a hollow fuse box. But it would have done the job—I know I'd never have found it—if Carp hadn't covered it up with the wrong kind of books.

The only stash was a small ledger, about three inches by five. I stuffed it under my belt in back and began trying to put Carp's office back the way it was.

I wasn't finished when I heard the door to the outer office softly brush the carpet.

My first heart-thumping instinct was to scratch around for another way out. But I had let my uninvited guest box me into a corner room with only a window barred from the outside.

Chapter 17

 You corner an experienced burglar, he'll climb as high in the room as he can. It's human nature to look eyeball height or lower when you come into a room searching for somebody. Almost nobody ever looks up at the tops of the walls. People figure to find the burglar crouched in a corner or huddled under a desk.

You can get your head hurt figuring that, I know for a fact.

The best B & E man in Newark taught me the hard way, when I was still a rookie. He spidered himself from the wood ceiling molding for over ten minutes. When that adrenaline is pumping away, anything is possible, I guess.

It's even possible that the searcher will turn the wrong way, let you get a jump on him. I scrambled to the top of the file cabinet beside the door and flattened myself against the wall like a shadow. Nothing happened; not a creak, not a sigh from the outer office.

Felt like I was stretched out on that cabinet top for forty minutes, though the clock probably ticked off three. Whoever it was had talent for the game we were playing. Outwait that foxy old burglar. Just sit yourself down out there and let him sweat. I concentrated so hard on controlling my breathing and freezing my muscles that my whole body started shaking. Nobody can freeze totally still against a wall for more than five, ten minutes.

At least not when he knows somebody's getting ready to come at him.

Bastard sure was taking his sweet time coming in.

Carefully, I wiped my perspiration-soaked palms onto my pants leg and tried swallowing, but my mouth was stone dry. My legs were pea vines. That damn doorknob took to bouncing up and down as I focused in on it.

Come on, you mother. Let's get on with it.

It happened fast, the door bursting open, a large shape lurching into the room. A big man in a combat crouch, practically silent. I could just pick out his movements. He pivoted sharply to the left. Then to the right. Searching for me. Looking at eyeball height, I prayed.

Dizzy by then, but halfway calm too, I could just feel that waiting half a second longer would cramp my body up.

One, two, three, without ever deciding, I was flying off the cabinet top, swinging my arms at the middle of the

118

room. Both feet came whamming down into the intruder's neck and head.

The explosion sent him diving across the room on his stomach, slamming up against the wall. The wind wooshed out of my lungs, but though it hurt I shoved myself onto my feet. All my instincts, surer than mother's love, told me it was Ray Velnarsky spilled out on the dark floor. And told me not to dawdle, no matter how I ached to kick his teeth in and drag him to a cell. My story was still just a story, whereas the big cop had caught me neck-deep in a felony; backup troops could be pouring in any minute, for all I knew.

"Ray?" I heard somebody whisper on the opposite side of the connecting door. I yanked the handle with my right and tagged a second man off-guard with my left fist. Before he could react, I popped up and shivered him under the chin with my left forearm. He went down like pickup-sticks. I shot through the outside door and stretched it for the stairs.

Behind me I could hear them regrouping. But I blew out of the little side alley before they could hit the back door. I'd take no chances fumbling with my truck keys. Sprint west on William Street, away from my vehicle. No matter if the two heavyweights come huffing and yelling behind me. I grew up in this neighborhood; I'd lose them but quick.

An engine roared and tires screamed. At the same time, I could hear gasping and the heavy footslapping of one man still at least a hundred feet behind me. William Street drops straight as an arrow down the hill, not good cover, so I cut sharp to my right through a vacant lot of crushed glass, concrete chunks, and car parts, where a whole neighborhood of apartment houses stood when I was a boy. At big, wide Springfield Avenue, I timed the traffic right, not missing a stride across and past the old Music Supply House. By the time I'd grown to be a cop, when we'd radio-car to the semi-regular burglary calls from there, we'd always hear trumpets screeching and drums banging in the next-door tenements down Springfield Avenue.

119

At the Music House, I glanced backwards. Back across Springfield Avenue, Velnarsky was threading between cars coming two ways. His windbreaker was unbuttoned, and the white turtleneck beneath it accentuated the bulges of his chest and the slimness of his waist. Still a decent gap between him and me, enough of an edge for me to cook him up a nasty surprise. Where his partner in the car was, I had no clue, but me staying off the road would neutralize him.

Behind the Music House were filed the backyards of single-family houses still holding on. If I ran through them, I'd come out on Stirling Street. I didn't.

I cut left instead, ran behind the tenement where I grew up, along the backyard fences. When I was ten, Mrs. O'Boyle, tired of screaming at us tenement boys cutting through her yard to the Belmont Avenue school, had an eight-foot stockade fence installed across her back boundary, which was only ten feet wide. I say stockade, but I don't mean those pretty pointy top prefab things they stick up in the suburbs. I mean inner-city stockade, vertical two-by-fours, whitewashed, spiked to heavy posts and braced by a horizontal four-by-four at the top.

There it was, still standing, looking much the same, though probably the below-ground posts had been replaced sometime. The fence had never stopped us, being more in the nature of a thrilling challenge, of course, to a bunch of grade-school boys. But I was going to make use of it now.

At the foot of the fence, I peered behind me, and didn't actually see Velnarsky so much as smell him. He'd be running with his gun in his hand, most likely, here where he wouldn't draw much attention.

I sprang straight up, grabbed the top brace with both hands, and pulled my waist up to the top. Got a foot up and slung myself down the other side.

I could have used either the bird bath or the trash can for my purpose. Bird bath was closer. I lugged it by its base right up to the fence, stepped in the dead middle of the bowl, got my balance, and squatted down.

I was hardly in place before the chugging sounds of a runner came up two inches from me, behind the fence.

Didn't take Velnarsky a second to figure that I must have gone over. Just over my head and a foot to the left I could see one fist clutch the rail, then the other come up and wrist it, because of the gun in its fingers.

Just as a shock of Velnarsky's hair appeared above the top, I drove upwards, legs, chest, and arms, and smashed a right hand into his face as it came bobbing up. I doubt he ever glimpsed my face or the fist that walloped him.

I socked him pretty damn hard. Would have been harder still, but the bird bath teetered and then spilled me over, spoiling my follow-through. I do know Velnarsky's face and hands just wiped away from the fence top.

I slapped the dirt off my knees. That's two you ate, sucker. You want some more lunch? You got to come over here, because I am not about to climb back after you.

Before whoever was living in Mrs. O'Boyle's house could horn in a police alert, I hoofed it past the house out to Stirling Street. Up and down, it looked dead. If Velnarsky's partner in the car had lost us, I was betting he'd circle back to William Street where they'd picked me up.

So, the opposite direction for me. I walked fast, not quite trotting, west on Stirling, south on Prince Street, west again on South Orange. The next cross-street was Howard Street, the area where half the drug traffic and all the radical politics were brewed in Newark back in the 1960s. After that, Springfield Avenue was all vacant lots, eight blocks of them, down to Belmont Avenue.

As I hustled down from Howard Street, the traffic died off like when you shut the door on a windy day. All that empty space along Springfield Avenue was piled high with mounds of garbage that out-of-town contractors unload in Newark under cover of darkness. Twenty feet high some of them were, rowed one behind the other, roughly fifty feet apart. Some had been in place so long, they'd stopped smelling altogether; the fresh ones knocked you back worse than sewer gas. Through the spaces between them, to the left of me, I was catching glimpses of the old derelict Kreuger Brewery, glowering like a clutch of mountains over foothills and an asphalt prairie.

The hills of trash saved my life. They were what kept the car from just charging across the empty lots and smearing me into the blacktop.

I swan-dived onto cans and knobby bags, then, when the car torched rubber past me, I churned to the next pile in from Springfield Avenue. While there was space between the piles for the car to maneuver, he couldn't keep track of where I was because I kept circling those garbage hills. I could hear the roaring engine, and planned my dashes. Every time I split from behind one rubbish heap to the next, I'd glimpse the unmarked sedan poking its searchlight, then swerving at me. The searchlight meant the wheelman had his hands too full of light and wheel, for the time being, to hold a gun ready. If he put the light down, he could never spot me. Sooner or later, he'd decide to get out of the car. And I didn't like those odds. I decided to lose him altogether.

So when it felt right, I zigzagged to within eighty feet of the brewery. Wanted to get the huge brewery buildings between me and the cop car, then break for Belmont Ave and fade inside some diner or bar.

Would have worked, too.

When I broke into the open, as if towards Belmont Avenue, I listened to the car roar up behind me, and stamped my lead foot into a very hard ninety-degree turn. The pursuit car just rocketed past, tires shrilling bloody murder as it fishtailed to head me off.

Too late, my man. I'd reach the Brewery and stroll down one of its litter-strewn alleys before you recover.

Except for the crack of a handgun. Which came, not from where the car still squealed, but behind, where I'd run from the trash piles. How far behind, I had no idea.

Velnarsky had picked himself up and muscled right after my ass while I'd played dodgem with the vehicle.

For a long instant, I instinctively swerved towards the cover of the nearest garbage hill, but with a chill I realized that would amount to suicide. Instead, I pumped it again for the space between two brewery buildings, lungs sorely burning now.

The forty feet blurred by in two seconds, long enough for Velnarsky to squeeze off a second round. And long enough for the pursuit car to bear in on me just at the alleyway mouth.

There was time to take one veering stride to the right, frantically trying to skirt the back of the car and get on up the alley.

But as soon as I heard Velnarsky's pistol fire again, I changed my mind.

And tossed my chest right onto the roof of the car as it skidded by.

The next bullet exploded into the rear passenger's window, blasting right through and out the other rear glass. Shortly thereafter, I came sliding headfirst down the far side, directly on the warehouse doorstep.

It wasn't until much later that I had leisure to find any joy in those dirty cops shooting up their own vehicle.

What registered at the moment was the brewery door in front of me, nailed together of paint-chipped wood panels. No extra boarding across it, just a rusty padlock on a hasp holding it shut. That's all I saw, with no time to study the situation.

I just muscled up from my crouch with my knees and thighs, and drove my shoulder into that door. No awareness in my head that it's impossible to break down an outside door with your shoulder.

Like a dream, the whole thing smashed right off the jamb, rusty old hinge-screws screaming out of the wood. Panels splintered all around, as the door and me both landed with a "whumpf" on a cold cement floor. Ribs sore, what the hell, I was glad as an angel to be inside that building.

Dark as evil in there. Jerking up off that door, I humped it through what had to be a museum of old machines. Years of rust had frozen them in place. And they hurt when you bounced off them. I took maybe five steps, then threw myself down, behind something or other.

Chapter 18

The two silhouettes showed up immediately against the watery light coming through the doorway. One of them started emptying his revolver, whanging shots off the weird metal hulks in every direction in that hell of blackness. All I could do was duck my cheek against that cold floor and pray.

Then I heard them step inside and spread out in either direction. I pitched myself to my feet and worked further into the building. One of them silhouetted again, scurrying out for the flashlight, most likely. I would have maybe three, four seconds to search out a pathway in the dark through that damn mechanical maze.

But a prize could be had for walking that puzzle. Under that warehouse, like a fat worm, an enormous tunnel lay. My daddy used to tell us stories about it when we lived in the neighborhood. So also sang the popular tune around the West Precinct house, when I was a cop. Story was, around the turn of the century, Kreuger Beer's top brass dug that tunnel between the brewery on Belmont Avenue and the Kreuger Mansion on High Street so they could travel the half-mile or so underground on rainy days and not dampen their patent leather and spats. I had never seen it, though. The whole place had been locked up since Prohibition. Not the first brewery to die in Newark and, God knows, by no means the last.

An early radio-car partner, who claimed to have explored the tunnel, had described a series of circular steel staircases leading to the old basement.

As the searchlight stabbed at the dark behind me, I dropped to my hands and toes and crawled. By the time Velnarsky and company had worked half their way through the junk on the main floor, I had elbowed real soft to the spiral stairs. And then slithered it on down.

Below ground, I could hear footsteps thumping on the concrete floor over my head, at first hesitant, then faster and faster. A searchlight would speed up moving through the metal wreckage. Waving it so freely, they must be positive I was packing no gun.

I bumped shins around that basement for more than long enough, until, in between the wooden beer trucks and carriages parked there, I found what must be the tunnel doors along the back wall. The heavy iron bar that shut the two doors together was chain-wrapped, too much for my shaking hands. I threw my whole weight against the thick planks as heavily as I could, but no more hinges were giving way for me that day.

Like evil thunderclaps, the footsteps overhead banged then rumbled down the metal steps and grew, crossing two hundred feet of basement floor. The hunters were closing in for the kill.

Shoved my arm and shoulder through the crack between the doors, but no farther.

One of the chaser's yells suddenly boomed off the high cement walls. Too close. Raw fear clawed at me from the roof of my mouth to the center of my guts. Exactly where they were I could not tell, the echoes were so spooky.

When I fumbled again with the chains, this time an end flopped over. I kept flipping it until the whole thing slid off. The cross-bar stuck, then pivoted up; the double door grated inwards on the rough floor.

Inside, the tunnel was colder than the basement, damp and covered with slick mossy growth. Water drops rippled into a pool somewhere ahead. The slime made my progress a clown show in the blackness. I slipped a hundred times, until my ass was hurting so, I could cry.

I fingered along the stone-coffered walls, though every shuffle echoed a mortar-barrage. Every ten yards or so, the walls were ribbed by brick archways. Best as I could reckon in the dark, that tunnel was maybe five yards wide, and sloped downhill plenty quick. Twice more my feet skidded from under me on the slimy bricks and I banged on the seat of my pants, each time sliding a few feet.

Second time, the breath was rapped clear out of me and I wheezed on my back until the air seeped back into my lungs. Groans and bellowing rolled in from behind me, probably the gunmen cursing the day I was born. I never knew sounds like that existed, beginning faintly, then echoing off stone walls past me and on down the empty tunnel, weird enough to stagger me back onto my feet.

Maybe twenty minutes' worth more slipping and skating along on those slimy bricks. Now I was splashing through invisible icy water up to my ankles.

At the bottom of a dip in the floor, where the tunnel made a wide bend, this scummy pool blocked the way. Oh, I couldn't see it, but I could hear that pool, drops of water dripping from the broken main overhead, smacking the water and echoing off. Ticking off all the seconds that I stood there, my imagination picturing the water miles long and yards deep. God knows what on the bottom.

What was there to think about? Drown or get shot. When it comes to that, I'd rather die by my own doing. I fumbled two strides into the pool.

And promptly sank up to my knees in the filth at the bottom. Heart scrambling up my neck, I saw myself sinking powerlessly until the ooze covered my head forever. But all that happened was my feet stuck flypaper-tight. Over my waist in liquid that felt thicker than water, and colder. Then one foot sucked out so I could grope forward again. But when I leaned hard on my right foot to yank up my left, I just drove that right foot deep into the cold scum again. So I shifted weight back onto my left to suck out the right foot, and kept it up. The mechanical rhythm I struck helped turn off thinking about how murderously slow I was moving.

With my buzzy head, I almost fell to giggling. Saw myself like a huge fly tugging at a monster strip of sticky tape.

Water was sloshing around my chest, frigid-cold and smelling of dead things. The chill probably kept me from fading out altogether.

That pit couldn't have been more than thirty yards

across. One fine miracle, though, if I had kept my balance all the way across in the dark. As it was, I got halfway across before I tipped over. Leaned my weight on one foot, and when the other was too quick to suck free, I just slid in over my head.

Exactly what I needed, too, because I clawed through that scum like a madman, violated to be drenched in it, dragging myself out onto the scummy bricks on the far side.

First thing, I got done panting, I strained my ears for news of my hunters. No idea how close they had crawled up behind me while I was yanking my feet unstuck in that foul pool. Nerve endings in my eyes started to sparkle as I focused hard on the dark down the tunnel. Only damn thing I could see was blackness.

A push-up put me on hands and knees again. Best I could manage was to crawl straight away from the pool. Every part of me was protesting—the point of my shoulder from body-blocking the warehouse door, calves and back from the strain they'd absorbed all night—but especially my knees, so raw from crawling on bricks that pretty soon I was resting for a couple seconds every time I dragged one creep forward. All I could hear was the breath tearing at my throat.

My inchworming slowed still more when I pushed a palm down and mushed a soft furry lump that screeched in pain, then squirmed away. Something else bit my thumb. Then I saw them. Hundreds of glitter eyes staring back all around me. In front of me, on all sides. A sea of them behind me too, between me and the slimy pool.

I tried flapping my hands. I swear, not one pair of pink pupils even twitched.

The scuff of feet told me the death twins stood on the far side of the green sea, waving that damned searchlight around, maybe sixty feet away. I lay flat on my belly, pressing in the muck to keep from shivering. Rats scurried light-footed over my body; one tried to burrow up the leg of my pants. Burning with disgust, I grit my molars, but didn't flick a muscle to stop him.

Slowly, the searchlight played out over the filthy pool.

Then I could hear one man start wading in. Whoever held the light was careful never to silhouette his partner, just illuminated a route for him along the opposite wall from where I had sloughed. The water must have been even deeper there. Before he mucked even halfway out, the wader was practically eating water. He yelped in fear. His partner laughed. The man in the soup sucked out a foot, then the other one, but in reverse. Pretty soon his chattering teeth were back on the edge where he started.

They went back to playing that deadly light on the water and across the pool. Seemed to land on my body two dozen times. Or was I dreaming? The tunnel bent in a huge curve right there. Could be the light beam didn't reach me at all. Except that every time the beam landed, the rats stopped their constant nervous stir and froze.

The wader mumbled something, in which I heard the words "fuckin' cold." To which his partner told him to shut up. Then he must have hefted his revolver and pointed it right down the tunnel where I was laying. Wham! Six demolition explosions would have been quieter. All I could do was cover my head with my arms and dig my toes deeper into the scum. With the slugs slamming off the tunnel's floor and walls, the racket was terrific. The echoes went on for an eternity. I clenched, like the center of a spinning universe.

Finally, I creaked my neck back up. The tunnel was totally black and silent as a tomb.

Chapter 19

I froze as long as I could, until my heart slowed to a gallop. If the gunmen were still waiting across the pool, they were making not a sound. Maybe they had retraced their steps.

Somehow or other I hoisted back up on hands and knees, and flinched when a swarm of light points backed off, making little tapping sounds. They graciously yielded me a few inches of room.

Some trick to stand on my feet without those rat eyes to pin down where the floor was for my spinny head.

The tunnel was climbing here, first gradually, then pretty damn steeply. Here the fungus carpet was less slippery. One step at a time, taking a decade to do it, I crept along that tunnel, braced against the wall for balance.

When my hands touched an iron rung on the wall, I could have wept for joy. Felt like a ladder going up a manhole shaft. Just the ticket, since my persevering companions would surely be camped by now at both ends of the tunnel. I hand-over-handed myself up twenty rungs fixed in cement.

At the top of that cistern was an iron saucer that weighed a ton. First time I pushed at it, it didn't budge. Clenching my teeth, I braced my aching shoulder on it and heaved with my legs. The lid raised up slow, then flopped over with a crunch. My head was poking out into perfumed fresh air. Even the stink of garbage sucked in sweet.

At three A.M. the Ponderosa is quiet as a church on Saturday, but the faint city noises popped loud and lovely in my ears. The weeds tufting through that empty paved lot smelled strong and good.

My head and shoulders stuck out of that hole like a groundhog while I revolved for a look. Under that sickening gray haze before dawn, I flopped out of the hole, onto my back, feeling the soggy little book from Carp's office pressing into my spine. I'd forgotten I had it. The fresh air rearranged my bearings some, enough to weary to my feet and wobble to the curb of Belmont Avenue.

No idea where old Death and Destruction had taken themselves off to. But this black man was not about to loiter. When a yellow garbage truck growled up and idled at a traffic light a block away, I yelled out to the driver, flagged him down.

Crew hanging on the back watched me limping up to

them without saying a word. They'd have a story to tell later at the barn about a crazy man.

"Need a ride," I told them. "All right I catch a lift with you, crosstown?"

"We not going where you live, man," one of them answered tonelessly. "Doing the Weequahic today."

"Suits me fine."

They just looked at each other. While they were doing that, I hoisted myself up on the lip of the hopper.

"Really appreciate it," I said.

One of the crew waved a hand up front at the driver's mirror, and we steamed on off.

So I don't look uptown to the junkmen, huh? Still, that destination couldn't suit me better. I had a date with a Weequahic lady. As far as I was concerned, I had a date, that is. Better eight hours late than never. Not to mention the questions I was itching to pop on the woman.

The crew shook me awake when the truck chugged near Weequahic Park.

Close to five A.M., I smacked down the knocker on the front door of Ruth Epps' house.

She took one hell of a long time answering, but I didn't mind, busy as I was hiding Carl Carp's dirty ledger behind a juniper bush. I was not sure yet what the little book would say, but I resolved that nobody else, but nobody, was going to find out it even existed.

When Ruth finally pulled the door open, I could have sworn a faint smile rippled on, then off, her face.

"Oh," she said. "Was the traffic that bad?"

A blue watered-silk bathrobe covered Mrs. Epps to her ankles, except that at her throat some cream-colored ruffles were trying to peep out. Nightgown. Shortie? Or full length? I took my time deciding, looking the lady over real close for possible evidence. Too close to call. She was wearing matching cream-colored high-heel shoes, though.

My opening line could have been sweeter. "I been out working for you tonight, lady," I said. "You know what the evening's entertainment was? First, I sit watching while a Homicide cop takes your late husband's accountant and smashes his head like a pumpkin on mischief night. Next, some breaking and entering, in which I was the breaker. A chase through a filthy, wet tunnel, in which I was the chasee. Followed by a lot of target practice, in which I was the target."

"Why don't we get you inside before the early trash pickup comes around?" she said, as if I'd remarked that it might rain.

"Trashmen made the rounds already," I said. "Dropped a pile off on your front porch. It's here still."

"I couldn't help but notice." That came with her first real smile. "You probably need some breakfast."

"All right!"

"You certainly need a bath."

Her kitchen was top shelf all around, appliances I'd never seen before, separate ones to grind the coffee, beat the eggs, roast the ox, and probably hand you the right fork for your salad. All brand spanking new and a bit too shiny. From what I saw of Ruth Epps in action, she was the kind of homebody who put the emphasis on body. Her idea of breakfast was instant coffee and a toasted English muffin. I'm not complaining; what I saw of her long body moving under that silk robe more than made up for her shortcomings as a cook.

She waited for me to wolf down my third muffin. "So, the important news that made you stand me up?"

"The good news is your husband was murdered. The bad news is I can't prove it, not yet anyway."

"How did you find this out?" Ruth said, working hard to show no reaction.

"The old-fashioned way. I risked getting my ass shot off for it." I sipped the Nescafé. Even tired and wet as I was, the water in the tunnel pool had tasted better. "You could have mentioned your husband was targeted by a federal Grand Jury, you know. Would have saved me walking around without a Seeing Eye dog."

Ruth shook her head. "That's news to me." She spread butter, then honey, then jam on a muffin, put it on a pretty china plate, and ate it in big, slow bites.

131

"Your own husband got subpoenaed to testify about fraud in the agency he directed, and he never mentioned it to you?" When she gave me the raised eyebrow treatment and bit another big chunk of her muffin, I said, "I don't believe you."

"Well, you should. Shady dealings are a way of life in the federal projects. You know that. The investigations go on continually, year after year. Walter had testified before."

"This time he was armpit deep in hot water, lady."

"Really? And you think the business trouble led to Walter's murder?"

"I know it. He ever mention any names of people he was involved with?"

"Legal involvement or illegal?"

"Is the list so endless? You know what I'm talking about."

"Who killed my husband," she said. "That's all I paid you to find out."

I stayed careful. If you don't watch yourself, you can overreact to a beautiful woman, let her get the upper hand.

"Your husband cooked methamphetamine, the chemical they found in his blood the night he bought the ranch. You know, right after he caught his johnson in the U.S. Attorney's zipper?"

Ruth put her polished nails through the muffin ritual again. Everything on it: butter, honey, both yellow and red jam.

I was having trouble hitting a punctuation mark with her.

"His partners in the drug ring thought he might try to trade them in," I tried. "He'd do that, to buy his freedom, you know."

"Walter might have liked prison," Ruth smiled. "All those gay men."

"Horseshit. Nobody wants cancer, nobody wants prison. Walter had some big names to trade with. He'd chirp like a sparrow, when the time came."

"You've no doubt about this?"

132

"None whatsoever. I saw the lab last night. What's more, I watched somebody else get wasted."

"And that's why you were shot at?"

"Not even that." I drained my coffee to milk her interest. "Nobody spotted me at the lab or at the murder scene. It was after that I got chased."

"Who chased you?"

"The same killers that did your old man."

Virginia Slims menthol light cigarettes were on the table, with a Bic lighter. Ruth took one out and lit it. I'd smoked two since I got in the house.

"Who?"

"Cops. One of them at least a Homicide detective." If I hadn't been watching her eyes, I would have missed the flicker she couldn't control.

"Disappointed?" I asked.

"No, I'm pleased." Ruth shrugged lovely shoulders. "I was the one who knew it was murder, remember?"

"Lady, I didn't fall out of the trees yesterday." My turn to laugh at her. "You were worried it was somebody else offed old Walter. That lover of yours, did you think it was? Too many scruples to make love to your husband's murderer? That a little too heavy-duty for you?"

Ruth's steady look burned holes in my pupils. Then she surprised me. She leaned back in her chair and looked almost friendly.

"Does it make such a difference why I hired you? Can't I be more complicated than that? Whether I loved him or not, Walter never deserved to be murdered. If I also worried that my lover had killed him, does that make me a monster? I for one was pleased to find I *had* scruples like those. Besides, I didn't exactly lie to you, I—"

"Just didn't tell me enough to stay out of the wolves' lair," I finished. "Don't get me wrong, Mrs. Epps, lying to your private eye is one of privileges a client pays for. I just wish you hadn't let me chase your ball out of the playground, baby. Who am I supposed to trust now? When I came here tonight, I sure didn't trust *you*, I'll tell you."

Tired as I was, I was too keyed up to sit still. At the sink, I drank a glass of water. Couldn't get it to run cold enough.

"Can't you just drop the investigation?" Ruth stepped up behind me, then touched me on the shoulder. They sure do miracles with perfume these days. My head swam.

"Those badasses that chased me knew who I was. They had to. They don't know how much I'm on to, but they're out there with their noses to the ground. If I sit still for ten seconds, they'll find me."

Inside my head was cotton candy, and my eyeballs felt coated with vaseline. "I'm done in," I told her. "You got a bed I can sleep in?"

Ruth reached out a shapely arm and brushed my cheek with the back of her hand. "You must be exhausted. I'll wash and dry your clothes while you shower upstairs. Then you can catch some sleep, and we will talk about what to do when you've got a clear head."

The shower was off the master bedroom. I stripped quickly at the sight of myself in the mirror and tossed my rags outside the door. In the shower stall, when I lathered up, everything felt and smelled specially rich and luxurious on my aching body. That hot, hot steaming water, the scented soap, the rough loofah sponge I rubbed my back with were all making me feel like I could doze off right there under the water-jet.

But the minute I stepped from the stall to towel off I was glad I stayed awake. Ruth was standing just inside the little room, in the tiniest of nightgowns. Shortie, all right, short as they come.

It only took me one step forward to reach her and put my hand behind her neck. The kiss started where we first touched and kept growing as I cupped her buttocks and carried her into her bedroom where we pressed our bodies together, still slick and soapy, her leg curling to stroke mine. Then we each reached down a hand, to tease and then to hold. I undressed her shoulders with my other hand, kissing her long neck, bending her backwards to run my lips and tongue along the upper curves of her breasts. Popped open one tiny button at a time of her nightgown, to nuzzle all that soft clean skin.

I moved her the few steps to the bed and laid her on her back, undoing the last couple buttons to free her legs, rolled next to her on the bed, our mouths both rushing at each other and just about missing. That tempted me to laugh, but her hand was bringing me to the point of making a decision. I made one and positioned both of us.

I guess it was the right decision. Ruth Epps sure seemed to think so. I know I never had a woman love me back like that in my whole life.

After a while we both got to playing the same game. Working to make the other one come first. She almost won that game, too.

Except that all of a sudden I rolled completely over, pitching her onto her back. And she gasped and hung on for dear life, arching her back, no way of controlling herself any more. That squirming pleasure of hers was infectious, too, because I started to shudder along with her and then spill over.

Afterwards, I yawned and kissed Ruth Epps' hot mouth. She ran a finger down my cheek and reached for a cigarette. She looked like she wanted to talk. Me, I went under like a cement innertube.

Chapter 20

First, the light was different in that bedroom when I opened my eyes. Second, my mouth tasted evil and rings of fire circled both eyeballs.

Best thing I noticed, though, was the widow Epps draped across my chest, lazily tickling the hair there. The

135

yawn I gave off was a giant one. Ruth Epps smiled at me and reached farther down. I ran one fingernail down her back. And she took to purring like a cat.

We were lying without blankets or any coverings on her four-poster bed. She had turned up the room heat so it was toasty and comfortable.

I liked looking at her. The height of her game, she was, late twenties, and she'd been taking care of her body. Let me tell you, I truly appreciated it. She was one great lover who'd learned that the only sure way to reach pleasure was to give it out, without holding back.

She was giving out pleasure again now. Our full attention was on my body.

I fingered along that curved back of hers, and down below her back. That cat sound turned throatier and more demanding.

"You let me sleep all day," I said. "It's after four."

"Seemed a waste of valuable time," she agreed.

"I was just dead, I guess." I stretched and then winced when the big muscles on my thighs bunched so tight my knees locked open. The muscle knots were stabbing into my flesh.

"Want me to rub that for you?" Ruth volunteered. "If I hadn't seen you in action, I might have reached the same conclusion. That you were dead, I mean."

"You saying I'm a stiff in bed, lady?"

"Well, at the moment, you've got several parts that answer that description."

"Just what time is it?"

"Why? This won't take long," she said and started exercising the rest of my body.

She was right. Didn't take all that long.

When she was finished with the physical, I caught my breath. Rolling out of the crib stretched my soreness.

"You washed my clothes!"

"You're welcome."

"Thank you, ma'am. For everything."

"Well, you'd never fit any of Walter's clothes. You are way too big. Where will you go now? To the police?"

"That'd be tricky. At least one Homicide dick is running the show. How do I know more cops aren't hooked up?"

"The detective I met—Dorey? He seemed very nice."

Dorey was many things, but nice wasn't one of them. I didn't bother to set her straight. "Nice guys like to finish first, too, you know. Last night one of Dorey's Homicide stablemates wasted Walter's accountant. I got to check Dorey out before I'd trust him. Good thing I still have one old friend in Homicide."

"You said you had no evidence. How will you convince your friend?"

"He knows me. He'll listen for a while anyway. I do have one card I can play."

Ruth sat up in bed. Her breasts showed above the blanket.

"What is it, honey?"

"The name Carl Carp ring any bells?"

"No, should it?" Ruth got out of bed, picked up a cotton blouse, then slipped into a bulky pullover sweater. My mouth went dry watching her.

"Carp was the creative writer of the accounting books for your husband and his partners. I got a ledger I'm pretty sure covers the meth operation." After all, I told myself, she might recognize a name or two.

"Where is it now?"

"Your front flower bed."

"May I see it?"

In the kitchen, Ruth and I pried the pages apart. Carp must have scribbled with a laundry marker; the ink was still legible. But we couldn't make heads or tails of it.

"All these columns of figures," I complained. "Who knows what they mean? Carp used codes for the entries, see? It'll take an expert accountant to decipher these numbers."

"But you are sure these numbers document an illegal drug operation?"

"Has to be," I said. "The ledger's the only thing Carp tucked away in his hidey-hole."

"The policemen trying to kill you tends to confirm that, doesn't it? Make sure they never take it from you."

"You know some place they'd never think to look?" Maybe I sounded nonchalant, but I watched her reaction real sharply.

"Oh, no you don't," she snapped. "I've got troubles enough as it is. I don't need murdering policemen breathing down my neck."

"Just a thought. There's enough safe places."

"Be sure it's very safe. If push comes to shove later, and you can't find another place, then I might consider hiding it, but not until then."

"Yeah, sure, I understand." Maybe I sounded nonchalant, but she'd passed the acid test, and I was relieved. "Wait until I'm calling some shots in this game instead of running all the time, hiding and watching."

"Just don't get killed or lose that book. I still plan on collecting on Walter's death policy, Mister Detective."

"Whew," I wiped my brow. "I was beginning to think you liked me."

"I do." She leaned over and kissed me good. "But let's not confuse business with pleasure, buster."

"Where's your phone?"

She handed me a pink cordless telephone with an antenna sticking out of it. I started dialing Dale Mooney's work numbers.

Chapter 21

When I couldn't reach Mooney, I asked for Eddie Dorey. But the deadpanned cop voice reported those two out together on a murder call, a body dumped last night in Weequahic Park. I pictured Carl Carp's fat mortal remains stuffed in Velnarsky's car trunk. My message asked

Dale to call me pronto. I left both the number Marlene would answer at my office and the number of my answering machine at home. Urgent, I added, just before I hung up.

Ruth was dressing for the evening viewing of her husband's body at seven P.M.

With time to kill and me too antsy to sit still, I decided to tag along. Epps was public figure enough that significant faces might turn up, the way Mafia bosses pay their respects to a rival they've iced. A peek at the guest book of Walter Epps' mourners might prove handy down the line.

Dressed to kill in a black designer dress with a little cocked hat and veil to match, Ruth swayed downstairs. I wondered if she realized she looked so striking for her husband's wake. I didn't tell her so.

Outside her door, we agreed to split up. Bringing a date to her husband's wake seemed tacky, she pointed out. No matter, I needed to pick up my truck and stow Carp's ledger somewhere safe. She'd be walking to the funeral parlor on Chancellor Avenue, she told me. Maybe I'd get to drive her home tonight, if I played my cards right.

First stop was for my pickup. I flagged down a cabbie who pried a beer baron's ransom out of me to run downtown to Lincoln Park. Miracle of miracles, my Chevy was still across the street from Carp's office, untouched except for a parking ticket under the wiper. I fired up all eight and growled off, flapping in the breeze for a block or two.

Next stop, Cosmo's cigar shop, downtown. Halfway there, I remembered how late it was and rerouted to Cosmo's apartment in the Ironbound section, a center-city island ringed with railroad tracks, elevated and otherwise. It was turning into a warm cloudy day's evening—cold and clear, I mean. The late sun came out just before I drove into the Ironbound and brightened up the rows of neat shops and neighborhood markets, always with three floors of apartments above them. It's a Portuguese district now, with the lowest crime rate in Newark. The Portuguese take care of their own.

I caught my man bustling out to the Meadowlands for night racing. Cosmo is my bookie, also my old friend. He asked no questions, promised to hide the little notebook some place good and waved me off.

The Gates of Heaven Funeral Home and Mortuary sat only five blocks north of the Eppses' house, which gives you an idea of how quickly Newark neighborhoods change tone. When I pulled up across the street, I remembered seeing the joint before and was surprised that a wealthy man like Walter Epps would be laid out in such a low-rent way. One jump north of a pauper's funeral was the style they featured.

This evening, though, a fleet of Mercedes, Cadillacs, and Lincolns lined Chancellor Avenue and its cross streets. The show was in full swing early. For future reference, I strolled carefully around, notebook in hand, jotting down every license number on every car.

The neighborhood had once resembled where Ruth Epps lived, but up here nobody'd been sandblasting loose paint or employing any landscapers. The funeral home was a wood-frame, three-story Victorian house on the corner, with the pointy top turret on one front corner balanced by the big circular sitting-porch on the other. A double driveway dipped to basement depth on the less conspicuous side where I sat. Two car ports jutted out for backing in the hearses.

Ruth had said this ritual would be over at ten. I waited until a lot of the crowd left, then zipped in for a peek at the "Dearly Beloved" book. The funeral home doors were painted pearly white, naturally, and inside the parlor was done up in hushed tones of red and brown. I flicked through the condolence book pedestaled at the viewing room entrance. Several pages of names, a few I recognized on the spot. The mayor had not seen fit to stop by. Nor the governor or president, for that matter. I raised my head; no one was noticing me. They hadn't caught a good look at the rips and stains on my clothes yet, is all. I stuck my notebook in my pocket and carefully tore out the pages of Epps' guests, folded them, and tucked them in my pocket, too.

Then I glanced for Ruth inside the "Deliverance Room" where Walter was laid out. The O'Neal Twins singing "Jesus Dropped the Charges" was just audible through hidden speakers. A considerable number of mourners still chattered and clinked glasses, the noisiest damn wake, actually, that I've ever seen. The circus atmosphere was easy to figure, though. Mixed in with all the politicos that Walter Epps had rubbed elbows with, were all the other movers and shakers he had rubbed the rest of his body against. Included in the sideshows was Angel, of course, at the moment chatting with the widow. Chewing her ear off about what a prince dear Waltie was, no doubt. Well, Angel had known Walter Epps for lots of years, which sometimes counts more than you'd think to a street character like Angel.

While I was letting old Waltie rest in peace and slipping back out the front door, the Deacon Elmo Toledo walked into the opposite end of the parlor and made like a host bidding the guests farewell. This I could not pass up.

I stepped up behind him.

"Mr. Gabriel," he said over his shoulder. "Friend of the deceased?" He was smiling tearfully and holding old ladies' hands with both of his.

When I said nothing, he whispered, "No, I think not. I am astonished at your perseverance, traveler, not to mention your poor taste, in pursuing a purely business matter at a spiritual juncture." He turned enough so I could see his mustache was shiny with cocktail drops.

"The other night, Mildred's two hundred dollars *was* a spiritual affair to you," I said. Deacon Elmo kept his dignity for the stream of departing mourners.

"So you own this place," I nodded. "You got your thumb in everything, don't you? That why Walter Epps' widow had his funeral at a dump like this? Fancy casket, all those flowers. You're in for eight, nine grand, aren't you? You have some kind of an edge with her? Or maybe with Epps himself?"

"My assistants," Deacon Elmo hissed.

"Call them," I said. "They're a sociable crowd. Maybe they'll talk to me about you and Epps."

"Scram," the Deacon said. "Leave the House of God, you sinner."

"So, any place you hang your hat is sacred, Deacon? I'll be going, right enough, but I'll be sticking to you like hot blueberry pie until I got you."

As I spun to leave, the name KELVIN STOKES poked me from the scheduling signboard. The boy's viewing was the next morning, burial at noon. Well, a teenager from a welfare family was more the Deacon's usual clientele.

Outside, I sat in my pickup for forty minutes more, watching the mourners leave and, mostly, waiting to go home with Ruth. Angel wiggled out the funeral parlor, wearing jodhpurs, midnight black to match his leather boots, and over them a gorgeous black cape.

When I highbeamed him, Angel señoritaed down the block and hopped into my passenger's bucket, clucking about how I was just too much sometimes.

"Papi, why you hiding in your funny truck like you some kind of pervert?" he demanded, rummaging through his purse for a cigarette. When he couldn't find one, he slipped his hand into my jacket, then wrinkled his nose when all he pulled out were Chesterfields.

"Take one," I said. "I think it's the filters that give you cancer anyway."

A hearse pulled down the funeral home driveway and into an unloading port. I half-watched them, listening to Angel's fashion chatter, until I recognized the attendants unloading the plain wood casket.

Fahriq's Blues Brothers, dressed as always in little round short-brimmed hats, tuxedos, bow ties. The short, broad dude must have a better head: he'd taken off his sunshades for the eleven P.M. lighting. His co-worker still hid behind his.

What would mobsters be doing, making a delivery to the good Deacon Toledo? I nudged Angel as the garage door opened and they wheeled the yellow pine coffin into the mortuary.

"Why are we watching?" Angel demanded after they hearsed off again.

"Delivery boys," I said. "Something fishy in that package."

"Easy, you remind me." Angel unsnapped his purse and reached inside. "Eddie Dorey says I got to give you this." Angel handed me the tweed cap I hadn't seen for a couple of days.

"I forgot it at Beverly's apartment, huh?"

"I think you lose a friend," Angel said. He fiddled with the radio until he dialed in a Spanish Schaefer beer commercial. Dorey had not exactly been my buddy; I hardly knew the man. But I liked talking to him plenty. More important, I'd hoped he'd be a friend at Newark PD these days when I needed them pretty damn badly. On top of it all, I felt a greasy icing of guilt about sleeping with his girlfriend. He was the type of dude would take it hard, I realized that now.

Get on with it, Barnes. "You up for a little bit of fun, Angel?" I asked.

"Fun?" Angel brightened. "Angel is always in the mood for fun. We go dancing, Easy!"

"Not what I had in mind. I got a job for us."

"What is that?" Angel peered at me suspiciously.

"Remember that flick with Ingrid Bergman and Cary Grant?"

"Oh yes," Angel nodded with his whole body. "She is so much in love with Mister Cary and he asks her to spy on Nazis in the jungles of Brazil and she knows it is so much danger but she is so in love with Mister Cary that her poor heart is breaking and she must make much love to that Nazi pig so she can steal secrets for Mister Cary who loves her too but don't know it."

"That's the one." I had to smile. "I'm asking you to carry out a very perilous but important mission for me."

"Yas, Easy," Angel lifted his chin stoically. "But I hope you gonna realize you in love before it is too late."

"Keep it in mind," I said. I needed this favor.

Angel looked profoundly at me.

"Listen, go back into that funeral home and loiter until everybody's cleared out and gone home. Hide out in the ladies' room or something, wait for the Deacon and his helpers to lock up tight and turn out the lights."

"Papi," Angel said sternly. "Angel has never played with no dead bodies. Don't like them."

"All you got to do is open the door for me to slip in," I said, pointing to the metal side-door by the car ports. "Whatever you do, don't turn on any lights, or the neighbors'll call the cops."

When I shoved Angel out his side of the pickup, he pouted, but dragged himself back up the block to the funeral home. There he glared at me one last time before disappearing inside.

In less than an hour, the remaining wake partyers had departed, Ruth Epps last of all. She had been waiting for me, like as not, until the last ride was fixing to leave. I watched her climb into a long, dark car with friends and felt more than a twinge of regret. But I couldn't risk blowing my cover or creating a scene. Ruth had never seen my truck, so she didn't give a look as her friends drove past me. She looked great in black.

The interior lights winked out and then the Deacon locked up for the night. He walked past flanked by two men in suits who towered above him like cathedral spires. Probably two of the boys I'd met Tuesday night.

Not long enough after they motored off, Angel's orange mop of hair popped out the basement door. I walked quietly but directly down the driveway to him.

"Is it clear inside?" I asked.

"Yas, now Angel will guard your little truck from vandals." Angel tried slipping by me, but I grabbed his arm. "Oh, no you don't, partner," I said. "You'll draw a crowd, like always. Go home."

Angel shook his head emphatically.

"In with you, then."

I half-tugged us both into the cool dark passageway. "Is spookay in here," Angel whispered, hanging onto the back of my jacket. The basement corridor had no outside windows, so a light would be safe, but I couldn't for the life of me find a switch. I whacked my thigh on a stretcher cart resting along the tile wall. Feeling my way around it, I couldn't help but wonder if the thick canvas straps I was running my hands along were stained with blood. Epps' blood, Stokes' blood, Carp's blood? Could be any or all.

"Where you taking us?" Angel tugged hard. His head was practically buried now in my back. "I think we go to jail, Easy."

At the corridor's end, my hands touched two doors. Both closed.

"You want to split up or hang together?" I whispered.

Angel informed me too loudly that no way was I going to leave him alone down there. He was like my shadow, only closer, he told me.

"Well, then I say we take the high road." Felt for the handle of the door on the right and opened it. Cool rush of air let me know pronto I'd picked right. So we tugboated our way into the refrigerated room that housed the bodies, Angel still clutching my jacket. This room had an outside window and enough light to see five lumps in plastic bags stretched to the far wall.

"Why you stopping?" Angel said, still clinging to the back of my jacket.

"We're in the right place."

"What is right about this, Papi?"

"Dead right?" At Angel's woeful expression, I couldn't help laughing.

"You mean these lumps is people?" Angel's voice thickened.

"Was people." Before I could finish, he'd spun around and was clicking little boot heels for the door.

"Look here," I called encouragingly. "Now we know where we stand so far as bumping into any stiffs. There's probably more of 'em out in the hall you'd bump into without the flashlight. Am I right?"

That reeled Angel back. I had to risk flicking on the overhead lights. The sight of those bodies in a row made Angel suck in his breath.

A couple of the plastic bags were caked with clots of dried blood, but most were coated with a cloudy film of grease. The corpse on the end nearest us was cherry red. No coroner needed to ID that cause of death—every cop is taught to recognize a dude who punched out on a lungful of carbon monoxide gas. Probably used a vacuum cleaner hose to run exhaust from his car into the passenger's compartment, while he just sat back and went along for the whole ride.

At the far end of the room sat a varnished yellow pine box, the super-economy model, it looked like. The lid was sealed by three heavy screw clamps, wing nuts fastened over the top brackets; hinges anchored the other side. Slowly I untwisted the wing nuts and one by one the clamps popped clear of the brackets. Angel pressed so tight against my back you couldn't slip a newspaper between us. I filled my own lungs up and cracked the lid a hair or two to peek inside.

Just a body bag like every other. A cardboard tag wired to a canvas handle confirmed it was Kelvin Stokes. Through the filmy plastic bag the boy looked frozen in ice. Considering Dr. Butterfield's description of the body's condition that day in his office with Mooney, I had no stomach for zipping open the body bag for a closer look.

Still, Fahriq did not have his men drive Stokes' body around just to do his grandmother a favor.

Left hand holding my nose and mouth, I used right thumb and forefinger to unzip the body bag. That was when Angel hit the floor with a thud.

Chapter 22

In the El Camino's bucket seats, I tried hushing Angel about how I saved him from death.

"Would you kindly put your Mister Cary and Ingrid Bergman on ice?" I said, shifting into drive.

"Well, is true," Angel said, looking hurt. "What happen in the movie happen to us, Easy."

"You're making it up," I said. "What happened was, you fell out at the sight of Kelvin Stokes' corpse."

"You find what you looking for?"

"Not really."

"Those delivery boys smash Kelvie's head like that?"

"Uh-uh. That happened when he died. What Fahriq could want with that corpse is spooky, alright. But I'll be checking it out tomorrow."

"You going home now, Easy?"

I remembered the canopied bed with Ruth's body in it. But I didn't dare wake her again in the middle of the night.

"Not home. Velnarsky and whoever else he's working with will be staking out my place."

"Where you sleep tonight, Easy?"

"Your couch, probably."

"Yas, you can sleep my place," Angel said earnestly. My best friend.

"I'll be on the couch, get the picture?"

"Yas, everything so mixed up, Papi," Angel breathed. "You got to do thinking for both us."

I roared, but damned if I could get Angel to crack a smile on that. If it wasn't Cary Grant and Ingrid Bergman, it was Bogart and Bergman. Must be Ingrid Bergman week on channel nine.

At Angel's direction, I steered to North Newark and dropped him at the Pimlico's door, where he handed me the key to his apartment on Orange Street. Eight stories above the street clutter below, Angel's place was wall-to-wall thick cream rugs, overstuffed sectional couches, and robust art works on the wall. All the latest conveniences of modern love in the bedroom. When I woke up, every muscle like a stubbed toe, after a fitful night's snooze on Angel's loveseat, he still hadn't come home.

Angel's refrigerator supplied only banana yogurt for breakfast, but his telephone came in handy. Marlene's phone at my office rang and rang until I recollected that it was Saturday morning. No matter, when I rang my apartment number and beeped the answering machine with the little box I keep in the glove box, Dale Mooney's voice told me it was six P.M., he'd got my call, and what did I want? Call him downtown. Then Mooney again, going home, call him there, and the number. Next Ruth Epps came on and informed me that being stood up a second time doubled her life total. She was prepared to forgive me, though, if I would care to come over any time that night? On the most recent recording, Dale, with real concern in his voice, wondered if I was okay, buddy, and I should try to reach him ASAP.

Ruth picked up her phone first ring. I hard-sold her my excuse; she was buying only in small lots.

"Well, when can I see you again?"

"Why don't we just cool it down? When I invite a man to my bed, I expect him to respond before the next morning."

"What are you doing today?"

"My husband's burial is this afternoon."

"I'll pick you up afterwards."

"Don't bother." Icy.

"Deacon Toledo presiding over the burial ceremony, too?"

"I suppose so."

"You don't think that funeral parlor of his is an awfully cheesy operation to handle Walter's funeral, all the big shots turning out?"

"I was astonished at what a crummy little place it was."

"Smelled like cabbage."

"I thought sweat socks and vinegar."

"That too. Why'd you pick the place? Deacon's not that savory a character, either."

Ruth paused to think. "Oh, I've never had to use one before. I asked for suggestions."

"Who?"

"Well, the doctor, for one, who operated, that's not the right word, on Walter's body."

"Butterfield?"

"I think that's his name."

"Maybe the morgue does lots of business with the Deacon. He say?"

"I hardly exchanged two words with him."

"Okay. I'll pick you up after the burial, okay?"

"We'll see." She hung up.

I punched the receiver button and dialed Dale at Police HQ. Sloppy as always, he wanted the whole story out of me right there on the phone. Nothing doing, I said. Eleven o'clock, in front of the Central Jersey Bank, the corner of Broad Street and Raymond Boulevard. Two and a half hours to set up protection for the meet. Since bumping into the Deacon behind Walter Epps' funeral, I had already decided to cultivate more suspiciousness. Who knew how big this circle of drugs and murder was already? Not me, that's for sure.

Driving to my own neighborhood, it dawned on me just how important Dale Mooney was becoming to my plans. Should have warned him to cover his ass on his way to meeting me.

By the eight-thirty daylight, I figured it was relatively safe to scoot over to the Branchbrook Park area. Velnarsky would never bother to stake out my apartment in the daytime; no way a white man, cop or otherwise, is going to loiter in a black neighborhood without drawing a whole pile of attention. Anyway, most of my friends spend all their time in the immediate neighborhood. They would tip me to any stranger hanging out there.

The Newark Sharecroppers were just what the doctor ordered. Besides, the big day for our community garden was coming up tomorrow, and I hadn't been by for two days. Tomorrow, Althea would be showing the national judges around for the finalist competition. Pictures in the *Star-Ledger*, the whole deal. I felt bad about neglecting my share of the gardening chores, but how could I have helped it?

At the 2200 block curb, I almost didn't recognize our garden. Mrs. Washington, in a flowered housedress and shin guards, was cracking the whip on Ernie Horton, who was shoving a wheelbarrow of blue stones up the central footpath between the vegetable rows. Lavinia Everett was on her hands and knees spreading the stones over the dirt path.

"Ezell, where you been? You like the sprucing up we've done?" Mrs. Pasquale beamed from between the rows of pigeon peas and *calabaza*, maybe the only Puerto Rican legumes and squash anybody was growing in Newark.

"Neater than most people's living rooms. Where on earth did all this stuff come from?"

Pink flamingos now framed a garden gate to Laurel Garden Avenue. The Field Marshal, uniformed, was lawn-chaired just outside it, eating his breakfast. The first Sabrett's dog of a new day.

"Who brought the flamingos?" I said to everybody.

"My Ramone got these pretty birds for us. *Las miras*," Mrs. Pasquale waved her hands enthusiastically. "They are donations from the local stores that Ramone talked to."

Across the garden, Ramone was mounting a glass globe on a cement pedestal. "Ramone," I hollered. "I want a word with you, man."

"Sure thing, Mister Barnes." Ramone peacocked over, proud as I'd ever seen him. The garden was doing wonders for him.

"Where'd you lift these things from?" I asked, shouldering him out of his mother's earshot.

"I didn't lift nothing. I ain't into stealing no more, these was donations from grateful storekeepers."

"Grateful about what, Ramone? That you weren't going to torch their businesses down in the middle of the night?"

"That's arson. I ain't no firebug, neither." Ramone spat, but carefully, not on the melons. "I only tell them how I know the kids in the neighborhood and I can make sure they don't get broke into no more."

"I'm going to wring your neck, you know that? You've graduated from stolen cars to extortion. Your probation officer is going to love this, man. And me the one who convinced the judge not to send you up to the reformatory. I only did that as a favor to your mother."

"I did it for the garden, Mister Barnes." Ramone pawed at the dirt with his hightop sneakers. "I didn't make no money off it and you got to admit the place looks great."

150

Snake in the Grasses

"A charm all its own, like a racetrack. As soon as the contest is over, this stuff all goes back. We understand each other?"

"Absolutely," Ramone said.

"When are the judges coming to our garden, Ezell?" Mrs. Everett had crush-stoned her way up to us.

"Tomorrow afternoon at two. Everyone got to be here in the flesh, for the judges to see, or we're disqualified."

"We'll all be here." Lavinia Everett's glare took in Ernie Horton and Ramone. "But where is that good-for-grief lizard?"

"The Snookman be snoring one off behind the fact he tasted too much of the grape last night," Ernie offered.

Mrs. Washington stepped in. "You all make sure that nappy-headed no-good get his worthless self here by two o'clock tomorrow, or else I'm goin upside his head with this shovel, so he ain't got to worry about sleeping late no more."

"I vote no more women in this here garden." The Field Marshal rose from his chair sputtering mustard and hot dog all over the front of his uniform. Ernie and Ramone looked like they might vote that way, too.

"Sit down fool." Mrs. Washington balled up a fist. "Fore I give you this to chew on."

"Everybody shut up and listen," I shouted. I'd been trusted with the job of coordinating the team, because that was easily the toughest job in the garden. And lately I hadn't been there for them.

"Tomorrow, our garden is going to be judged in the following categories: number of gardeners, number of vegetables, which we got, health and vigor, which we got, freedom from pests and disease, which we pretty much got, correct labeling, which I will double-check before we go, use of space—we're dynamite on that—and appearance of the plants. Which reminds me, Ramone. Althea warned me we can't vaseline up the cucumbers, eggplants, or tomatoes, like they do in the markets. Judges will take points off."

151

"Don't we score no points for beauty?" Mrs. Pasquale stuck her top teeth over her lower lip and wagged her head from side to side.

"Of course we do. That's the last category, general beauty. And that's where we have all the other gardens beat."

"Looking gooood," Ramone howled, and there was a hearty chorus of approval.

"What do you mean, 'before we go'?" piped up tiny Lavinia Everett.

"That's another matter," I said. "Need to borrow five of you to help me with some surveillance work, downtown."

"Now?" Lavinia was dubious. "We got plenty to get on, Ezell."

"Back by noon," I promised. "Who can come?"

"I'm good at street work," Ramone volunteered.

"No thanks, man," I said. "Beat cop sees you standing in one place downtown, he's going to call in the national guard for sure."

"I'll go, Ezell," Mrs. Washington said grimly. "You, Vini?" Mrs. Everett nodded and began untying the orange bandana that protected her hair from the garden dust.

"How about me and Snookie?" Ernie's masculine pride was touched.

"Good, you two, the Field Marshal, Mrs. Washington and Mrs. Everett," I said. "Ready to go?"

"We take my truck," Ernie nodded. "Pick up old Snook on the way."

"We ladies aren't going to sit in the bed of that nasty truck," Lavinia said. "It's all rusty. Can we ride up front with Ernie?"

"No," Ernie said indignantly. "Snookie rides shotgun."

We compromised by arranging bales of peat moss in the truck for the two ladies. I offered the Field Marshal a ride with me, but he preferred setting up his folding chair in Ernie's truck bed even though it was next to the women. I led the parade downtown.

An hour was left to position the Sharecroppers before my meet with Mooney went down. Cosmo was standing at

Commerce and Broad Streets when we drove up. As quickly as possible, I ran them all through their assignments.

"Everybody got it?" I asked and everybody nodded. "What's your job, Snookie?"

"I am standing here on Commerce and Broad. I see a dude with a Perry Como sweater and white shoes, I tips my hat to Cosmo, one time only."

"Right. What else?"

"But if I see a great big dude with red hair that smells like a cop, I flaps my lid a bunch of times at Cosmo."

"Good. And what else?"

"Nothing else."

"You're keeping your eyes on Lavinia, too, right? She's on the corner of Raymond Boulevard and Broad Street, right down there by the sidewalk clock? What if she starts flapping her hat?"

"Then I pass the signal on to Cosmos."

"That's it. Cosmo's going to relay the signal to me."

"One shake of the raccoon's tail," the Field Marshal piped up.

"'Bout time you finally remembered something, fool." Mrs. Washington poked the Field Marshal in the shoulder with a long finger.

"One last thing," I interrupted, before warfare could break out again, "soon as you finish giving the signal, I want you all to pile back into Ernie's truck and go about your business. Go back to the garden. Any bailing out needs to be done, Cosmo'll be here."

The women looked at each other. I said to them particularly: "Any trouble goes down, anything happens to me today, I don't want you to remember you knew me. Hear what I'm saying? You don't know nothing about nothing."

I shooed them off to their posts at both ends of the block coming off Broad Street. Cosmo sauntered a ways down Commerce Street and took up station there.

The Central Jersey Bank, where I'd told Dale Mooney to meet me, was two-thirds of a block down Commerce from Broad. Across from the bank, the whole block was swallowed up by a dozen-story white elephant of offices and ground-floor shops: the Raymond-Commerce Building.

First I walked the perimeter. Snookie on Broad and Commerce, Lavinia Everett on Raymond and Broad, the Field Marshal on Raymond and Commerce Place, Mrs. Washington on Commerce Street and Commerce Place.

Then I made one more half revolution to the middle of Raymond Boulevard, and cut right underneath this big arch, through revolving doors, into the Raymond-Commerce lobby. Lined with shops, it split the block-long building, so you could walk straight out to Commerce Street. You could see the Central Jersey Bank fine from the Commerce Street entry, I found out. On the other hand, this lady security officer was stooling behind a desk right at that point. My biggest smile came out when she looked over her newspaper to stare me up and down.

Okay. No standing in the lobby, but Raymond Street, via the long arched lobby, would be my back door, any trouble came up.

Since the lobby wouldn't do, I tried the Coffee And . . . shop off the lobby. No tables, nothing but two horseshoe counters. More crowded than I wanted. Window angle on the bank was a bitch, too. On the plus side, lots of citizens were scattered around the counterspace. The shop "L'd" at the back, so a second door opened out into the lobby. The Coffee And . . . had one or two other features I needed, too.

The streetfront window would do but only because it had to. The Central Jersey was almost out of view, but over the window muffin trays, I could see Cosmo patrolling up and down the block better than I'd have guessed from the outside.

For the next fifteen minutes, I faded with the decor while the cat sitting closest to the wall phone mopped up his gravy with bread.

"There are plenty of seats further down," yelled a tall, brassy-haired waitress. Everybody at the first counter turned to look at me.

"Oh, I don't mind waiting for *your* counter," I said

smiling. Waitress set her jaw. Couple people kept staring nervously at me.

Four folks left empty seats at that counter before the right man stood up, slung his jacket around his shoulders, and walked off. I hustled up and dropped my newspaper on the counterstool, then draped my jacket, completely covering the pay phone. Where I sat was five feet away from the phone.

"What's the idea?" snapped my waitress. "Why're you acting like this for, anyway?" From force of habit, she started pouring me coffee while she was bagging me.

From my wallet I pulled two Lincolns. "I hear you don't rush a man's lunch," I said. "These are for you."

"Take your time," she said. "What's the big deal about the phone?"

"I'm needing that," I said. "Don't you give it a thought, ma'am."

Without reading the menu, I ordered soup, dinner salad, club sandwich, cream pie. One after the other, I said. And take your time.

When she brought my bean and bacon soup, and not before, I strolled outside again and dropped a quarter in the *Star-Ledger* box. Sticking my nose in the paper like I was scouting the classifieds, I made sure Cosmo noticed me, then walked back into the coffee shop. Now he would know where to broadcast his signals.

Back inside the Coffee And . . . it was ten-fifteen. "Darlin'," I said. "Give me ten dimes for this dollar, will you?" I put a third five alongside the other two.

By eleven o'clock I knew every car and parking meter you could see out the diner's window. The breakfast crowd thinned, but I still had to menace off one cool breeze from dumping my jacket to get at the phone.

I ordered another piece of pie and a fourth coffee. Settled my bill and gave the waitress her tip. Chatted her up a little tiny bit, not too much, keeping one eye on the bank. Waitress warmed up to me enough to start squawking about her second job in the evenings.

Cosmo walked in front of the coffee shop plate glass

window for the twentieth time and pretended to stop and admire his hat in the reflection. This time, he lifted the gray fedora off his bald head just once, and set it back at a rakish angle.

When he did that, I jumped up and searchbeamed up and down the block. Bingo. Old Dale was posted like a wart on somebody's nose, slumped down in the driver's seat of his red Plymouth, exhaust smoking away in the cool fall air.

Felt good to see him, too. Old Dale might be less than awesome at police work, but I needed to hook up with somebody in the cops I trusted. "Trusted" being a relative term, I guess, seeing how I'd set up this little test for Dale. Now to wait fifteen minutes or so. If none of the Sharecroppers gave the Velnarsky alert, I'd walk out to his car and spill my guts to Dale.

Everything looked good for fifteen minutes. Then I saw Mooney scowl at his watch. Time to make my move, before he gave up on me, went home.

At the counter, I was scooping up my jacket and dimes when I glimpsed Cosmo hustling back by the window, tipping his hat like a lunatic at ladies passing by. Taking this opposite cue, I dashed out the coffee shop's back door, tracked down the lobby to the Raymond Boulevard revolving door, and turkey-necked it up and down the block. My left toe was practically out the door when I spotted Velnarsky plunked in the last chair of the shoeshine stand on the corner of Broad and Raymond. Dear old Lavinia Everett had given the signal to Snookie, who'd relayed it correctly.

Velnarsky had the top, Mooney taking the bottom. Time to play both ends against the middle. I revolved right around again into the lobby, back to the Coffee And . . . , where I pulled my coat off the phone and fished a ten-cent piece down the slot. I punched out 9-1-1. The dime clanked back out. So sometimes I overplan.

"Police Emergency," said the kind of receptionist they snip out of sheet metal for the job.

"I want to report a crime."

"This an emergency crime?"

"In progress."

"Where?"

"Uh, this is Mr. Peterson, at the Central Jersey branch office on Commerce Street? We've had a man just walk into our lobby. He showed everyone this shotgun under his coat?"

In the background, the police voice was relaying the holdup to a dispatcher now.

"Got a description of the gunman?"

"Tan raincoat and brown jeff-cap. Oh, and his partner is driving a get-away car parked up the street."

"Give me what you got on him too."

Did I ever give that cop a good description of Mooney and his car, right down to the missing pieces of grill, front of his radiator.

Cops did a good job too, got that description on the horn pronto. Before you could say false alarm, old Commerce Street was swarming with more cops than Atlantic City at Miss America time.

Two hulking plainclothesmen crabbed up behind Mooney's car and tore him out of it at gunpoint, had him spread-eagled in the street before he could say a word. When they discovered his revolver, one gorilla pinned Mooney's face to the street with his boot.

By then I was strolling out the Coffee And . . . and down Commerce Street. Behind me an army of cops stormed the bank's front door. City the size of Newark, chances are real good that a batch of radio-car cops won't recognize a homicide detective like Mooney by sight. That's why I picked him out for them. Velnarsky, on the other hand, probably everybody knew by sight, goddam orangutan.

Taking a super-deluxe roundabout walk back to my pickup gave heaps of thinking time about how Epps, Carp, Fahriq, Velnarsky, Mooney, Deacon Toledo, and Kelvin Stokes ever became partners in the methamphetamine business. And the murder business.

Well, I knew the answer-man for that question. For the price of a big meth candy machine, even Hassan Fahriq would have to talk. Damn him.

Chapter 23

At noon on Saturday, Pennsylvania Station in Newark is an oversized tomb, so I told Fahriq over the phone to meet me in the main concourse by the arrivals and departures board.

The old train station had just been facelifted, and, although it was never in a league with Grand Central Station, it still wore the stateliness of an era gone by. The loudspeaker voice boomed off the marble walls and vaulted ceiling as trains rumbled in and out, on or behind schedule, but never ahead of the game.

Hassan Fahriq was ahead of time, though, sandwiched by the Blues Brothers. The threesome was dressed identically, in full-length black outercoats, white shirts with bow ties, and circular black hats that sat on their heads like pill boxes. In the far corner, I folded up my newspaper, then walked out to make the meet.

"Brother Barnes," Fahriq smiled. "News of your recent exploits has reached my ears."

"I've got even more good news for you."

"Talking in public is for fools." Fahriq swiveled his head about. "Why don't we retire to one of my offices?"

"No, thank you. I go there, I might just get retired permanently."

Fahriq grinned. "Where then? You pick the spot, *amigo* my man."

"Soon as you tell Gog and Magog to meet you back here in one hour."

I had him follow me through the interconnecting marble passageways of the old station to the Raymond Boulevard platform for the Newark–Belleville trolley. Two white-haired ladies slumped under shopping bags waited

158

for the trolley. I remembered that the downtown merchants were promoting a weeklong sale bonanza called "Downtown Shopping Days."

Fahriq's laugh rang out. "You really tickle my funny-bone, old buddy. We going for a trolley ride?"

A green and white trolley, noselamp glowing, rolled out of the tunnel and screeched to a halt in front of us. The cars are quaint as an amusement park ride, but neat as a pin, and in better running condition than the Amtrak trains. More and more commuters are parking their cars in lots out around Belleville and shuttling in and out of center city on the trolleys.

Hassan was looking at the trolley as if he smelled a trap.

On the running board, I turned.

"Jump now, Fahriq," I yelled. "Or you lose that meth lab your partners were running."

Fahriq grimaced, then swung on-board.

I dropped two tokens in the till and we shaky-legged to the back as the trolley rumbled along the tracks. We hung straps next to one another, though almost nobody else was traveling with us to Belleville at that time of day. Fahriq grinned at me again. He knew he was lucky I wasn't patting him down. I would have, except that as an ex-Federal-con, Fahriq could get sent back up for life if he got caught with a firearm. Nowadays, Fahriq pays his goons to carry the guns.

"Stupidity offends me," Fahriq deliberately spat out the side of his mouth. The gob landed on a seatback. I reached over with my handkerchief and wiped it up. "If your brains were electricity, Barnes, they wouldn't power a flashlight."

"Must be brain damage from boxing," I said.

Fahriq reached inside his coat and pulled out a cigar, but refrained from lighting it. "I hear from every low-rent in Newark how you are out banging on doors, asking questions that rile some very powerful and dangerous people. There is no profit in it for you."

A long time since Hassan Fahriq had had to chase after the likes of me for anything, and his anger showed.

"Just hear me out," I said. "Could be there's a nice profit waiting for you. A whole methamphetamine lab full of profit."

The sarcasm slipped off Fahriq's face, and his eyes narrowed down still more.

"Methamphetamine." He savored the word, rolling his cigar between his thumb and fingers a little. "That is a white man's drug, brother. Very popular down around Philadelphia. Just catching on here in Newark."

"You should know."

"Where did you come by this half-cocked idea I have partners in the meth business?"

"Who's zooming who?" I returned, shouting as we rattled over a rail-switch. "Meth's speeding through Newark these days like a runaway express. You know it, and what's more you know who's making it."

Fahriq's eyes didn't deny a thing, so I risked stretching what I knew.

"Your end of the action is to ship the meth all over the country. Who else has the nationwide connections for it, and the muscle? I watched two of your boys make a delivery to the Gates of Heaven Funeral Home."

Fahriq finally lit his cigar and let blue smoke ooze around the end of his mouth. The trolley pulled up at the Rutgers University stop and a herd of students with backpack-bookbags hustled aboard. Hassan snaked his free arm around my shoulder and grinned at me.

"Well, I must admit. I am most pleasantly surprised at you, old buddy. You are wising up. Drugs was never your line of work before."

"Just a little something I stumbled across investigating the Walter Epps murder."

"And stumbled across what else?"

"Getting tired of racing around in the dark, Hassan. You got what I need, the names of your meth partners. And I'll pay you by rolling over the meth kitchen to you."

"What makes you so sure I do not know already where the lab is?"

"You forget how long we go back together, brother." I

smiled. "I know your style; as soon as you don't need a partner, you dump him. Remember the ambush behind the Ritz Theatre?"

"History repeats itself, do it not?" Fahriq chuckled.

"You'd never do business with them clowns, if you didn't absolutely have to. The only reason they're still alive this minute is because they're keeping you at arm's length from the lab."

"If this is a double-cross, turkey," Fahriq blew smoke at me, "I will ice you, personally, I guarantee."

"These eyes have seen it," I said. "Complete with all the trimmings. And that's including a fifty-five-gallon drum of P-2-P."

"Sounds like some new kind of laundry detergent."

"You're selling woofing tickets," I said. My turn to lean back now. "You'd come in your pants for some P-2-P. Crucial ingredient in manufacturing methamphetamine, isn't it? Very illegal, and just about impossible to get any more? Crooked doctors used to get it, until the good narcotics folks found out just how limited the legitimate medical uses are. These days I hear the cooks got to smuggle it in from Europe. Awful hard to find."

Fahriq just beamed at me.

"You had that drum, man," I said, "you'd be grabbing the black meth market by the balls. Shit, you'd *be* the black market." Fahriq eyeballed me some more. I stared back at him. "That scam's through, Hassan. Too much going down. Might as well let me in on it. You're going to have to start over, anyhow."

He bent to peer out the trolley window.

"Sounds reasonable, Barnes," he said finally, still not looking at me. "Damn, I like talking business with you better than what we have been talking, man. Just what did you want to know?"

"Run the scam down for me from the top," I said. "Epps do all the manufacturing?"

"That's it, Epps made the drugs. He and the Deacon started cooking meth a couple years ago. Old Walter embezzled the seed money to get them started, and back then the Deacon had access to the P-2-P, for embalming purposes."

"Half the ballgame, wasn't it? I heard they stopped the flow of P-2-P like you squeeze blood dripping from your arm."

Fahriq opened his hands and cocked his head.

"How did Velnarsky shoehorn his way in?"

"That I was never sure about. Meth stinks to high heaven when you cook it up, maybe that big rat sniffed it out one night." Fahriq's nostrils flared at the thought.

"And you?"

"My idea to ship the meth inside stiffs to dealers outside the state. The Deacon kept up appearances by burying boxfuls of rocks, after the wakes was done, naturally."

"Tell me something. Why'd Epps want to cut in an accountant? You pinheads couldn't keep your own books?"

Fahriq got a rich chuckle out of that. "Old Carp was more than our accountant, baby. You think whitebreads like Velnarsky, toms like Epps could buy their condos and their Cadillacs with street money? IRS's got to make a living, too, you know. That Carp had a thousand clients. By the time he mixed and sudsed all that money around, your cash was steam-pressed and smelled like a sunny day."

"What about Kelvin Stokes, Epps' boy?"

"He was the courier," Fahriq tied it up. "Ran the drugs from the kitchen up to the funeral home."

"Everybody's dead but Velnarsky and you, that it? What other cops does Velnarsky have in this with him? I know one name: Mooney. Who are the others?"

"Don't know a thing about that end," Fahriq said. "Velnarsky's a tight-lipped bastard, you see."

"How do I fry these scumball ex-partners of yours for whacking Walter Epps?"

"You a bigger chump than I been worried you were!" The old street-wise Fahriq came out whenever I riled him. "You think anybody would shit over who offed Walt Piss-ant Epps? The lovely Widow Epps got you thinking with your one-eyed snake, chump?"

"Epps means nothing to me," I protested.

"You bet he don't. The man had his spoon in Uncle

Sam's sugar bowl alongside ten thousand other politicians. Irish did it soon as they opened the boat doors. Then the Eye-talians and the Germans and the Yids. And right on down the line. The brothers' turn now in the sun, the American dream, if ever there was one. Any youngster, any race, creed, or color, can grow up to be a politician and steal himself a fortune from the people."

I shook my head at so much cynicism.

"People don't even give a shit," Fahriq went on. "They used to it. Smokie's turn now, they tell themselves."

"Recent American history as told by Fahriq." I looked around. "Any of these Rutgers kids taking notes?"

"This city is flat ass broke," Hassan protested. "Old money's gone. Only money oozing into this town comes from Uncle Sam himself. You was here, brother, you know. Riots come, pimps in Washington figure to pump the conscience money into the cities. Soothe all the savage beasts." Fahriq chuckled sourly.

"What's this got to do with Epps' murder? Feds didn't ice him, I know that."

"Of course not, my man. But they gave him enough rope to hang himself. Look here, the Feds have made it too damn easy for most folks to resist the temptation. As long as folks don't pocket the money outright, the Feds don't mind looking the other way. All they ask for is camouflage; if nothing is blatant, then they do not have to stir up the mess, get in Dutch with the Democrats."

"How did Epps get grabbed then?"

"Income tax. Man was greedy, you know, and careless. Strictly an amateur after all those years."

"So who wanted to kill him over some income tax humbug?"

"Different humbug. Everybody knew that when Epps got caught in the wringer, he'd start squealing like a little pig about all his old cronies."

"You were his partner, too. You sure you didn't do the job on Epps yourself? Who did? The cop, Velnarsky?"

Fahriq gave me a judicious nod. "Velnarsky, all the way, brother."

"How do I squeeze his balls, Hassan?"

"Listen good," Fahriq said. "We make a trade here, this is your payment in full. Your choices are slim and none, buddy. You want to hide out with me, you got it. But you pigheaded enough to go after Velnarsky, you do it by your-self."

I nodded.

"Another thing. You sing about me to the Feds, and I'll weep at your grave."

I shook my head again. "You know I have to stay clear of the Feds. Even if I could force the U.S. Attorney to take on a full investigation, they'd hamstring me one of two ways. Either they'd order me off the case, warn me to sit tight, in which case, slow as they are, I'd get dead long before the Grand Jury hearing. Or else they'd stick me in that witness protection program they got for cheese eaters. Change my name, relocate me to some miserable place like Des Moines, Iowa, different line of work entirely. Rest of my life, I'd never rest easy, worrying that my whereabouts had leaked out."

"Shit," said Fahriq scornfully. "It'd never get that far. These are white cops, black politicians you are scrambling after, buddy. A political can of worms, the kind the Feds just hate. Only thing they love is picking on the Eye-talians, gets them good ink in the newspapers. With Epps dead and gone, can of worms he crawled out of is closed. No witness, no case."

"What do I do?"

"Go public," Fahriq said. "And listen, I don't mean crying your heart out to some newspaper reporter. That'll just hurry up your funeral."

"What then?"

"Epps is getting buried today, four o'clock in the Holy Ghost Cemetery. Crack open that coffin of his in front of all the bigwigs that're gonna be there."

"They'll drag me off in a straitjacket. It's body-snatch-ing or something."

"Got to be a body for body-snatching. Ain't no corpse in that coffin."

"That your end of the meth operation?"

"Epps went out this morning with a load of meth sewn inside his chest. His coffin's full of New Jersey granite, and nothing but. The Stokes boy also went out carrying a load. But his casket's already planted by now."

"Just Epps' name and a box full of rocks are getting set in the ground this afternoon?"

"Trust me, man." Fahriq leaned closer and lowered his voice. His breath oozed spicy Havana tobacco. "You pop the lid on that coffin, and find no Walter Epps inside, all hell breaks loose in this city. No way they will get all that toothpaste back in the tube." Fahriq rolled his head back in a baritone laugh.

On a note sheet in my shirt pocket I had scribbled the location of the meth kitchen at the Port of Newark. I reached it over to Fahriq, then pulled it back. "What about you? If the stink gets too big for Velnarsky and Mooney to stay clear of, how do you keep outside it, Hassan?"

Fahriq wasn't smiling when he said, "Those cops have got nothing solid on me; we were two or three steps removed from doing business directly. Those shitheads cut their own lifeline when they killed both Epps and Carp. Velnarsky's too smart to risk trying a whistle-blow on me—he knows what'd come down in prison if that happened. That Mooney dude and any others, they will be scared too, if they have the sense. If not, they will not last long."

Fahriq reached across me and tugged the note from my fingers.

The stop cord was pulled by three high-school girls in Livingston pep-club jackets.

"Thanks for the help, Hassan." I started shuffling to the exit door behind the giggling girls.

"Where you going?" Fahriq looked as if I'd tricked him.

"End of the line for me," I said. "Sit tight, the trolley turns around in about another mile and heads back to town. Trust me."

Where I jumped off was the Park Avenue shop, west side of Branchbrook Park. Fahriq's face watched me from the trolley windows, cigar between his teeth. When he was out of sight, I jogged through the cherry trees to my apartment.

Chapter 24

Cosmo Delesandro had driven my truck uptown to my apartment and waited in the garden helping Mrs. Pasquale in the zucchini patch. Cosmo, sixty and Italian-shaped, is a kind man who wears a kind expression. Mrs. Pasquale, who has been a widow since Ramone was a baby, flirts like a sixteen-year-old whenever Cosmo comes to the garden. Usually, it is fun listening to them, but today I motioned Cosmo to the sidewalk with a wag of my head.

"It went better than I expected," I told him. "This case'll get laid to rest this afternoon if I hustle." The Sharecroppers were all scurrying about the garden, some with tools in hand, some just scurrying.

"That ledger's hid good in my apartment," Cosmo reported. "Just give me the word and I'll dig it out."

"No need for a little while. What I do need, though, is info about coffins."

"Search me," Cosmo shrugged.

"Snookie know," Ernie Horton volunteered. He had worked close enough to eavesdrop. "Used to be a undertaker."

When we dragged him over, Snookie confirmed it. "I was a younger man, I worked as an undertaker's assistant. Devil of a time getting dates with the girls, always with that formaldehyde stink on me." The fond memory made his face crumple.

"What tools I need to pop a coffin, Snook?"

"We needs to bring a prybar, some vise-grips, and a extra-long screwdriver, not any old kind, a cabinetmaker's."

It was after three by the time I'd hunted down the

tools. Worse than that, it was pouring. Cosmo, Snookie Izard, and Ernie Horton tailed me in Ernie's jalopy truck. If all went as planned, those three would buy me the time to blow open Epps' coffin and the case.

We reached Holy Ghost Cemetery just as the funeral procession entered the gates, a long line of black sedans droning by, carrying Ruth Epps and the dignitaries. Bureaucrats sure do turn out for their own. My new silver pickup made the last item in the motorcade.

At the gravesite, most of the crowd was dressed in official black, except me. Naturally I had on my raingear, beige raincoat and wrinkled golf hat. Car doors began slamming shut and umbrellas popped open. The rain was really sheeting down now; you could hear the herd slosh its way across the soggy turf to the red dirt mounds surrounded by drenched flower tributes.

For ten minutes everybody stood around, waiting. Then six somber-faced men squished across the lawn to the grave with Walter Epps' coffin and positioned it on a shiny bronze frame covering the pit. Mounds of rich red clay heaped around the rectangular hole let water trickle down the sides and run into the grave. An inch of water had already collected at the bottom.

The crowd stood like deaf-mutes as somebody said the usual about how kind and generous the deceased had been to his family and friends. Ruth Epps sniffled and boo-hooed at the appropriate spots, tearful but tasteful. Like I said, she looks terrific in black.

Then the most sanctified Deacon Toledo took over, braying resonantly about Walter Epps starting out on a long and wonderous journey. At which point I started easing to the front row, no small job, what with a prybar stuffed down my pants leg. The clanking of the screwdriver and the visegrips in my raincoat pocket wasn't helping any, either.

Over my shoulder I checked that Cosmo and Snookie were in place at a plot immediately across the road from Epps' gravesite, raking and clipping like a cemetery crew grooming the grounds. Ernie Horton idled in his ancient delivery truck about a football field down the road.

When I popped open the Budweiser golf umbrella I carried, Ernie spotted the signal and set his wheels in motion. The old truck came backfiring down the road full steam, swerved toward Snookie and Cosmo, who hurtled clear, and skidded off the road, knocking down two headstones. Snookie dummy-chucked to the ground and screamed horribly in pain. Ernie flopped forward on the steering wheel so the truck horn blared nonstop.

A horrified gasp ran through the crowd.

"Someone help that man!" I bellowed. Most of them poured obligingly across the road. Those that didn't stared in their direction.

At that, I yanked out my prybar and screwdriver and darted up to the coffin.

Snookie had estimated three minutes flat for twisting out the screws, but just finding them could take longer. On the expensive Kinney casket, he remembered, the screws were accessible only from the underside. With the vise-grips, I manhandled off the ornamental cap over the first screwhead. Then, thin-shanked screwdriver in the slot, I twisted that damn screw for all I was worth. Rain slipped the handle in my hand. But so far nobody was saying anything to stop me. I managed to pull out the two eight-inch screws on one end of the coffin and the two along the side before the diversion began to dissolve like snow in the rain.

"Hey you, stop that!"

A mourner was watching me in outraged disbelief. I ignored him and started on the last two end screws.

The vise-grips were latched to the last screw cap, when Deacon Toledo spotted me.

"What is the meaning of this?" he shrieked, shaking his Bible at me, sodden white surplice flapping. "This is sacrilege!"

"Stay back, Deacon," I snarled. "I'll shoot you if I have to."

Then the shit really grew wings.

"Ezell, for God's sake, what are you doing!" I thought I heard Ruth Epps scream. Of course, by now everybody else was joining in the fracas. Ernie was still napping on the horn. You'll never hear such pandemonium outside of hell.

I made hard faces at them. The politicos were looking plenty pissed, but they lacked the intestines to take a run at me.

The Deacon was a whole 'nother smoke, though. He had the Lord at his side. "I'll put a stop to this," he roared, then charged, vestments ballooning in the breeze, for all the world like a drenched gooney bird trying to take off. The last screw was open to the screwdriver. I unhunched, let the Deacon set his sights on me, and at the last second matadored to the side. As he lurched past, I grabbed the man's pants seat from behind and heaved him gently in the air. The Deacon flew clear over the coffin, arms and legs flailing. He almost caught his balance, too, just not enough to keep from landing face first in the mud.

"That will be all, we've had enough," one take-charge VIP hollered. "Stop it now or I'll brain you." The man reached in the mud, grabbed my dropped prybar, and swung it above his shoulder.

"Meet Smith and Wesson," I said. "One more step, froggie, and you'll really be in a snit."

At the sight of my gun, the crowd gasped collectively and shoved back. Not a hero among them. I put the .38 back in my raincoat pocket.

My forearms were aching but I kept turning until the last screw loosened, and the coffin lid snapped open. My audience began to inch its way forward in grisly anticipation. Digging in fingernails, I pried up the lid enough to get a finger grip, then, with one gut-twisting grunt, I tipped the bronze-sheathed cover onto one of the mud piles.

The shriek those grievers let out was loud enough to wake the dead. But Walter Epps didn't hear them; he just lay there quietly inside that satin-lined box, hands clasped placidly over his chest.

I swear a dead man's smirk was pasted on his ashy face.

"Somebody call the police," the Deacon blubbered through mud-caked lips.

Chapter 25

At Police Headquarters, the atmosphere was church bazaar, except it was my goose they were cooking. By the time it was fully dark outside, Ruth Epps and I had been shunted into a smallish interrogation room with Eddie Dorey, who had picked up the assignment because the Walter Epps suicide had originally been his case.

Part of my story I had already told three or four times. Now I put my last ace on the table. "I can take you to the meth lab," I told Dorey. "Then nobody can pretend nothing happened."

"You just finished telling me you didn't know the whereabouts of the meth kitchen." Dorey looked like he could use some sleep.

"I was hoping you'd buy my story without it. You know the friend I told you doped me on the rocks in Epps' coffin? Well, I traded the kitchen to him for that pearl. He crossed me up, but he could have killed me instead, just as easily. I was hoping to keep him out of the story."

"Who is this friend of yours?"

"I'd rather not say."

"The only thing with rocks in it is your head," Dorey snapped, for about the third time. "Each version of your story has a new angle to it. Doesn't exactly inspire confidence, you know?"

"That boy scout shit doesn't matter, at this point," I said. "I'm going to say it again, watch my lips move this time: the drug conspiracy that got Walter Epps killed is still on the rampage. Some of your fellow cops are in it to their ears. More people are going to get dead over this, man."

Dorey warned me, as if he hadn't listened, "Do you

understand that, if it weren't for me knowing you, and Mrs. Epps refusing to press body-tampering charges against you, your ass would be in jail right now?"

Ruth was giving both of us that cool stare of hers. As always, Ruth's looks were tricky to read: could have been her idea of staunch support, could have been fear of rabies. She hadn't said much, that's for sure.

"Is that true, what this character claims about a book?" Dorey asked her again.

"I've told you." Ruth lit a Virginia Slims. "He showed me a notebook full of code words and figures. He said they referred to drugs."

"But you believed him?"

Her ironical smile was as much for me as for Dorey.

"She thinks you're a certifiable nutcake." Dorey leaned across his desk to leer intimately at me. "You lost your last shred of credibility in this town, Barnes."

"Come on, Eddie. One last bite at the apple, huh? My friend's boys may be tearing the kitchen down right this minute. Just drive there with me, you'll see."

Dorey's look was sharp, but after a second he nodded.

"I don't suppose you'd care to come along, Mrs. Epps?"

"No, Officer Dorey, I've had enough adventures for one day." Ruth finished the cigarette and stood up. "I think I'll go home." I watched her hips and shoulders move out of the room, hoping for some kind of high-sign. Didn't see one.

When I wriggled out of Police Headquarters with Dorey, it was nearly seven o'clock and still pouring.

"Stop and think about this a minute, Eddie."

"I'm afraid to. I've always been proud of my judgment."

"I'd feel safer if we were bringing a couple radio cars along, too."

"Not on your life," Dorey said devoutly. "Anybody hears I'm humoring the rocks-in-the-casket fruitcake, I'll never live it down. Ten years on the force down the toilet."

"Then spring my .38 out of impoundment."

"After you threatened half the mucky-mucks in Newark with it? Just let's go."

"How about we stop by my apartment, pick up some firepower?"

Dorey looked up to heaven and heaved his shoulders. But he drove me home.

Trudging ahead of him up the stairs, I said, "Last time I saw the meth kitchen, I watched Ray Velnarsky snuff out a little dude's lights, and all I could do was stand by because I was packing only a pea-shooter."

"Watch your mouth about Ray Velnarsky. He's a homicide detective, like me. Just because he's one tough cookie doesn't mean you get to accuse him of every murder in Newark."

I shook my head. The signals from Dorey were mixed. He agreed to check out the meth lab, but then insisted on driving me without backup to the Port. Now evidently he was letting me pack some heat. Strangest of all, he had not said a word yet about me sleeping with his girlfriend.

Inside, the place stank of stale butts and unflushed kitchen drain. No ventilation for most of a week. I made straight for the bathroom and sat sideways on the porcelain throne.

A panel door, no higher than two feet, was built into the wall beside the commode, concealing a crawl space that housed the water valves to the toilet, sink, and shower. This was also where I stashed my war chest.

Behind the copper tubing, I fingered until I touched the plastic bag that covered my little footlocker-shaped chest. Just about two feet by one foot, and you had to angle it just right to yank it out past the pipes. No trouble this time dragging it onto the pink tile floor, or up and into the kitchen.

"I haven't seen one of these since I came stateside from Vietnam," Dorey said, looking over the chest.

"I didn't know you were a vet."

"Sure, how many cops our age do you know who didn't get drafted? Did my two-year tour and got the hell out."

"Goddamn jungle war made men our age a different breed," I said. "Left its mark on most of us."

Dorey raised an eyebrow.

"Think about it. I came back with this chest," I said. "And a lifetime of bad dreams. Used to scare my radio-car partners half to death, when we'd snooze on night patrol and I'd wake up screaming. Velnarsky, he came back with killing in his blood. That M.E. of yours, Butterfield, went to Nam all set for a rich suburban medical practice and came back slicing people's bodies up for the rest of his life. The hell did you come back with, Eddie?"

"I came back with my hands empty. What I left there haunts me."

"What's that?"

"My kid," he said, letting me toast in his angry eyes and set Irish jaw. "A daughter I had by this Vietnamese girl."

I tilted my head sympathetically.

"I always planned on getting the two of them to the States, but after I got shipped back and Saigon fell, I lost touch with them."

"I'm sorry, man," I said and meant it.

"If they weren't executed as American sympathizers, they're starving their lives away in some shitty hut. My kid in a hut." He lifted his face to drill me with those blue eyes. "That's why the kid I got with Beverly is doubly important to me."

"Angel gave me your message."

"We settle that score later," he said, as if we'd already agreed to do so. "Get suited up so we can go see this meth kitchen of yours."

Resting on the kitchen counter, the chest was beautiful as always. Cut out of seasoned mahogany, scenes of warlords carved on all its surfaces, antique three-pronged oriental lock fastened through this ornate brass hasp that sealed its lid tighter than a clam. The lock was really a pretty simple mechanism, once you understood it. But its oriental nature kept it an inscrutable mystery to every American I ever tried it on.

From my powdered sugar box on the kitchen shelf, I drew a long T-shaped prong and slipped it into the lock. The lid cracked open. After nearly ten years, the fragrance of the camphorwood lining still cleansed the air.

That chest and I went back together all the way to Saigon, where I'd had it specially built. For ten dollars in army script, GIs could watch tuberculosis-ridden coolies carve them up a chest half like this one. But only half. Coolies'd get a bowl of rice for their labors and a metal shack to sleep in, next to a dozen others. GIs got a box rough-cut of green wood that cracked in a month or so, when the soft wood dried up. Only the slavers that hired the coolies and cheated the GIs made out pretty good.

MPs always did just a little better, though. Whenever we'd put a slaver behind bars, usually for pimping on U.S. Military Territory, his competitors would present us with gifts. Top quality jewelry and fancy food and such. That's where I got this chest. Fifteen years later, it was still solid as a rock.

"You took a chance waiting so long," Dorey was saying. "Why didn't you give me a ring as soon as you found the drugs?"

Inside the chest, my old police-issue bulletproof vest was folded on top, ballistic cords glistening under the kitchen's fluorescent bulbs. Underneath were quite a few more items that I'd thrown together when I quit the police department. More out of some vague itch of insecurity than any real need, like some men buy life insurance policies.

I stripped off my shirt and, lifting the vest out by its shoulder straps, slung the front then the back plate over my shoulders. Each plate was fourteen inches square, about a quarter-inch thick. Even though the whole vest weighed only about three pounds total, that ballistic nylon made it impregnable to everything but a high-power rifle shot. When the front and back plates were cinched tight with Velcro straps, I felt like a Roman warrior ready to bully into battle. I pulled on a navy blue turtleneck and tucked it in my pants.

"Well?" Dorey said.

"Wasn't sure who I could trust," I said, not looking at him. "Velnarsky works with you, and he murdered Epps' accountant. I thought I could trust Dale Mooney—I've known him for years—but he hunted me in a pack with Velnarsky."

"Wait a minute—Jesus Christ, Barnes! Now Mooney is a murderer, too?"

"I don't know about murderer. But he is Velnarsky's accomplice, for certain, and probably an accessory to murder. I don't know just how deep Dale has dug himself."

"So you figured I was crooked, too, huh?"

"I never made up my mind. But can't you picture yourself in my shoes? When Angel gave me my hat back last night I wasn't going to put my life in your hands. You might burn me just to even the score about Beverly."

Unraveling the straps of a Bianchi quick-draw shoulder holster, I wriggled into the harness. My prize Charter Arms .44 caliber "Bulldog" revolver came out wrapped in a silicon cloth. I had modified it with a custom grip to control the recoil, loosened the action on it, built up the trigger with a shoe to hair touch. The carefully oiled cylinder popped out with one flick of my middle finger. I held the barrel up to the kitchen light and checked the bore out for obstructions. Then I quick-wiped the piece with the silicon rag one last time before I dry-fired it to gauge the trigger pull.

Twenty rounds of 200-grain hot-charged hydroshock .44 caliber ammunition was standing upright in a Styrofoam container. Dorey picked one out and hefted it. "Damn things cost pretty near a buck apiece," he said. I plucked out five rounds, plunked each lubaloy-finished bullet into the cylinder, and snapped it shut. Old Bulldog felt pregnant in my hands, ready to blow a hole in anything, the drop of a hat.

Now a .44 is a awesome weapon to start with. But you load one up with the water-filled hydroshock bullets, that gun will knock a Cadillac sideways. Bulldog got holstered under my left arm. Then I threw on a dark nylon windbreaker cut extra-baggy to hide the bulge. Loaded up a spare cartridge spindle with bullets and pocketed it in the jacket.

175

Uniform and equipment routines used to be important rituals when I was a cop. They steady up most people, just before they hit the street. Gave me half an ounce of grit that night, which I sorely needed. Mental readiness through physical preparation, they used to preach at us. But I never saw a cop who didn't just automatically take one long, silent time getting ready in the locker room.

I nodded to Dorey on his kitchen stool. He would understand what I felt.

"You ready?" he asked.

"What time you got?"

Dorey glanced at his wristwatch. "Seven-forty-five."

I exhaled. "All right, let's move out."

Outside in the drizzle, walking to his car, Dorey said, "That isn't my style, you know." He sounded disappointed somehow. "I make an absolute point of never letting my personal life interfere with my job."

He waited for me to respond, so I said, "How did I know that? I thought I knew Dale Mooney and I called him instead of you, only to find him in this scam up to his freckled nose."

"I thought you'd be a judge of character," Dorey said. This was bothering him plenty. "You're an ex-cop, and the kind of work you do . . ."

"Hard to figure Mooney, isn't it?" I wondered. "Fourteen years a cop, five kids, fat wife, happy as a piss-clam."

"It isn't hard to figure," Dorey said. "Mooney's a clown, harmless by himself but a real go-along. He worships Ray Velnarsky."

"You sound like you believe me."

"I'll believe you when I see the lab. You lead the way and I'll follow." He motioned me away from his car, towards my truck.

I shrugged, unlocked the passenger's door, then the driver's, and climbed in. Part of me wanted to trust the man. But I felt a whole lot better now that I wore a bulletproof vest.

Chapter 26

The old warehouse stretched out in front of us. The strong breeze shoveled salty, fishy stink into our noses. Overhead, streaky gray clouds went racing across the round moon. Rising out of the water on its forest of supports, crusted at the bottom with shells and low-tide slime, that warehouse looked like a prehistoric mud-flat beast in boots. Not another car in sight. No rumble of trucks bouncing by, either, probably due to it being Saturday night. Just the powerful whoosh of bay breeze smearing our faces flat and puffing out our jackets.

Dorey motioned me with his head to go ahead. Circling widely around the street lamp shining on the parking spaces, I kept to the left of the railroad spur paralleling the waterfront, cut across at the far side, and soft-shoed along the pier apron to the fire escape ladder. Dorey me-and-my-shadowed until I paused and I jerked my thumb upwards.

He scowled. "Tell me this is only a stupid joke, Barnes," he hissed.

"Only way in," I shrugged.

"The only way in for you, maybe."

I squinted real sharp at Dorey. No sharper than he was squinting back, though.

"I'll be waiting around the side for you to scramble up that ladder and open the door for me," Dorey said. I glanced up. Above three stories of spidery fire stairs, the catwalk door looked hours and hours away.

"I don't like it. Whyn't you be a man, go in with me?"

"Two things: You're the one that knows the layout inside. Second, you shake anybody out of there, I'll be here watching the outside doors."

Dorey was using the flat police-procedural voice all

cops get issued. No special stress notes that I could hear.

"My back's gonna make a mighty broad target all the way up those stairs," I complained.

The wind was picking up. Dorey had to half-holler:

"Check. The third reason I stay out here is to cover your back going up."

A couple more seconds of eyeball-wrestling. I still couldn't read a clue in that damned Mr. Potato-Head face.

I pushed it. "That what you'll be doing? What's to stop you from blowing me off those stairs halfway up? Smells like a frame, man, you know? Drug kitchen inside'd tie a real nice ribbon around my corpse, wouldn't it?"

"Jesus Christ." Dorey had that disappointed look again. Did he think the whole world could just see the color of his hat? "Get the hell up the ladder, Barnes. You dragged me out here, besides which I am cutting you a break by even listening to your horseshit story. I'm at the end of my rope with you."

"Just so it's not the same rope that dented Walter Epps' neck."

"Christ," Dorey spat. "Just climb the goddam ladder. I'll be covering your ass."

Not liking it, I stacked two crates, clambered up, and leaped to snare the folding iron ladder. When I reached the first little zigzag landing, I shot a glance down. Dorey had disappeared. On the top landing, I stuck my arm through the glass pane I'd broken before, pushed the release bar, and slipped inside. Nobody screamed. No bullet in the back, either.

I could see a little better than the last time I was in there. Streaky moonlight through the skylight switched the catwalk and the roof support struts into something's rib cage, on then off again. The empty middle of the warehouse floor was one minute well lit—like right field at a minor league night game. But then it would fade into the edges that stayed murky black.

While I was easing the door shut, the bar slipped out of my hands so that the latch banged. Whammed like a hand grenade to my ears. I froze. It took forever for everything to quiet down. Then it got too quiet, so I could hear that whole big metal box of a building whining and griping in the wind. Then, gingerly, I stepped out onto the catwalk and toed along it, one foot slowly and lightly in front of the other. Three stories below, I could make out the outline of the shipping clerk's room.

Ten minutes of creeping took me to the ladder at the opposite end of the catwalk. I had hooked my heels down four or five rungs when a voice from the bottom of the ladder boomed off every surface in the place.

"Police. Freeze!"

What I did was commence bumping knees and elbows scuttling back up that ladder. When I hit the catwalk again, I hit it hard, on my belly.

"Drop that gun or we'll fire," commanded the next echo. Now I knew the shit was going down. In that light, I was just an outline to them; no way they could see a gun, even if I had been holding one.

I cursed myself for a chump. While Dorey covered the outside platform, whoever was on the floor below had me treed like a cat. Velnarsky? Mooney? Fifteen others? I tried peering down at the warehouse floor, but the edges were dense shadow, and the center was empty. I reached into my jacket and pulled out the Bulldog revolver.

In a jam, you think too long, and you might freeze up. Without exactly ordering my muscles to go, I found myself banging to my feet and sprinting back the way I'd come. At least I'd be a moving target.

For about three long, bouncy strides nothing happened. My heart was tearing out of my chest, boots thumping, catwalk screaming like its tail was pulled.

Then everything blew up. Splinters of wood ripped my face, a split second before shotgun thunder boomed. A step ahead of me, the catwalk disappeared into fragments, the gust pinching my pants legs as the load flew by and spread, spattering like hard rain against the tin roof.

A second later, I had hopped over the shotgun hole and was tearing nearly halfway across, when the edge of a second full-choked load rasped across the back plate of my ballistics vest. At less than forty feet range, even the edge of the pattern twisted me around, rubber-balling me off the hand rails.

Somehow, the pistol stayed stuck in my hand. I caught my balance enough to spray four blind shots at different sections of the floor below, but I needn't have wasted my time. The thin moonlight bloomed into living color, the orange flash and the mulekick slamming me at once. I guess I took the whole steel pellet pattern on my chest. I know it blew me backwards and draped me across the thin safety rail like a dish rag on a hook.

Chapter 27

Stars and stripes wheeled in my head. If every cell in my body hadn't hurt so much, hanging off that catwalk, I'd swear I was an angel hovering in the twilight zone above my killers.

Sounds staggered back into place first. Below me, and far back, somebody was pounding on the warehouse door like a kettle drum.

I heard the door lock click. "Eddie, it's us," a familiar voice shouted. Old Dale Mooney. "I'm gonna open up now, Eddie. Keep it in your pants." The hinges shrieked.

"What the hell happened?" On the word "happened," Dorey's voice suddenly filled the space, when he stepped into the terminal, as if a volume control got spun.

By the time Mooney finished with the "Geez, it's good to see yous" and the "We really got 'em now, don't wes," I was already having trouble hearing. My head, hanging straight down, was throbbing with blood. I knew I was somewhere over their heads, but what was holding me from a swan dive was not easy to figure.

I was hanging head down, arms dangling. That much I

could figure. I tried clenching and unclenching my hands. Both worked; both were empty, though. The Bulldog must have flopped over the side when the blast blew me backwards.

My ribs screamed from the bruising they'd taken, but I tasted no blood, so my vest had caught most all the pellets. The pressure at my groin filled in the last clue. Knocked backwards, I'd half-spun, hit the safety rail at belly-buttom level, and dumped myself facedown, legs and thighs still on the catwalk, upper body suspended in mid-air.

Tenderly, I wriggled one shoe towards the opposite edge of the catwalk planks, found it, hooked both toes over it, and flexed stomach muscles to raise my torso. I immediately rolled over on my back, stripped off the windbreaker, and hung it back over the railing as a decoy.

Dorey and Mooney were closer now. Too busy palavering to fix on me, I prayed. I strained to fine-tune their voices.

"What was all the friggin' shooting about?" There was a rasp in Dorey's bark.

Mooney said nothing. They walked underneath the catwalk. A third figure strolled out to meet them from the shadows at the foot of the iron stairs.

"Barnes drew on us." Velnarsky pointed up at my jacket. "You probably heard it from the outside. We gave him a warning, told him to drop his gun, but the crazy buckwheat started firing."

"How'd you even know Barnes was bringing me down here?" Dorey asked.

Up top, I started crabbing towards the fire escape door. "Griff filled us in," Mooney piped. "He overheard you two sitting in the squad room. Said Barnes was laying this line of shit on you, how a meth kitchen was cooking down here? Ray and I put two and two together, didn't we, Ray? Figured Barnes was sucking you down here to waste you."

"Griff wasn't working," Dorey said. His voice sounded very far away. At the fire door, I groped up to press the release bar, eased the door open a crack, and poked my head outside.

From inside, Velnarsky's voice shuddered the tin walls. "The fuck he wasn't! Came on duty just before you walked out with Barnes. You didn't notice?"

Slithering out on my belly, I heard Dorey buy that part of the package.

"I guess you're right. What do we know about the meth kitchen Barnes claimed was down here?"

I paused in mid-wiggle.

"We checked it out, soon as we got here." Mooney sounded as if he were showing Dorey his clean hands. "Nothing. Want to see?"

That was the last I heard for a while, because I dropped my feet onto the outdoor fire stairs and vibrated my way down. With my feet on the last rungs of the swing-down ladder, I began to take stock. My chest blazed and ached, as if two heavyweights had socked me at once. But inhaling was no longer white fire. Could be I'd get away with no more than a few bruised or cracked ribs. I had lived through worse.

The big problem wasn't me, anyway. It was Eddie Dorey. Unless he was the type to keep his suspicions to himself, he would never walk back out of that warehouse.

My heart sank. Face it, Barnes, Dorey was surely not that type. He'd speak his mind. Down the length of the pier I made like Marcel Marceau, then flattened against the corner and peeked quickly around it. I mean *quickly*. I almost snapped my head off yanking it back so fast, because next to the parking lot, separated from me by just the warehouse facade, Dorey, Mooney, and Velnarsky stood cupping cigarettes and arguing.

I never heard a word of it, what with the wind zooming like a jet blast from behind me. But when I peeped around again, all three were gone.

One, two, three, shit, I whipped around the corner, streaked along the facade, and braked in time to sneak a look around the other corner. They'd gone back inside. When my ear to the heavy metal door picked up nothing, I turned the knob slowly and tugged gently. Unlocked. It didn't figure that they'd bother to latch the door behind them, and they hadn't. I slipped in and concentrated to pick them out in the gloom. Nearly at the clerk's shed, I could see them; their voices boomed back clearly to me.

"That's the way it always is, with nuts," Velnarsky was saying. "If it's real to them, then they sound so damn convincing."

"The way I figure this mess, Eddie," Mooney contributed earnestly, "Barnes wasn't wrapped too tight to start with, got hooked up with Epps in some scam, and when Epps got nabbed by the Feds, Barnes whacked out and iced the little dude."

"The Medical Examiner says Epps died by suicide." I felt my heart stutter. Dorey was too smart to buy the crude frame, too simply honest to fake buying it.

Velnarsky dropped an arm around Dorey's shoulders, the way he had around the late Carl Carp's. In the other hand he still gripped the pump-action shotgun he'd fired at me. My lungs stopped pumping air.

"What the fuck does that idiot know, anyway?" Velnarsky chuckled. He was affectionately massaging the back of Dorey's neck with his big hand. "Butterfield's a coroner because he couldn't hack it as a surgeon. This way, he don't have to worry about all the parts working right when he sews bodies back together."

"Isn't that the truth?" Mooney sniggered. "Besides, suicide or murder, makes no difference now that Barnes has bought it."

"Are you two so sure Barnes is dead?" Dorey shrugged Velnarsky's hand off his back. "How about I climb up there and find out? If he's alive, probably he's got something important we need to know."

Dale Mooney looked frantically at Velnarsky. "He ain't got anything important to tell us." Mooney's voice was thin. "We know the whole story already. Let Barnes drain up there. He's dead already."

"Shut up," Velnarsky told him. Then he turned to Dorey: "Save it, brother. First, we show you there's no meth kitchen here."

Just before the shed door, Dorey kicked something.

"This his gun?" He stooped, picked up my Bulldog revolver, and sniffed it.

For a split second my heart thumped hard when I saw Dorey holding that big pistol. But it fell an instant later when Velnarsky reached over, friendly like, and took the Bulldog by the barrel out of Dorey's hand.

"Been fired, ain't it?" Velnarsky said reasonably. "Like we said, Barnes opened up on us. Making sense to you now, Eddie?"

I didn't hear Dorey's answer, if he made one. I was busy sneaking up the shadowy wall to get nearer.

Velnarsky tugged open the shed door and waved Dorey in. By his pause, Dorey was making up his mind about something. "No, not before I see if Barnes is still alive," he said finally. "This isn't right, Ray, and you know it."

"He's a murderer." Mooney was losing it. "Barnes tried to kill the two of us. He would have killed you too, we hadn't drilled him. Forget him, Eddie."

Dorey swung around and stared down Mooney, then turned his look on Velnarsky. "This smells worse and worse," he said flatly. "I'm going up to check on whether Barnes is dead or alive. I hope to God you called it in, like you said, Ray." He looked up at my jacket bannering the catwalk, then back at Velnarsky. But maybe he half-knew what would happen; he didn't move a step.

Velnarsky sighed. "Stick them on your head, Eddie," he said softly. He raised the shotgun to waist level. The Bulldog dangled in his left hand. Mooney pulled his revolver out, too.

Dorey said steadily: "You gonna put a gun on *me*, Ray? One of your own?"

"You don't have a fucking clue what 'your own' means, do you, Eddie?" Velnarsky's voice was soothing, almost sympathetic. "You're the one that didn't do the right thing, went against your family. You think anything in this life's more important than that? I feel sorry for you."

"What do I do, Ray?" Mooney said. Nervous.

"Pat him down."

My mind throttled high. I could count on Mooney

slopping up the weapon search, like everything else he ever tried. I had a split second to figure a move. I figured one.

What I went for filled me with regret that I'd snuck up so close on top of them. I had to hope the shadows and the echoes would hide me long enough.

While Mooney was fumbling under Dorey's armpit for his holster, I turned and bounced my voice away from them down the cold concrete floor.

"Freeze, motherfuckers!" The echoes snarled from everywhere. "One move, and you're dog food."

All three of them, even Velnarsky, involuntarily jerked their heads up to stare at my jacket, hanging unmoving above them, shimmering a little in the moonlight.

Then, while Velnarsky hopped into a spread-legged squat like a frog, Dorey grabbed Mooney's elbow, stuck out a leg, and tripped him down hard onto the floor. Still sliding, Dale Mooney fumbled up his service revolver and began pulling the trigger wildly, setting ricochets off the hard floor. Faster than I could see, Dorey dove into a prone combat position, bracing his right wrist on his propped left forearm, pointing his own pistol squarely at Mooney. It popped twice, flames spitting, then licking back along the muzzle. Mooney jerked back like a puppet sprawling off too-loose strings. A chunk of something hit the wall behind his body, which twitched in a ragdoll heap.

"Freeze, Velnarsky," I screamed again, doing what little I could. Then I dove flat on my stomach further back in the shadows. If I hadn't, the blast from his shotgun would have taken me out. As it was, it punched a manhole in the wall where my head had been.

Stretched on the floor, under the skylight, Dorey swung his upper body in a blur, bringing the revolver up to train on Velnarsky. For a second, I thought he'd pull it off before that animal could repump his .20 gauge.

But I was forgetting about the Bulldog pistol in Velnarsky's other hand. The crimson spark from the hydroshock cartridges lit up Dorey's fierce expression, before his entire body jolted off the concrete floor as it caught the slug from the gun I'd prepared.

Chapter 28

While Velnarsky nudged Dorey's body with a shoe tip, I tried sliding in the shadows along the wall towards the door.

"Ready, Barnes?" he boomed without looking up. I froze, in the idiotic hope he hadn't pinpointed me. "Exactly what was it you planned on doing, Barnes?"

I stood watching him pump out a smoking shell and load in new cartridges. He actioned a fresh round into the chamber and walked right at me. "Out here, where I can see you."

I slithered towards the middle where moonbeams snowed on the vast empty floor, hands stretched out, palms open. I had to step around Dorey's body, stretched out on his stomach. Five steps away, Mooney lay on his back, a terrible grin on his dead face, spittle and blood dribbling down to stain his shirt front.

Velnarsky stood there with indifference painted all over his face. He was bored. That gave me an idea.

"Your partner's shot, too," I pointed out. "You gonna toe him with your boot?"

Velnarsky laughed. "Nah, Dorey finished the blabber-mouth off. Good riddance. Saved me the trouble."

"That's right, you been a busy beaver, these days," I said. "Counting Epps, how many scalps you put on your belt this week?"

Velnarsky grunted.

"Tell me something. You pop a nut fixing up Epps like that, stripping him nude, tying the string around him, and all?"

"Dale did that," Velnarsky said calmly. "Give credit where credit's coming."

"But *you* wasted Epps first, didn't you? Break his neck with your hands?"

"Sure. But you were Johnny-on-the-spot. So while I was out settling your hash, Dale fixed up the suicide, best as he could. Guess he figured the bare-assed body would look right for a pervert."

"You settled *my* hash? Why, I kicked your ass upside and down, until you pulled a sneaky Pete like a damned weasel."

Velnarsky's face really got interested in me then, like a man seeing a good breakfast after an all-night shift.

"If you hadn't suckered me twice, in Carp's office and behind those tenements," he said, "I'd have your ass on my mantel a long time ago."

"I cleaned your clock, chump. Even after you back-jumped me at Epps' house."

Grinning again, he told me: "You're not in shape, coon-cake. You don't even train any more. No way you'd last two minutes with me." With each sentence, he took one step closer. Now the shotgun barrel was maybe a foot from my nose, looking like the Holland Tunnel. My straining eyes saw Velnarsky's shooting hand just draped over the trigger-guard.

The shotgun clattered to the cement, and he kicked it out of reach behind him.

"You beat me," he challenged softly, "you get the gun."

He might have been betting a six-pack on the NFL playoffs. But I didn't stop to shake on it. Instead, I suckered him with a haymaker and followed up quick with two jabs. He shook them off like mosquito bites. Then he rang my chimes with a stiff right hand.

I backed out and circled, shuffling a little. Velnarsky knew how to counter that. He bore down on me, like he was cutting down a ring, working me side to side, until the huge warehouse wall loomed close behind me. That red-haired ape was even quicker than I'd figured. I kept trying to slide off the wall, but he kept picking up my fakes and jumping first.

Along the wall, the piss-poor light was deceptive. I ate

a second vicious right hook that I never saw coming. I kept him off with my jab, until my head cleared. Then I sparred and parried, locking in my elbows to protect my tender midsection. I swung in a meathook right I knew he'd block and danced starboard, edging closer to the outside door. What I hadn't noticed before was how that route was blocked by a mountain of pallets rising higher than my head in the gloom. In the time I took to take that in, a third head shot lit blue flames in my skull.

Still, years of counterpunching had taught me a few things. This time I rolled off the shot, and played his over-committed strength against him. I leaned in, hooked an elbow around his waist, and spun around him, into the clear, before his fist levered back again.

Two chopping rabbit punches to his neck, and a twisting right dug deep into his kidney, and I danced back on my toes. Velnarsky made his first sound, a little snarl. He pivoted to square off with me, lips curled on that stone marker face. I didn't care: it was his turn in the corner now. I stung him hard with flicking jabs. I owed him that for Dorey. He was stronger, but I was quicker. If I didn't have the muscle to pin him there, I would pour on the speed. Cut his eyes up, bash his nose, my rhythm went. Make that mother crazy with hate.

Who knows if he crazed with hate, but I know I hurt him. Still, he did not go down. Every time he tried to rush, I danced off, then backed him up with chin jabs. My combinations bounced off his head like tennis balls off a re-bound wall. Was I outboxing him, or was he just letting me hit him? I was flicking my hands now, just snapping my elbows, two lefts, a right, not fresh enough to get much shoulder into the shots.

It was hard to tell what Velnarsky had left. He was taking a lot of punishment to his head. I sorely wanted to drop him, but to hit any harder I would need to shuffle in closer for more leverage.

Did Velnarsky maybe look a little punchy? I took a chance and shuffled in. The minute I did, he belted me through my guard as fresh as if he'd just finished warming up. My left hook to his cheekbone landed the same time his left reached my ribs. He didn't scream. I did, seared, dropping my arms like a second-act curtain. Then hard rights and lefts to my head. I covered up and blocked, got the old elbows up and peekabooed him, vintage Floyd Patterson. But I wasn't hardly holding my own. Just covering up felt equal to hefting two brick-filled suitcases waist-high.

With my elbows tucked in to protect my ribs, my head was vulnerable. Three times, like John Henry driving stakes, Velnarsky whomped overhead rights down on my head and shoulders, each one threatening to cave me in. My arms were burning hot as coals, protesting what I needed them to do.

Velnarsky saw the opening and brought his left fist off his hip for the cross to my chin. Set 'em up with the rights, then cross with the left. Classic combo, nothing fancy, straight-up boxing.

That was the reason I didn't go for it. That and his feet. The man's feet were set up wrong. You can't throw a left hook, weight off your left foot, and power out a fly. I didn't consciously process the information. You spar enough, something like that just *looks* funny to you.

So I rode out the fake. Velnarsky pulled back the left hand, rose up on his right foot, and whipped his left leg around, head-high.

If the kick had hit me, it would have killed me. It didn't. As the boot rocketed past, I timed it, leaned outside the arc of his swing, and felt the ferocious gust of air.

Something unexpected happened then. Crowded by the pallets, Velnarsky caught a hitch in his pivot, had to short-hop back on his right foot to clear some space. And that's when, without thinking, I stepped in on top of the man. All the way from China, I pulled that left uppercut. I let him eat every smudge of muscle I had left in my legs, chest, and arms.

I was aiming to drive his balls clear up to his tonsils.

Velnarsky's face screwed up in agony, though he never

let out a sound like any normal human would. Like a bat-
tleship torpedoed in the gut, he listed to the right, smashed
into the wall of pallets, and fell.

I wobbled back a couple steps and watched him. Then
I sank down cross-legged. But not like a Buddha, mind over
matter. I was clenched up in knots of pain that no quantity
of adrenaline, morphine, or meditation would ever dull.
Breathing was a job to occupy a man fully twenty-four hours
a day. Moving another inch felt totally out of the question.
For a lifetime, all I saw was the red blood in the pain-
swollen lumps that were my eyeballs. And seeping through
it, the sight of Velnarsky's hump of flesh on the floor.

I concentrated on forcing my tinker-toy body back onto
the slinkies I was wearing for legs, a blue-pained effort. The
ache in my ribs seemed to have spread, numbing the nerves
in my legs, back, and shoulders. My body was a new
damned enemy, fighting me for every inch.

Velnarsky lay four paces from me, as silent and un-
twitching as the bodies of Mooney and Dorey out in the
middle of the moon-splashed floor. He was so deathlike, I
almost forgot about him.

I got up on both feet and clenched my knees with my
hands. Catch my breath, let the fire seep out of my side,
maybe I'd walk out of there under my own steam.

Or so I reckoned until I heard Velnarsky stirring from
the dead. A Japanese horror flick star, he lumbered to his
feet and periscoped for me.

Now, maybe I was punchy, but for a loony minute I felt
fine and feisty. The sight of that hulk hoisting himself up
and trying to move brought a wicked grin to my teeth. So
what if old blue eyes beat me out for the standing-up-first
trophy? I could see by how he limped that his testicles were
close to a ten-count. He could barely move his thighs. No
way he could punch or kick with that pair of blue coconut
balls. I would just wait until Godzilla staggered up, and
then Mrs. Barnes' little boy would let him soak in another
shot to the nuggets. That would hold even him.

It was a good idea, except that Velnarsky wobbled, not
towards me, but away from me, like a bowlegged cowboy

doing the twist six inches at a time, angling towards the middle of the enormous floor. One foot after another, not a look at me, every scrap of prehistoric muscle focused on his painful locomotion.

For about twenty steps, I watched him, fascinated, wondering how far he'd get before he dropped. Then I realized what he was after.

He was dragging himself, with unerring precision, to the loaded shotgun he'd tossed down as a challenge to me.

By the time I'd wired that right, he'd already made too much of the distance. Insanity for me to stagger after him, even if I could have.

Get away, my brain screamed.

My legs remained way too shaky to trust. Instead, I banged down onto my knees and crawled in the opposite direction, straining every muscle. Even so, nothing could keep me from glancing over my shoulder to monitor that human wreck twisting that inhuman journey. Forty feet from me, Velnarsky all at once slumped to his knees, then onto his hands. When he raised up his torso again, the shotgun was cradled across his chest.

By then I had a reasonable knee and palm trot working. I hardly felt the rough cement floor scour my hands raw and rip patches off my knees. I was crawling faster than he could limp. I beelined down the black shadows along the wall, heading for the door to the outside and freedom.

But after only a few seconds my fingers brushed the raspy, splintery wood of the pallets. Left turn only out of that corner. Worse, that heap of pallets made a wall stretching twenty-five, thirty feet out towards the center of the warehouse floor. Even as slowly as he was twisting along, Velnarsky still had a terrific angle on me.

Velnarsky was only fifteen feet away, still limping, cutting the angle so that if I went any further now, I'd be moving towards him. I stopped. Against the dark pallet mountain, I was a huddle of black shadows near the floor. Velnarsky stood half bent over, knees bent, breathing like a chain saw.

He surprised me by whispering, low and hoarse, "Think you kicked my ass, Barnes?"

I figured my answer would be my last words. I said: "You know I did."

Velnarsky's laugh was keyed to shake the bats out of the warehouse rafters. He levered up the shotgun barrel until it pointed roughly between my belt and my crotch tape. I dug in my toes and hands to push off for the rush I knew I had nothing left for.

The explosion of a handgun stopped everything. At the range of twenty feet, the hydroshock bullet from the Bulldog shattered Velnarsky's disbelieving face. His body jerked back once, then again, and finally spread-eagled on the cool cement floor.

Chapter 29

Let me set the scene for you. Some night watchman in a neighboring warehouse must have heard the fireworks and called in the police. I was the one and only black man in a warehouse with three dead white cops. No surprise to me when the uniforms who answered the call weren't more sympathetic about my wounds. First they cuffed me tight, then barbecued me with questions. You've got to expect cops to be cops.

My savior stood there like a great white hunter. Doctor Raymond Butterfield in his bushwhacking outfit, leather aviator's jacket, and Indiana Jones hat. The cops huddled around him so that I didn't know what Butterfield was telling them. I do know they cuffed me so tight on the ride downtown that my hands blew up like catcher's mitts. Up in the homicide squad room, they flopped me down on an icy aluminum chair in a postage-stamp-sized interrogation cubicle. My body ached all over, but I needed to stay keen. I was prepared to turn down a pain killer, but none was offered.

The hurt only faded when I dozed off in the chair while waiting for the rubber-hose boys to dance through the door and work me over. Doze off I did for a couple hours at least, until the heavy door flew open with a thud, and a detective I'd never seen before slouched in.

"Stand up, Barnes," he mushy-mouthed.

"What for?"

"Don't be such a pain in the ass." Every "s" sound was an adventure in diction. He laid his big red paws on me and yanked me out of the chair. Doll-like, he spun me around, and the next thing I knew he twisted a little key into the handcuffs and freed my wrists.

"Rub 'em real good," he ordered. "Takes a few minutes for the circulation to come back."

The look on my face would have stopped a traffic accident. "Don't just stand there gawking," the big cop grunted, swinging his weight for the door. "Follow me."

"Where?"

He didn't bother to answer. I limped behind through the homicide room, then down two double flights of fire stairs. On the first floor, we passed through the main lobby to a side corridor with just one big door at its end. He swung to one side and pulled the door open for me.

"Go on," he jerked his head toward the inside. "They're waiting for you. Pull yourself together."

Two steps into the office and the door closed with a hush behind me. A combination of weary legs and deep-pile carpet wobbled me across the room like a drunken sailor. This was a triple secretaries' office, empty now and dimly lit by just one reading light. At the far end of that room was an open passageway, and I hobbled through it.

A big oak desk barely put a dent in that giant office. All wood paneling, walls and ceiling. Persian rugs on bare floors. Big United States and New Jersey flags flanking the desk. A face from the newspaper photos was sitting between the flags. Old hardass Commissioner Randall Man-ouso.

He was not alone. Lounging in a facing armchair was daisy-fresh Doctor Raymond Butterfield. He had found time to change clothes. Cream-colored suit and shirt, deep blue tie, tassled cordovan moccasins. Legs crossed. Bastard looked ready to go club-hopping at the drop of a hat.

Butterfield raised his coffee cup to me as I dragged it to the front of Manouso's desk.

"Take a seat, Mr. Barnes." The Commissioner reminded me of Mario Cuomo, polished but hard as stainless steel. His rain-colored eyes ran over me like a plantation owner at a slave auction.

I turned to eye Butterfield, who just smiled and nodded back like we were old homies. "Doctor Butterfield tells me you saved his life last night," Manouso said. His voice was unexpectedly high and penetrating in such a big man. It never lost its edge of irony.

"You got a window in here?" I asked. "I want to check, see if I'm on the planet earth."

"Doctor Butterfield reported last night's tragedy at the Port of Newark," Manouso said impatiently. "You prevented his murder." He tugged at his loosened tie, which went nicely with his nondescript gray suit and unfastened collar. He might have been unbuttoned because it was the seven A.M. of a long night, but you got the feeling he'd look the same at any hour of the day or night.

"That so?"

"Yes," Manouso's voice was full of the final, official version of the facts. "You could be commended for your courage and tenacity in this unpleasant incident."

"You sure you understand what went down last night?"

"I understand plenty. A Police Commissioner is obviously not going to rejoice that Edward Dorey was a bad cop. We take full responsibility for his illegal acts. Our chief regret, though, is that two of Newark's best detectives lost their lives in the line of duty, trying to apprehend Dorey."

"You got it ass-backwards, Manouso," I said. "Velnarsky and Mooney were the ones teamed up with Butterfield here to push drugs. Not Eddie Dorey."

"Drugs?" Manouso glanced at Butterfield, who shrugged.

"What are you talkin'—*drugs?*!" I jumped to my feet. "Methamphetamine, by name. Butterfield, along with Velnarsky and Mooney, was cooking methamphetamine in the warehouse down the Port where you found us."

Butterfield shrugged a second time. Manouso wasn't even looking over at him. He was saying to me:

"My investigators went over that warehouse with a fine-tooth comb, Barnes. There were no traces of any drug operation in that building."

Inside, I was groaning and kicking at myself. It had been my cute idea to call in Fahriq to clear out that warehouse. I stuck to my guns anyway.

"Commissioner, you remember when this civil servant named Walter Epps got killed?"

"Another name from the homicide lists."

"Well, Epps was managing a federal family planning agency that he skimmed money from. They used it as seed funds for the meth operation. His partner was Butterfield. Butterfield came up with the chemicals to make the drugs and the corpses to ship the finished product around the country."

"Hold it. Epps committed suicide." Manouso was annoyed with me. "I routinely review all homicide reports." He tugged at his withered tie again.

"Can't you see the cover-up?" I was practically yelling. "Butterfield was chin-deep all the way, along with Epps and a funeral parlor director named Elmo Toledo. They used the bodies of indigents and people that had no families to pay attention to what happened to them."

Manouso was glaring at me to finish.

"After Butterfield sews the drugs inside the corpses, Toledo puts the bodies on display, then ships them out to different cities. It's the safest way to ship drugs known to man, all the legal papers, the right trucks. It can't fail. Then Toledo plants caskets full of rocks in the ground."

To my left, Butterfield uncrossed his legs, then crossed them the other way. He looked ready to say something, then he sipped again at his coffee.

Manouso said it for him, irony dialed all the way up: "It seems to me you proved the rocks-in-the-casket theory yesterday, didn't you, Barnes?"

"They outfoxed me, is all," I protested. "Why is that so hard to see? I'll tell you right now, you dig up the casket of a Kelvin Stokes that got buried yesterday too, you'll find rocks for certain. How about it?"

Manouso drummed his thick fingers on the desktop. "You know anything about judges, Barnes?" He smiled. "Even if I believed you—which I do not—there isn't a judge in all of New Jersey who will issue a court order to exhume a body solely on your say-so. You've been nipping at the edges of the law for a while now. After yesterday's little performance in the cemetery, you just plain have no credibility left."

Manouso was right, of course. I had cried wolf, real loudly, once—and once was too often, in this town. Hassan Fahriq had set me up, and the kick was I knew he meant it as a special favor to me. If he had not been an old friend, and maybe felt a little in my debt, not just my credibility would be dead.

I kept a small edge by keeping Hassan's name to myself. The way Manouso was shoveling cat litter over the whole mess, he'd most likely prefer not to even hear Fahriq's name. But if he ever did make trouble for Hassan, it would also be trouble for me. I had been warned.

"I got something else," I said slowly. "A ledger that I found in the office of Epps' attorney, Carl Carp."

"Now a name from the missing persons list," Manouso said coolly. "What kind of ledger?"

"It lays out the entire operation, soup to nuts."

"Complete with names?" Manouso looked suddenly interested.

"Code names," I conceded. "But a good financial investigator could take that book and crack the case."

"So you don't actually yourself know *what's* in it?"

I said nothing, sorry I'd brought it up.

"Nevertheless, we'll take a look at this ledger," Manouso said crisply, reaching for the telephone. "Where is it located? I'll have it picked up."

"Not without a subpoena," I bartered grimly.

"I can make life very unpleasant for you in Newark, Mr. Barnes."

I had very few cards left. I played one.

"Not unpleasant enough to take that ledger from me without an evidence subpoena. To do that, you'd have to admit there was probable cause to think it was evidence of a crime and maybe the lid'd come off the whole stinking mess."

"You could find yourself out in the cold, Barnes, grubbing for a living." Manouso bored in on me full throttle. "I can see to it that your private investigator's license hops the shuttle to Kokomo if you don't leave this nonsense alone."

"Do it," I said. "Now there's one hearing I can't wait to testify at. I'll mouth off plenty, then."

"Keep the ledger," Manouso said, in disgust. "Take it home and cuddle it in your sleep. You're sick, you know that? You know how much evidence disputes your story? We've a complete signed statement from your client, Mrs. Ruth Epps, fully backing up Doctor Butterfield's version of the facts."

I opened my mouth, and was surprised when no words fell out.

"Their story makes perfect sense to everyone but you," Manouso began patiently, the tin man explaining the facts of life to the scarecrow. "Both Edward Dorey and Doctor Butterfield were deep in love affairs with Ruth Epps."

I started to complain. Manouso said, "The lady claims you were enjoying her affections, too."

At the way he put that, it was Butterfield's turn to make protesting noises.

I could feel the fix go in like a stiletto between my ribs.

"You weren't aware that Dorey was Mrs. Epps' lover, were you? That's why you've got it all wrong, Barnes. It's the age-old story of two men competing for a beautiful woman's attentions. According to Mrs. Epps, Dorey became insanely jealous of her relationship with Doctor Butterfield. In fact, after her husband committed suicide, Dorey ordered her to stop seeing Butterfield altogether. When she refused, Dorey unhinged and gathered matters into his own hands."

"Oh, the man was insane, all right," Butterfield chimed in. "He called me last night to notify me of a homicide scene at the Port of Newark and gave me a warehouse address. It was Dorey's intention to lure me to that secluded spot and murder me."

Butterfield gave me a superficially chummy grin with a seasoning of mockery Manouso maybe couldn't pick up.

I sneered back at the little creep. "Who'd believe that pitiful line of crap?"

Manouso leaned in: "Evidently, two top detectives, Officers Velnarsky and Mooney, believed it when they heard Dorey had summoned the doctor to the Port. Their instincts suspected his motives, and they soon laid bare his plan. But regrettably, Dorey got the jump on them and gunned them down like mad dogs."

"Mooney was killed with Dorey's gun," I said sourly.

"Oh, that's right, Velnarsky was murdered with *your* weapon, wasn't he, Barnes?"

"How about Butterfield's fingerprints on it?" I persisted. "You run a nitrates test on his hand, see if he fired the gun?"

Manouso's eyes flicked over at Butterfield, then back at me. "I've taken over direction of the case myself. All the standard forensics tests are being run in due order."

"Jesus!" I grimaced. "The man runs the lab where those tests are going down. Butterfield killed Velnarsky to cover his traces."

Both Manouso and Butterfield were staring at me. Identical looks.

"You don't even want to hear any more about this, do you?" I said to Manouso. "You already decided how it's gonna read, and it ain't based on the truth."

"I have heard enough." Manouso sighed, and reached to his intercom panel.

"Not the last of this, you haven't heard." I stood up and leaned on Manouso's desk. "I'm prancing to the Feds with this. Count on it."

"With what evidence?" Manouso almost yawned. "They'll think you are a raving lunatic, friend."

"You are something, you know that, man? To you, this is just a cat pile you got to sweep under the carpet."

"This is a big city police department I'm running," he said smoothly, already looking over papers on his desk. "Not a boy scout camp. Don't slam the door on your way out."

Butterfield touched a finger to an eyebrow, then flicked it towards me.

A second door from Manouso's office opened directly into the enormous marble courthouse lobby. Empty on a Sunday morning. Out there, in the light and sudden echoes, I eyed the row of telephones and momentarily contemplated calling Ruth Epps. There were knots in my shoulders and I shrugged to loosen them.

What would I say to her, be serious now. I'd just end up screaming how she was a pork-chop-eating bitch, and she'd find some superior icy way to put me down. No thanks. I'd already eaten at the all-the-pride-you-can-swallow buffet.

Hobbling out, I shouldered against an imaginary Sunday flow of lawyers, witnesses, and defendants pouring through the Broad Street door. The eight A.M. sun was still cold, and already I felt swimming against the traffic.

Nearly out the arch, my eye fell on an old favorite of mine, old Lady Justice, twice life-sized and all woman. Her clinging robe hinted of a body that could flaunt itself or melt coy. The heavy sword in her hand warned oglers like me and other amateurs to stay clear. The scales in her right hand had been loaded with balls of gum and cigarette butts. Some wise man had inked two eyeballs onto her blindfold.

An idea hit me about some homegrown justice.

Chapter 30

Frost was on the pumpkin in the Laurel Gardens garden, and I wondered if my plan would simply wither on the vine. In the meantime, I kept a profile so low a worm wouldn't even notice me, taking care of business as usual downtown. Althea drove off to college, amidst the Sharecroppers' promises that we'd win the national contest for her next year. Our eighth-place finish earned us one thousand dollars that we all voted towards building a solar greenhouse. All except at first for Snookie and the Field Marshal, who wanted to throw a party. After I described how it would be like a sun-heated clubhouse in the winter, even those two went for the idea like it was their own. I think everybody had begun to worry about how they would spend their days once the gardening was all through for the winter. They hadn't realized until then how the garden was giving them something to wake up for every morning.

Angel got so many compliments on his dancing at the Pimlico that he answered an open casting call for a fifty-showgirl revue backing up Paul Anka at Harrah's Casino in Atlantic City. Naturally he got picked out of the crowd to dance in the front row, which took him off the streets of Newark and gave him a taste of glamour for a month. After that, Angel long-legged around chuckling practically non-stop for another month.

Night thoroughbred racing repaid Cosmo for twenty-five years of fidelity by wiring three Exactas for him in five days, to the tune of sixty-five thousand dollars. Cosmo promptly donated a five-thousand-dollar tax deduction to the Sharecroppers' greenhouse, enough for us to apply for matching funds in the program sponsored by the nation's premier greenhouse manufacturers, Noble and Fyrham.

Mrs. Washington talked them into donating the assembly labor, too, with some help from us. Then the city surprised us by offering a twenty-year lease on the vacant lot for one dollar a year. Next thing we knew, Noble and Fyrham had trucked in heavy equipment, excavated a huge hole, and poured a slab. The sample pictures made the greenhouse-to-be look as big as a Newark bungalow and ten times as light filled and colorful and comfortable. On-site assembly of the prefabricated kit was scheduled for the second week of November.

All these were good and welcome events, and I tried to get involved in my friends' pleasure. But all the while, I was nursing another feeling, something that squirmed inside and threatened never to quit. An inner-city September crawled into the longer footstrides and stiffer street faces of October. I waited and watched, scoured every inch of the newspaper every day, kept warm a scheme that I played over and over in my imagination.

Finally, the Columbus Day edition of the *Star-Ledger* second-paged the signal I'd been tensed for. I was sitting in Al's Queen Street diner, nursing a platter of hotcakes and over-easies. At ten A.M., Al and I had the place to ourselves.

I read the headline, looked at the photo, read the headline again. The picture was a very recent one of Doctor Raymond Butterfield. Bow-tied and slick-haired, Butterfield held the world by the tail and showed how he liked that by his sardonic grin.

MEDICAL EXAMINER LEAVES OFFICE WITH BLAST, the bottom-left headline punned. In what was being understated as a suspicious death, the police reported that Doctor Raymond Butterfield had left the morgue late the night before and was killed when his Porsche blew to Laos during ignition.

Only a sizable fix could have kept that news off the front page, but I could not care less about that.

I'd played my next move so often in my mind that I just mopped up the yolk on my plate, tucked the newspaper under my arm, and stepped over to the pay phone mounted on the aluminum wall of Al's diner.

I stonewalled two different voices before the right speaker came on.

"How sweet it is!" I crooned into the mouthpiece.

"Jackie Gleason? Been a long time since you called, Jackie," said a streetwise voice.

"Just a grateful admirer. Calling to compliment you on last night's work of art. You're a regular Picasso with a pipe bomb."

"Sorry to disappoint you, Barnes," Fahriq said. "But that wasn't my signature. Bombs are not my style."

"You are much too modest, Hassan. Or is it because Franklin, Benjamin, and Isaacs are visiting with you?"

"No, for once the Feds don't have my damn phone bugged," Fahriq chuckled. "Straight goods, buddy. Wasn't me who gave the good doctor his hot foot."

"Who then?"

"Could be the black widow her very-grieving-self that did in lover boy."

"Hell hath no fury—" I began.

"Like a beneficiary scorned," he finished.

Behind all the jive, I knew very well Fahriq had done the job on Butterfield. And, what's more, he knew very well that I was hip. All the noise to the contrary was only to reassure Fahriq that his version of the story was okay by me.

"Police have a clue?"

"Just what their heads can see up their dark alleys," Fahriq whooped. "Anyway, they don't seem to be looking too hard. I'd say they prefer not knowing too much about old Butterfield."

"Can't say as I'm upset to see that ratbait get short fused," I said. "Justice walks in strange ways."

"Earth to Barnes," Fahriq joked, schoolkid-style. "Ain't you heard, spaceman? Justice ain't but a word in the dictionary. Comes between jackass and juvenile. Greed and revenge're what make this sorry world go round."

But the way I'd played the call had put Fahriq in a cooperative mood, relieved he wouldn't have to teach me another lesson. Did he feel the tiniest bit guilty about the graveyard humiliation he'd dealt for me? Or maybe he just missed pattering with me as an old friend. There weren't so many left.

So when I asked, "Butterfield have his assets stashed in Jamaica?" Fahriq didn't mind talking.

"That's it," he drawled. "Had this villa down there he planned to retire to eventually. Soon as it wouldn't look too sudden or final, you see. Widow's got it all, now."

"She stood to gain plenty, that's for certain." It was true: I thought of that letter from Doctor Raymond *Always* squirreled away in Ruth Epps' pretty bedroom.

Time to hear the dime drop.

"Remember you called me a month ago looking to tie up loose ends—loose ends other than Butterfield? You were wondering if I had the account book of your one-time business manager, Carl Carp? You ever find that?"

All the clowning flushed out of Fahriq's voice. "You got it after all, don't you, old buddy? All that innocent resentment was humbug, that it, flash?"

"That's it. Now I want you to sell me some revenge."

"God damn, I do love the way you say things!"

Five nickels later, after twenty-five minutes of dickering and skepticism, Fahriq finally said, "Shit, boy, you let me do it my way, we bring the whole house of cards down in a couple hours. Way you want to play it is risky, take a lot of work, too. No need for that risk."

"You get the ledger only when the package is delivered. After that graveyard fiasco, it's strictly COD with me from now on, my friend."

"Corpse on Delivery," Fahriq roared. "You're learning, Ezell. But, I tell you again, it'd be no-muss, no-fuss, you let me handle the entire transaction."

"Not a chance. The only way I want to do this is my way. How it happens matters more to me than even what happens. How soon can it all come down?"

"Well, I'm sad to say, Doctor Ray's blown away. Won't be shipped for many a day," Fahriq was snapping his fingers and laying on the Harry Belafonte drawl. He didn't stop there. "For news of that clown, I'll keep me ear to the ground. You'll be the first to hear when he is Kingston bound."

"I'll call in two days to firm up the moves," I promised. When I hung up, Fahriq was still humming "Jamaica Farewell."

Chapter 31

Outside Terminal A at Newark Airport, the cold sun gleamed through a late October sky. Inside, the clouds were brewing.

Ruth Epps stood in line, clasping her gloved hands tensely. She wore a short, dark-fur jacket, black suede skirt, and high heels. The line she stood fifth on was strung along one side of a huge, otherwise empty room, edged with one customs inspection station after another, like checkout counters in the world's largest supermarket. Two uniformed customs agents examined passports and stamped them. Three others unpacked and repacked the merchandise being shipped to Kingston, Jamaica. Two of them wore belt holsters and revolvers. That hardly mattered, because two security officers in different uniforms stood talking and smoking over by the wall, right next to their rifles propped against the tiles. The linoleum tile made the high ceiling room boom and pop in my ears as I walked up from behind and took the place in line right behind Ruth. I reacquainted myself with her perfume.

In front of all of us, neatly rowed, were the articles in question. First, a dark walnut casket on a stainless caster-cart. Then orange crate after crate bulging with small shrubs and bundled trees, branches poking out the tops. Next, a series of portable kennels, both big and tiny, containing two sad-eyed dogs, a yelper, and four assorted cats.

Then several more crates of plants, long and narrow, imprisoning the dwarf trees' rootballs. Finally, a second coffin, bronze-plated and glowing.

The line moved very slowly. For a few minutes I stood in back of Ruth unnoticed and unrecognized. She was holding her body very erect and still, head fixed on what was happening ahead at the customs table. Once she turned slightly to eyeball the last coffin, Doctor Raymond Butterfield's coffin, that is, but immediately she moved eyes back front and center.

I tapped her on the shoulder. She wheeled fast, earrings flashing.

As soon as she saw me, she gasped, "My God!" Then she turned on the ice. "What do you want?"

"Plenty," I said. "I want it all."

"All what? You'd better start making sense, buster, or I'll call on one of these policemen."

"You call them now, or I'll call them later, it's up to you."

"What do you want?" she repeated mechanically. I glanced up ahead. The party with casket number one was not through yet. I took my time. Not until he went through and the shrub lady was handing over her passport did I hand Ruth the first document.

She stared at it, mystified. Then her eyes narrowed and her face hardened. Her beautiful eyes lashed at me with more hatred than I thought I'd ever see.

The paper contained these words:

The bronze casket, being shipped by Mrs. Ruth Epps of 344 Weequahic Avenue, Newark, contains the body of Doctor Raymond Butterfield. It also contains just over two kilos (4.6 pounds) of methamphetamine, an illegal drug, sewn into the chest cavity of the body by Mrs. Epps.

"You wouldn't *dare*," she hissed. "It would be your neck in the noose, too."

"Oh, why's that? I'm just an informant. A licensed de-

tective. I heard a drug rumor on the street and ran to tell
the authorities like I'm supposed to. Me, I'll probably pick
up a citation from the mayor's office."

The shrub lady thanked the customs officers in a clear
soprano, wished everyone a nice day, and bustled off to the
international flight lounge, both arms stuck through purses
and straw bags.

The cat and dog man stepped up to bat. I took the note
from Ruth's fingers and replaced it with a stapled sheaf of
tissue-paper documents

"What is *this*?" she demanded.

For reply, I handed her a Bic pen.

"Damn you! You better tell me what's going on."

"Sign there," I said. "And three other places where you
see X's."

"And what?"

"And you pass complete ownership of Butterfield's villa
in Jamaica to the one and only me."

"You are insane, if you think—"

"I do think. You don't have much time, baby. Ten,
maybe fifteen minutes, I'd guess. You have any idea how
much time you can do for smuggling drugs *out* of the U.S.?"

"How much?" Give the beautiful lady credit. She managed a sneer.

"Fifty years." I grinned. "A real good lawyer might
chisel it down to twenty. You'd be paroled in eleven to thir-
teen, is all."

"Damn you," she repeated through clenched teeth.

"You'd barely be forty years old when you got out."

Boxer's reflexes pulled my head back before her nails
could swipe into my eyes. One of the security guards
glanced at us, and I gave him back a big grin.

"Better pep it up, babe," I murmured to Ruth.
"Grizzly Adams there looks about finished."

Ruth stamped her high-heeled foot.

"Sign it," I advised softly. "It won't leave you broke,
will it?"

She turned the indignation up a notch in my direction.
Then, grasping the pen like a carving knife, she scratched

what could have been her signature on the dotted line on the cover sheet.

"And there," I said, turning the page. "And again there, and there."

When I looked up, Ruth was watching me carefully, sizing things up.

"This is nonsense," she said, deciding to patronize me. "No one can just type up a paper to take someone's property away."

"You can if you hire a couple good lawyers to study photocopies of the deed and title long enough."

Ruth stared at me.

"You probably never even knew your house got broken into. Twice."

The cat and dog man was squabbling with the customs agents, who were taking his dogs out of their kennels one by one and patting them down.

"Don't you feel anything for me?" Ruth tried, a note of tenderness in her voice. "What I feel for you is real."

"Why'd you do it?" I batted the question back. "Hire me, I mean. You had everything to lose if Butterfield went tumbling down. It's been puzzling me."

Ruth stood silently, calculating what to tell me. She started to say something, then stopped.

"Was Doctor Ray holding out on you? That it?"

Still, she said nothing.

"The only way I could figure it, when Walter died, his cut of the profits died on you, too. Butterfield was your last ticket on the gravy train. Did you think I'd rope him to Walter's murder for you?"

Ruth's eyes burned gravely into me. I thought I could see respect in them, but maybe that's wishful thinking.

"By the way," I kept my voice casual. "That line you fed me about not sleeping with your husband's killer. There anything at all to that?"

Now I could see her eyes fill with pleading and regret. But they were changing too often and too fast. And I was determined not to care.

"Of course, you had Walter's life insurance on your

mind, too. Isn't that so? Tell me, when did you find out Velnarsky and Mooney were going to murder Walter?"

"You've had your fun," Ruth lipped, sadly but coldly. "Leave me alone, for God's sake."

Instead, I rubbed my hands together. "Now for the liquid assets."

She jumped back as if somebody were stealing a baby out of her arms. "Don't you dare!" Almost all the customs folks looked at us then. So did the fruit tree man in front of Ruth—the last one on line before her.

"In your purse," I whispered. "The traveler's checks. Every last one of them."

Ruth had some cool left. I had to admire her. She actually got out a Virginia Slims and lit it before she zipped open her purse and rummaged. Then she hesitated.

"All fifty of them," I insisted. "All those five-hundred-dollar checks."

A noise from the customs table made Ruth glance over her shoulder. The fruit tree man shuffled forward. She was holding several thick stacks of Cook's Travellers' Cheques. "I can't possibly sign all of these!" she said scornfully.

"No need, babe." I reached into my breast pocket and flourished out yet another perfectly legal document. "One Jane Hancock on this and we are square."

"Bastard."

"Sign."

She signed.

"Let's see. Even forgetting that you connived with your husband's murderers, just remember that when Eddie Dorey and I set out for the warehouse, you immediately called Butterfield, who rang the alarm for Velnarsky and Mooney. Three men got killed because of you that night, lady. One of them was the best man I ever met."

Who knows exactly what her exasperated moan was intended to mean?

"And *I'm* the bastard? 'Scuse me, ma'am."

The fruit tree man was practically through. He was scooping up his papers and gabbing a mile a minute with the customs agents.

"Good-bye, Ruth. It was sweet while it lasted."

She poised for about a three-count, then coiled her head like a snake and spat in my eyes.

"Next," the agent was singing out.

I wiped the spit off with my palm. The hate in her eyes mixed with a sort of mean triumph.

"It's your turn, ma'am; we don't have all day."

With a fluid movement, Ruth turned to walk to the customs agents. She was prepared to freeze me out, out-class me down the homestretch.

"By the way," I stage-whispered, so she had to step back to make me hush. "You're probably thinking that at least you'll pick up your cut of the meth sitting where Doctor Ray's lungs used to be. Huh?"

She was not about to answer me. Still, she couldn't walk away.

"Well, think again. When you touch down in Jamaica, that coffin's gonna fade as fast as a winning lottery ticket."

She stiffened her shoulders, still beautiful in her fur jacket. Her mouth formed to spit something cutting at me. Then she changed her mind, and turned on her heel. The last I saw of Ruth Epps, she was explaining something to the U.S. Customs officials, head bent low and close and sexy to theirs.

Chapter 32

"This here's the lounge," Snookie Izard was telling me, waving his hand like a king. "Ernie's refrigerator going over there, we got a *genuine* poker table coming in that a friend of Ernie is donating."

The Grand Dedication was over. Today was Settling-In Day at the Sharecroppers' greenhouse.

When I had walked through the garden's raised beds,

the huge, double-paned greenhouse shone with yellow re-
flections of the sun and with the colors of clotheslines and
roof tiles from the neighboring tenements.

It glowed like a jewel.

"Over here, Ezell!" shouted Mrs. Washington from the
opposite end. The inside space had been argued over
endlessly until I finally stepped in and made some assignments. Snookie, Ernie, the Field Marshal, and Ramone—
with Cosmo as honorary member—were setting up the
north quarter as a combo television lounge/poker salon. Ernie and Snookie had first wanted to name the greenhouse
the Raccoons Poker and Social Club, then, as a gesture of
gratitude, Cosmo's Exacta Club.

The Field Marshal suggested The Hothouse, because,
as he kept repeating, "We hot now." Ramone Pasquale, still
hanging out with the Sharecroppers long after the garden
beds were shut down for the winter, had made his sarcastic
pitch for the Chick Coop. He didn't explain why, but I told
him anyway to forget the idea of bringing girls at night to
the greenhouse. The Field Marshal would be sleeping inside it at night, just to keep an eye on things. Not to mention that it was heaps nicer than the flophouses and
abandoned cars he too often slept in during the winters.

I took Mrs. Washington aside. "There's only enough
left over from Cosmo's donation to pump heat into this
greenhouse for one winter," I said. "Sun won't do it all, this
climate. Remember we agreed we'd raise the money for
next winter? You folks do any thinking about that?"

"Shut your mouth, Ezell Barnes." Mrs. Washington
glared. "We done took care of all that. Garden's getting
twice as big next year. All the extra tomatoes and corn we
raise are getting sold to keep the greenhouse going."

The women's lion's share of the space was already
mostly filled with sturdy homemade seedling tables, overhead pipes for hanging pots, scrap wood potting tables
mounded with compost and soil. Plus, Lavinia Everett's and
Mrs. Washington's latest project, a shallow rectangular bin
filled with eggshells and coffee grounds, where, they

claimed, millions of red worms and nightcrawlers were furiously breeding below the surface.

Mrs. Pasquale, on the other hand, had pleaded long and hard to set up a small chicken run inside the greenhouse. Snookie and the Field Marshal especially were dead set against the idea of filthy old chickens and chicken shit in the place until Mrs. Pasquale brought over a giant platter of Puerto Rican fried chicken one afternoon. After that, Snookie hammered together the chicken run himself.

A name for the greenhouse was settled when the women put their heads together and decided on The New Ark Sun House.

When I had seen everything, I called the entire group together.

"There's one thing we haven't talked about," I said. "That's vandalism. How long you think this glass house is gonna live without a rock coming through or something like that? This here's a tough neighborhood."

I saw Ernie glance at Snookie, who glanced at Ramone. All three wore sheepish expressions.

"What's up, Ernie?"

"Well, you see, Easy, this neighborhood's gonna steer clear of messing the Sun House behind the fact we been telling everybody that you swore to gun down the first dude that lay a finger on it." Ernie panted for breath.

"Yeah," said the Snookman. "Ever'body know you a ex-prize fighter, carry guns around with you. They ain't gonna mess with nothing about nothing, I'm telling you."

"Well, that's just great," I said. "So everybody in my neighborhood is going dodge me like a dragon from now on?"

"Now, now, Ezell," Lavinia Everett soothed. "It's not like that. This is a tough neighborhood, but it's *our* neighborhood, yours and all of ours. People understand how much the Sun House means to us. They won't cause trouble. Ramone has even been talking to the street gangs."

I glanced at Ramone with appreciation. He tipped up his beer bottle to avoid embarrassment.

"Besides," Lavinia continued, "Elvira and me went to see that nice Mr. Castillo, that owns the electrical store downtown? And he had this extra portable intercom/alarm system? We gonna fix it up between here and your apartment, so the Field Marshal can ring at night, if any problems happen."

"Only for anything big what I can't handle by my lonesome," the Field Marshal tittered.

Everybody was nodding and drinking toasts. Mrs. Washington hugged little Lavinia Everett.

"Hallo, Easy and everybody," sang Angel, ducking through the outside door at the other end. He was wearing floral tights that thrust his slender legs out from under a long hot pink sweater cinched around his waist with a silk belt.

Later, I was standing alone outside, chain-smoking my third butt in the frosty twilight when Angel finished his mile-a-minute greetings to the Sharecroppers and stepped out to join me.

He wanted to hear the story from top to bottom, and with a little coaxing I started talking. I guess I needed to tell somebody.

"Don't you truss that Fareaks no more," Angel stormed at one point. "He help you this time, but he does very bad things sometime."

"You know Fahriq?"

Angel nodded. By the time I reached the part about wringing Ruth Epps dry as a chamois cloth, darkness had dropped over the streets. But Angel's eyes shone like cats' eyes in a penlight. He stretched out a hand to squeeze my arm.

"The deed to Butterfield's villa I traded to Fahriq for ten cents on the dollar. He has the connections to negotiate a contract like that in Kingston; I surely don't. Eighty-five grand. On the traveler's checks, he gave me an even split. Another twelve thousand, five hundred."

"What you done is so wonderful, Easy. I love you for that."

"What else was there to do?" I shrugged. I tossed down

another butt onto the little heap of them at my feet. "Dorey's son was gonna be left in this world without a dime. What kind of future could the kid expect? The trust fund'll kick in for him when he's ready to head for high school. Providing Beverly sends him away to boarding school, like she agreed, there'll be enough to pay his expenses right through college, give him some kind of head start in this world."

The Sun House door cracked open and Mrs. Pasquale stuck her head out and called, "You two come in! You got to be freezing out there! Come have the pork roast and greens with us. Squash, too. Last fresh vegables from the garden, 'til the greenhouse get going!"

"Coming!" I yelled back. Angel was beaming at me. He touched my arm again.

"Angel is very happy to have you as my friend," he purred.

"You're a good friend, too, Angel. Thanks for listening."

"How about you come home with Angel tonight?" Angel lifted an eyebrow when he said that. "I could be so nice to you, all them sorrows just float away."

That hit me just right, so I laughed hard for the first time in weeks. "Not on your life, Angel," I said, wiping the tears away. "We've been through this, remember? I'm way too old to go changing my point of view."

☐ 25789-7 **JUST ANOTHER DAY IN PARADISE,**
Maxwell $2.95

Fiddler has more money than he knows what to do with, he's tried about everything he'd ever thought of trying and there's not much left that interests him. So, when his ex-wife's twin brother disappears, when the feds begin to investigate the high-tech computer company the twin owns, and when Fiddler finds himself holding an envelope of Russian-cut diamonds, he decides to get involved. Is his ex-wife's twin selling high-tech information to the Russians?

☐ 26201-7 **NOT TILL A HOT JANUARY,**
Adamson $2.95

Introducing New York Homicide Detective Balthazar Marten. Balthazar Marten finds himself on special assignment in San Juan, Puerto Rico, far from the cold New York streets. Things really heat up when three coeds are strangled and Marten finds himself on the trail of a psycho.

☐ 25717-X **THE BACK-DOOR MAN,** Kantner $2.95

Ben Perkins doesn't look for trouble, but he isn't the kind of guy who looks the other way when something comes along to spark his interest. In this case, it's a wealthy widow who's a victim of embezzlement and the gold American Express card she gives him for expenses. Ben thinks it should be fun; the other people after the missing money are out to change his mind.

☐ 26061-8 **"B" IS FOR BURGLAR,** Grafton $3.50

"Kinsey is a refreshing heroine."—*Washington Post Book World*

"Kinsey Millhone ... is a stand-out specimen of the new female operatives." —*Philadelphia Inquirer*

[Millhone is] "a tough cookie with a soft center, a gregarious loner." —*Newsweek*

What appears to be a routine missing persons case for private detective Kinsey Millhone turns into a dark tangle of arson, theft and murder.

Look for them at your bookstore or use the coupon below: